LONDON'S BURNING

'SUMMARY JUSTICE' SERIES - BOOK 4

THEO HARRIS

London's Burning
Book 4 of the 'Summary Justice' series

Copyright © 2023 by Theo Harris
All rights reserved.
Paperback ISBN: 979-8-391748-43-4

No part of this book may be reproduced in any form or by any electronic or mechanical means, including information storage and retrieval systems, without written permission from the author, except for the use of brief quotations in a book review.

This is a work of fiction. Names, characters, places, and incidents are either the product of the author's imagination or are used fictitiously, and any resemblance to actual persons, living or dead, business establishments, places of learning, events or locales is entirely coincidental.

Edited by Linda Nagle
Cover art by Keith Johnston (Keith Draws Cover Art)

PROLOGUE

The room was buzzing with its usual excitement as the auction continued to garner higher-than-usual bids. It was one of those rare occasions when there were two or more parties interested in many of the rarer items. Christie's was a world-renowned auction house, having auctioned billions of pounds' worth of goods in recent years.

It was time for one of the rarer and more unusual items on offer. The auction house had ensured that it was placed strategically between some of the more expensive items to raise its profile and hopefully increase bidding.

'Ladies and gentlemen,' said the auctioneer, 'we now come to lot five-three-six, a most unusual item that we hope will attract much bidding. The proceeds of the sale will go towards improvements and equipment for a charity that helps single women, including a gym and club that helps with their physical and mental wellbeing. The item has been generously donated for these causes by a London company that wishes to remain anonymous.'

He indicated towards a colleague, who was approaching the dais holding a crimson velvet cushion displaying a unique bejewelled eyepatch. It was made of gold and encrusted with diamonds and other gems of various colours. The leather strap had been worked so that it held several smaller diamonds along its length, except for the last five inches of each side, which was fabric used for the knot.

'This very unusual, one-off, jewel-encrusted eyepatch was made by Tiffany and Company in Paris, and is made with twenty-four-carat gold. It is magnificently encrusted with eighty high-colour Carre-cut diamonds totalling forty-four carats, four Zambian emeralds totalling six carats, eight Mozambique rubies totalling ten carats, and finally four black opals totalling two carats. I have online bids and will start the bidding at three hundred and twenty thousand pounds.'

There was a buzz in the room as the starting bid was announced, with many intrigued by such a curious item.

'Do I have three-fifty?' the auctioneer asked. He glanced to the side, where the assistants were dealing with online bidders.

One of them raised their arms.

'We have three-fifty from an online bidder. Do we have three-seventy-five?'

An elderly woman in the audience raised her paddle, indicating a bid.

'We have three-seventy-five on the floor, thank you, madam. Do we have four hundred thousand?'

One assistant stood up, raised her arm in the air, and called out, 'Five hundred thousand!'

There was a collective gasp from the audience.

'We have a bid of five hundred thousand pounds from

overseas, ladies and gentlemen. Does anyone care to raise the bid to five hundred and fifty thousand?'

He looked at the audience ahead of him, some shaking their heads, others wide-mouthed at the development. Looking at the assistants, he saw more shaking heads. The bidding seemed to be over.

'Ladies and gentlemen, this beautiful one-off item is unlikely to be seen again, so don't let it get away.'

He looked again, and there was no movement.

'Going once, going twice... and sold, sold, sold to our overseas bidder for five hundred thousand pounds, ladies and gentlemen! That will be a tremendous boost to the charities that it will help. Thank you all for your bids.'

There was a round of applause as the auction ended and the assistant removed the eyepatch from the dais. The buzz of excitement continued for several minutes.

'Moving on to the next item, never seen before, a small twentieth-century self-portrait by the master artist David Hockney, oil on canvas, circa nineteen seventy-four. The bidding starts at sixty-five thousand pounds.'

'GOODNIGHT, Winston; make sure to try those cookies on your break, Marion spent hours baking them yesterday,' the auctioneer told the security guard as he left the building.

'Thank you, Mister Crawford, and please thank Missus Crawford too, they look delicious,' the guard replied, saluting as the auctioneer waved one last time before exiting via the front entrance and onto King Street. He walked towards St James's Street as he took his usual route to Green Park tube station.

There was little daylight left and streetlights were now illuminating the now-quiet road. As he neared the junction, the scaffolding that covered the entire building on the corner appeared to be the only place the lighting hadn't penetrated, the pavement still in darkness under the wooden boards that surrounded the building. It wasn't helped much by the white transit van that was parked alongside it, which cast more shadow on that part of the pavement.

Crawford had used this route for more than seven years and had no fear about the unlit pavement. His mind was on the successful auctions he had conducted that day, which had exceeded everyone's forecasts and estimates by several million pounds. His bonus would be a good one.

Making his way under the scaffolding, he saw the van's sliding door open suddenly as he came alongside it and two large men jumped out silently, one either side of him. They grabbed an arm each. A quiet, well-spoken voice came from within the van.

'If you struggle, we will not be so gentle with Marion. Do you understand?'

Crawford's blood froze as he nodded and acquiesced to being led to the van. Within seconds he was inside, sitting on a bench between the two hulking men, facing a well-dressed elegant woman who sat opposite. She was fanning herself with a multi-coloured, intricately patterned lace fan.

'Now then, Mister Crawford. I need you to answer some questions for me. Then we can let you be on your way to your charming wife. Does that sound okay to you?'

Crawford, who by now was shaking as the adrenaline took over, nodded quickly.

That's a lovely art deco fan, that would fetch a pretty penny at the auction, he thought.

1

'What do you mean, you want to be a captain?' Kendra asked as she sipped her latte.

'If I want to use the boat, it means I should train up and get a Boatmasters' license,' Andy replied.

'So go and get one.'

'I will. I'm looking forward to using *Soggy Bottom*, but you won't believe how much paperwork is involved,' he continued.

'As an ex-cop, you should feel right at home with that, shouldn't you?'

Soggy Bottom was the motor cruiser that Andy had been left as a bonus from a grateful dark-web hacker who had gained tens of millions of pounds thanks to Andy's tip-off. The tip-off, which had been sold at an online auction, had cost the hacker a couple of million pounds, but the forty million he had gained as a result was such a huge mark-up that he had gladly given Andy the boat as a gift. The hacker was now sitting on a much larger, newer, motor cruiser that was moored at St. Katherine's dock in Central London, waiting to be taken out for the first time.

'Well, I'm not a cop anymore, so I'm entitled to have the occasional whine, okay? I've always wanted a motor cruiser; it would have been perfect if all it took was to switch the engine on and drive the damned thing, not have to take exams, get a license, various certificates and all the other bullshit.'

'And it's taken you this long to figure that out?' Kendra asked.

'Yeah, well, I needed some time to unwind since the last adventure. I've made sure we're fully stocked up again and we're ready for the next one. How's it going at work?'

'I can't complain. They've got me checking on some armed robberies they think are connected. It's not as boring as I thought it would be,' Kendra said.

'Is Rick still asking you to go back full time?'

'He asks every week, hoping I'll cave. He's trying to wear me down, bless him.'

'He's a good boss, K, you can't blame him for wanting you around more. I wouldn't mind that myself,' Andy said.

'Okay, well, we both agreed not to go there, remember? Or are you having another of those mid-life crises that you have every month?'

Andy laughed.

'Nothing wrong with that, K, it keeps me on my toes. Life would be boring as hell if everything was perfect, wouldn't it? It's the little things that you either can't control or don't want to control that make it interesting.'

'That's a human trait, we have to keep learning new stuff or we wither and die,' Kendra said.

'Yep, it surely is.'

'Getting back to the saggy trousers business...'

'It's *Soggy Bottom*, and it's a cool name for a boat,' he corrected.

'It's not. Anyway, getting back to the boat, how long is it going to take to get your license?'

'Probably a few months. It's not difficult, more a formality and a paper exercise; I'll do it in my spare time.'

'You might as well start; I've been looking for something new for us to take on, but nothing seems to stick out at the moment. It's all quiet on the western front, as they say.'

'Okay, that's settled, then, I'll start tomorrow. Is your dad still coming over?'

'No,' said Kendra, 'he's going to spend the day visiting one of the clubs. He's bought some new kit that he wants to surprise them with. Those clubs are starting to look very professional and slick now, thanks to our criminal donors.'

'Yeah, we've done well with that. Long may it continue. Our coffers are full, and we are fully stocked up and ready to go. God help the criminal fraternity, especially the ones that we pick on next,' he said, pumping his fist in the air.

'Don't get too excited; like I said, there's not much for us to do at the moment.'

'THIS IS GREAT, TREV,' Charlie said as he examined the new kit that was being unloaded from a van. 'The kids will get a kick out of this stuff.'

'Yeah, I'm very pleased with it, Charlie. It wasn't cheap, but it'll be well worth it if they engage with us more.'

Along with two very modern treadmills, each of which featured a large screen for users to view as they ran, Trevor had bought a rowing machine and two new boxing target trees that featured strike pads at various angles and positions. There were also several boxes of new pads, gloves, and even tape. He had thought of everything.

'One last thing,' he said, opening the boot of his car. He pulled out a Bose Pro PA system that had built-in Bluetooth connectivity, a smart speaker that would allow the club to have the very best quality sound.

Charlie laughed.

'You know they'll be fighting over whose music to listen to, don't you?'

'That's where you come in, Charlie. You play our music, not theirs. I want them to listen to something other than that foul-mouthed violent crap that they seem to like. Get 'em used to something nicer, you know? It will help their mental health as well as soothe their souls. Boxing shouldn't be about violence, it's more about routine and mental strength, and they should channel their energies into the bags and pads – not their heads.'

'Don't you worry about that, I'll make sure they get plenty of soul and jazz,' Charlie replied, 'and maybe the odd rock anthem.'

'Nothing wrong with some good old-fashioned rock. Now, show me that kid you keep talking about, the middleweight. Danny, isn't it?'

'Danny Baptiste, yeah. He's only seventeen but he boxes like a seasoned pro. He has a great boxing mind and is a future champ, for sure,' Charlie said. 'He's just over there, come and say hello.'

They walked over to the young man that was helping to place one of the treadmills. He was tall and thin, his hair completely shorn, and was wearing a tracksuit. He was still a young man with plenty of growing ahead.

'Hey, Danny, come here, son,' Charlie said, waving him over. 'Come and say hello to Trevor, the owner.'

'How're you doing, boss?' Danny replied, shaking Trevor's hand firmly.

'That's a good, powerful grip you have there, young man. How are you enjoying the club so far?'

'It's great. I'm between jobs at the moment so I'm spending more time here than normal. It's helping take my mind off the whole unemployment situation.'

'You looking for a job? Anything in particular?' asked Trevor.

'I don't mind. My last couple have been in fast-food joints, so it would be nice to try something different.'

'Have you considered anything in security? Like learning a trade or two in the industry?'

'Not really, but I'd give anything a go.'

'That's good to know,' said Trevor. 'I may have something that would be a good fit for you, if you're up for it?'

'Yes, sir, I'd be very interested, thank you!'

Trevor turned to Charlie. 'Bring him to the factory tomorrow. I'm looking to take on more apprentices and interns.'

'I'll bring him over in the morning, then, show him around until you speak to him,' Charlie said.

'Alright then, I'll see you both tomorrow,' Trevor said. He shook both their hands and went back outside. He stood there, looking around at the familiar surroundings, taking a deep breath.

'I love this place,' he said out loud, 'you just can't beat London town.'

∼

2

Kendra was two hours into her shift when she received a summons from her boss, Detective Sergeant Rick Watts.

'Pop to my office, will you? I have some interesting news,' he said cryptically, before hanging up.

As she was working in the intel office that day, she walked upstairs to his office on the third floor, where her old unit, the *Serious Crimes Unit* was based. She was now occasionally attached to the unit as a liaison officer. Working part-time had allowed her the freedom to continue working with Andy and her dad on bringing criminals to justice in a more unorthodox—and somewhat illegal—manner, but it also meant that she could work with the SCU and the Intel Unit collectively, allowing her access to intelligence that had assisted them greatly so far. As such, she still considered Rick her boss and was happy to maintain a connection with her old team.

'Come in, Kendra,' he said, waving her into the room.

'Hi, Rick, what's up?' she said, sitting down.

'A couple of weird things is what,' he said, grinning.

'Not sure I like it when you smile like that, it usually means something is wrong,' she said.

'Well, you'd be wrong in this case. I just heard from an old colleague of mine that Eddie Duckmore and Dave Critchley have both resigned,' he said, still grinning.

Duckmore and Critchley were two *National Crime Agency* officers who had caused them all a great deal of problems recently, including filing complaints against both Kendra and Rick Watts.

'The douchebag has resigned? You're joking!'

'I am not. My mate at the NCA told me that rather than wait to be demoted, or worse, they decided to quit so they could avoid it.'

'Wow, that is a surprise. Did your mate tell you anything else?' Kendra asked.

'We both knew they'd shot themselves in the foot when they were interviewed by the DPS, so the allegations against them were pretty serious and considered gross misconduct. Most of the time nowadays you get the sack for that, don't you? Well, according to my source, they both put their papers in at the same time, used up their outstanding leave, and have already left.'

'That is weird,' she said, 'why go so quickly when they'd be entitled to more pay by prolonging it?'

'That's the interesting part. They've both been head-hunted by a private security company working out of Dartford, *Hurricane Security Solutions*. I tried looking them up, but they're a new company and there's nothing out there about them.'

'Hmm, that sounds very odd,' she said.

'Yep. I think we'll keep an eye out, because taking on dodgy ex-cops can only be a bad thing, right?'

'If there's anything you want me to do, just let me know,' Kendra said, 'but it doesn't sound like I'll be finding much if they're brand new, does it?'

'No. Just stick a pin in it for now and check up every few months,' Rick said.

'I can do that, for sure.'

'There's something unrelated that I wanted to speak to you about,' he continued. 'It's also weird but in a very different way.'

'Fire away.'

'One of the auctioneers at Christie's was abducted the other day. They threatened to kill his wife, showed him pictures so he knew they were serious, unless he helped them find something he'd sold that day at the auction house.'

'What's that got to do with us?'

'Only that he lives in South Woodford, which is on our patch, and that his brother-in-law is our boss, DI Damian Dunne.'

'Whoa, that's an unhappy coincidence,' said Kendra.

'We're lucky to have any information at all. If it wasn't for the boss, we wouldn't have a clue it had even happened.'

'Damn. Is the man okay?'

'Not really, they beat the crap out of him and tortured him. He's lost a finger and has a bunch of broken bones. He's lucky to be alive.'

'What the hell did they want from him?' she asked.

'A weird, jewelled eyepatch was sold anonymously. They wanted to know who had submitted it for auction.'

Kendra froze. It could only have been Goran Qupi's eyepatch, which they had taken from him when they had fought —and won — against the Albanian gang leader in their first major outing as a vigilante-style squad.

'You okay, Kendra?' Rick asked when he saw her expression, 'you look like you've seen a ghost.'

'Sorry, Rick, I'm a little confused. Are you saying that a man was tortured because someone wanted to know who had sent an eyepatch anonymously for auction?'

'That's what he said. They dumped him at the end of his road when he gave them the information and threatened to kill him and his wife if he came to the police. That's why he didn't want to say anything and that's why this has come to us, because what those bastards didn't realise is that their victim's brother is our boss – who is a tenacious bastard at best.'

'Wow. Weird does not cover it,' she replied, trying to act as normal as possible while her heart was thumping at twice its usual rate.

'For your information, the eyepatch sold for half a million quid, so you can understand the interest in it.'

'Wow, that's a lot of money for an accessory.'

'Yes, it is, so we'll be working on this case too—quietly; just a few of us here will be aware so as not to tip anyone off. You okay to help out?'

'Sure. As a matter of interest, what did he tell them?' she asked.

'He couldn't remember the exact details of the donor, so he had to go online to get the records, which is when they cut his finger off, after he failed to give them the information. All he could tell them was the beneficiaries from the auction, as the item was sold to fund some clubs. They told him that the next digit they'd cut off would eventually lead to something much worse, if he went to the police.'

'Do we have that information? It would be a good place to start,' she said.

'Yes, here it is,' Rick said, handing her a slip of paper. 'It's a couple of boxing clubs and a single mothers' club. I had a brief look but there's not a lot on there about them, so if you can dig deeper, that would be great.'

'Will do,' she said, taking the piece of paper from Rick.

Kendra walked downstairs and past the second floor where the Intel Unit was based, made her way to the ground floor and then outside to the back yard, where she called Andy.

'We have a major problem,' she said, looking around to ensure that there was nobody within earshot.

'What's wrong? Are you okay?' Andy asked.

'Not really. Do you know what happened to the jewelled eyepatch that Dad took from Qupi?'

'No, I thought it was in the safe. Why do you ask?'

'Because it was sold at auction. Someone tortured an auctioneer to get information about where the thing had come from, and he gave them the names of the boxing clubs and also the single mums' club.'

'Shit, did your dad auction it off?'

'No idea, I'm going to call him now. See if you can find anything out on your end, this could get very messy. Also, call the twins and let them know we may be having visitors very soon, and to be very careful.'

She ended the call and dialled again.

'How's it going, my favourite daughter?' Trevor asked.

'Dad, what did you do with Qupi's eyepatch? Did you send it to auction?'

'Yeah, how did you know about that? It was supposed to be an anonymous donation to raise money for the clubs. What's going on?'

'Someone tortured the auctioneer to get information, they cut his finger off and beat the hell out of him. He told them where the money was going,' she explained.

'Who the hell could it be?'

'No idea, Dad. My guess is they're after the money raised, what else could it be?'

'Shit! That's not good, K. It raised a ton of money for those causes, but I wish I hadn't bothered now. I thought it would be a good idea; it was sitting there doing nothing. Sorry, love.'

'There's no time for that. If they have the information, it means they'll be paying the clubs a visit. Can you get back there and start prepping everyone, just in case?'

'Of course, I'll leave now. Thanks for the heads-up. Are you okay?'

'Yeah, I'm at work. I'll catch up with you later, I have a few more hours here, yet. Please be careful, Dad.'

'I will, darling, don't worry about me. We'll get through this, okay?'

'I mean it, Dad. If people start sniffing around, they'll find out who the owners and directors are, and you're down as a director at Companies House, aren't you?'

'Yeah, but my home address isn't on there. I have hardly any presence online, I doubt they'll find me.'

'I'm not so much worried about them, Dad, I'm worried about my police colleagues' investigative abilities, they're bloody good. If they dig deep enough, they may find out that you're my dad and start looking at me as well. I know we have different surnames, but it won't be too difficult to find out. We need to sort something out, very quickly. If Rick finds out about us, then our entire operation will have been for nothing. Not only that, but we'll all end up in prison.'

CHARLIE AND DANNY arrived at the factory bright and early the following morning, as planned. Charlie wanted to show the young boxer the front end of the operation, the legitimate end, which was *Sherwood Solutions*, a security services company that Trevor was building slowly into a profitable company. One reason he had started it was to find placements for many of the youngsters that he had kept off the streets at the boxing clubs, so they had a future and a trade to turn to as they became adults. As such, there were a good dozen apprentices learning about the security industry, male and female, all being given a wage as they learned their trade.

'This is how Trevor gives back to the community,' Charlie told the young man as they walked through the front doors.

'Good morning, Charlie,' the youngster at reception said.

'Good morning, Gregory. This is Danny; I'm showing him the ropes before Trevor has a chat about him joining us. Danny, this is Greg Petrucci, one of our brightest talents here and a middleweight, like you.'

'How are you doing, mate?' Danny asked, shaking Greg's hand.

'You'll love it here, Danny, they treat you like adults and you'll learn some good stuff,' Greg replied.

'Did you pass the CCTV exam?' Charlie asked Greg.

'Yes, I did. I'm taking the data protection one next week, so I'll be ready to manage a CCTV suite if required.'

'Good lad,' Charlie said. 'I'm just going to show Danny the front end today, so we'll catch up later.' He walked Danny past the desk and through another door.

'What do you mean by front end?'

'Good question, young man. The front end is all you'll see until you have officially joined the company. We don't want you discovering our secrets, now, do we?'

TREVOR ARRIVED SLIGHTLY LATER than he'd told Charlie. The incident with the auctioneer had troubled him and he wanted to make sure the clubs were aware that they may be receiving dangerous visitors asking strange questions.

Fortunately, that hadn't happened yet, but he wasn't ruling it out and so he wanted them all prepared.

Charlie had finished showing Danny around and they were in the canteen with their coffees when Trevor arrived. He shook hands with them both.

'So, what do you think, young man?' he asked the teenager.

'It's very impressive, sir. I'd love to have the opportunity to work here,' Danny replied.

'That's good, because I need more trainees now that the company is doing so well. If you're up for it, you can start on Monday, nine o'clock sharp. Greg will be your mentor; you can shadow him as you learn the ropes.'

'I won't let you down, sir, thank you!' Danny said, shaking Trevor's hand.

'Good. We'll see you next week, then. Charlie, I need a

word, so please show Danny out and come and see me in the canteen.'

'Will do,' Charlie said. 'Come on then, Danny, you've seen enough for today.'

A few minutes later, Charlie and Trevor were sitting opposite each other in the canteen, nursing a cup of coffee each. Trevor gave him a run-down of the incident with the auctioneer.

'I want you to go around the clubs and make sure they're being vigilant,' Trevor said. 'I have a bad feeling about these people, and I don't want any of ours to get hurt.'

'No problem,' Charlie replied, 'I'll do the rounds and report back to you.'

'Thanks, mate. We could've done without this, I was hoping for a break from all the action to focus on growing the clubs, so this is a right pain in the arse.'

'I wouldn't worry about it, boss, nothing's happened yet, and they probably know we won't have the money at the clubs. If anything, you're the one who needs to be careful because you're the boss who controls the bank account.'

'Yeah, I get that, but all they'll have is my name. There's nothing they can trace back to my address. I've been very careful with that.'

'Still, it pays to be careful. Maybe you should have one of us keep you company for a few days.'

Trevor laughed. 'Come on, you know that ain't gonna happen. I'll be fine, I know how to keep an eye out and I have a ton of back-up just a phone call away.'

'Okay, if you insist, but don't say I didn't warn you. If there's nothing else, I'll head back to the club. See you tomorrow?'

'Yeah, see you, Charlie.'

Trevor considered Charlie's warnings as he walked to his car.

'*I suppose it can't hurt to be more vigilant,*' he thought, as he drove off.

3

The silver Volvo SUV parked fifty yards away from the brothel. The driver and the front passenger both got out, the driver opening the back door for the other passenger—their boss. She wore an ankle-length black puffer coat with a white-fur-trimmed hood, ideal for the chilly East London night. It was cold enough and dark enough that there was nobody around to see them walk the short distance to the mid-terrace house.

The ground floor was in darkness but there was a light on upstairs, along with the faint but pleasant sound of Ludovico Einaudi's piano. The men looked for instructions from their boss, who nodded to them as they stood by the front door. The passenger glanced around one more time to ensure they were not being watched, before he rammed his shoulder into the door. The wooden frame gave way immediately to his brute strength, splintering as it flew open. Surprisingly there was little noise from the impact, and the two men led the way inside.

The woman turned and closed the door. She wanted no witnesses. The upstairs light illuminated the ground floor enough for them to determine there was nobody downstairs, but one of the men had a cursory glance, just in case. He came back and shook his head. The woman nodded up to the first floor and the men quietly ascended the stairs, with her following, her hands still in her coat pockets.

As they climbed, the music got louder, suggesting that whoever was up there would not have heard the front door being barged open. As the first henchman rounded the stairs onto the landing, he saw a middle-aged woman sitting in a chair by a small table, fast asleep. The music was coming from a Bluetooth speaker on the table and was loud yet soothing. The henchman called his colleague and boss over.

They noticed that only one of the four doors was closed; the others, two bedrooms and a bathroom, were ajar and empty. There was a faint smell of incense in the air. The boss nodded to her men and one of them approached and grabbed the sleeping woman, with one hand over her mouth, the other holding her tight. The other man turned the speaker off.

The boss crouched in front of the frightened woman.

'He will let you go, but if you scream or do anything stupid, he will break your neck. Do you understand?'

'The woman nodded, so the boss looked up at her guard and did the same. He slowly removed his hand from the woman's mouth.

'That's good,' the boss said. 'Now I'm going to ask you some questions and I want you to answer quietly, do you understand?'

'Y-yes,' came the reply.

'Is the room occupied with a client?' the boss asked, pointing to the one closed door.

'Y-yes. He should be finished s-soon.'

The boss looked at the other henchman and nodded towards the room. He went over and barged in, closing the door behind him. Within seconds, there came the sounds of a woman shrieking and a man shouting.

'What the hell are you doing?' the client yelled. 'I've still got five minutes!'

An instant later they heard a loud slap. The boss and the other henchman both smiled.

Seconds later the door flew open, and a half-dressed, middle-aged man came running out, one side of his face red. His shirt hung from one arm, and he held his trousers and shoes in the other. His modesty was saved by the white y-fronts that he had been allowed to put on in his rush to leave.

'I ain't coming here again!' he shouted, running for his life down the stairs.

They heard a woman giggling before their associate reappeared with a grin on his face and joined them once again in front of the seated woman. He carried a chair, which he placed opposite for his boss.

'Now then, we can talk freely, no?' the boss told the woman. 'Mateo, please check downstairs and make sure we are not disturbed.'

One of the guards promptly went back down.

'What is your name?'

'It's Janet,' came the reply.

'Janet, I am looking for someone, and I hope you can help me.'

Janet nodded.

'I am looking for the man who was in charge here a few months ago. His name is Guran Qupi. Do you know of him?'

Janet nodded again, slowly this time.

'Tell me, Janet, do you know where Guran is?'

'N-no, ma'am, I don't. He disappeared a few months ago. They all did.'

'What do you mean, they all did?'

'Mister Qupi and all his men just... disappeared. One day they just weren't there anymore.'

The woman stared at Janet as she pondered on the information.

'Listen to me very carefully, Janet. I am not a woman to be trifled with, do you understand? How is it that dozens of men can simply disappear?' She looked at the remaining henchman and said, 'Esad, please take her left hand and hold it up.'

Esad did as he was told. Janet started shaking with fear.

'Please, I have done nothing,' she cried.

'Esad, break her little finger, will you?'

There was a loud snap as Esad immediately followed his orders, and a piercing cry from Janet at the suddenness of the pain. Her shaking became more pronounced as she sobbed.

'I will break every finger and then move to your feet and break every toe. When I am finished with the toes, I will break your arms and legs. I will not stop until I have broken every bone in your body. Do you understand me?'

'Y-yes, y-yes, I understand. Please!'

'Do you know why I'm angry, Janet?'

'N-no.'

'I am angry because you are making money from Qupi's business, yet you don't know what has happened to him. Is that not unfair?'

'What do you mean?'

'Guran Qupi has been missing for months now. And you are profiting from his absence, Janet, like a leech. Now, you see why I am angry?'

'Please, ma'am, I'm not making much money here, I am just the madam. I get paid by the hour,' Janet replied.

'Hmm, so you just work here, huh? So, who is running this establishment?'

Janet paused just long enough for her captor to nod to Esad again. Another loud crack was heard as the second finger was broken. This scream was louder than the first.

'P-please, no more!'

'I warned you. Answer my questions or I break bones. It is not difficult.'

'It's Brodie Dabbs, he's the man in charge,' Janet screamed, 'go and speak to him, I'm a nobody.'

'Where can I find this Brodie Dabbs, Janet?'

'I don't know, I only speak with him on the phone!'

'Where is your phone?'

Janet reached into her pocket with her undamaged hand and pulled out her mobile phone. She unlocked it and placed it on the table in front of her tormentor, who picked it up. She went through the recent calls and found the one she wanted. She dialled the number.

'Mister Dabbs, I presume? No, this isn't Janet. Janet is here with me, we're enjoying a chat, aren't we, Janet?'

She nodded to Esad, who broke another finger. Janet screamed again.

'Yes, that was Janet screaming. I am happy I have your attention, Mister Dabbs. It's important that I do, as we need to talk, soon.'

She listened for a few seconds.

'Mister Dabbs, my name is Leandra Qupi, and I am looking for my husband. I will burn every house in this damned city until I find him, starting with yours and your family's. Do we understand each other?'

She nodded to Esad again and had to raise her voice over the scream.

'Tomorrow, we meet. Call me on Janet's phone. She won't be needing it anymore.'

THE FIRE BRIGADE turned up thirty minutes later when the blaze was raging out of control. The once quiet street was now akin to a war zone as the valiant firefighters battled with the burning house. Neighbours stood outside their homes, watching in disbelief, wondering what had happened to the quiet, affable middle-aged lady who lived there. There were rumours, mainly because of the frequent visitors, but there had never been any problems—apart from the semi-naked man earlier—and she had a good relationship with them all, so they were now worried about her.

It wasn't until a week later that a frightened Janet eventually resurfaced, her hand bandaged and useless. She had decided to look for a different job, something a little less life-threatening. The neighbours noticed her hand shaking when she sipped her tea, but nobody asked how the fire had started or how her fingers had been broken. It was best they didn't know.

Leandra Qupi wanted to send a strong message in advance of her meeting with Brodie Dabbs. She was angry, and she wanted answers.

Dabbs called the morning after the fire, having been

made aware of the loss of the brothel. The house was a rental, so it wasn't his problem anymore, it was just a business address that was no longer fit for purpose. He was, however, unimpressed that Qupi's wife had decided on that action, guessing correctly that she was showing her strength and that she feared nobody.

'You didn't have to do that,' were his first words. 'I told you that I was happy to meet.'

'I don't care that you are happy to meet, Mister Dabbs, I want you to know that my intentions are very clear. Now, where do you feel safe enough to meet me? I will bring two men and you can do the same. Name the time and the place but be warned. Any treachery will be met by a force unlike anything you have ever seen. I have dozens of men here and a list of all the premises that my husband ran. I also know where you live, I know where your family lives, your sisters and your brother, all of them. Do not do anything stupid when we meet. Do we understand each other?'

'Meet me in one hour at the Miller and Carter in Loughton, the one on the roundabout at the junction of the A21 and Epping New Road. It's nice and busy there, we can meet in the main car park as you come in. We'll be in a silver Mercedes.'

Dabbs ended the call abruptly. He wasn't looking forward to the meeting but wanted to get it out of the way. His gang had taken over Qupi's operations relating to sex workers, logistics, and more. He had grown his empire and was now flourishing in the relatively peaceful east end of London. There were few challengers, and he wanted to keep it that way, maximum results with minimum effort.

'Damn that woman, I was hoping that bastard husband of hers was well and truly in our past. Get the car ready, Ernie.

Let's go and see this witch and see what else she's threatening.'

DABBS and his men were waiting in the car park in their Mercedes when the Volvo SUV arrived. It stopped twenty yards away and the front passenger got out to open the rear door for his boss. Leandra Qupi stepped out, wearing the same ankle-length coat, the hood down and her hands in her pockets. She was an imposing woman: tall, with her mousey-coloured hair in a ponytail, and had a steely-eyed look. Her expression was grim as she walked towards the Mercedes alone. She stopped halfway and waited.

Dabbs got out and walked towards her. His camel-hair overcoat was unbuttoned and flared behind him slightly as he approached.

'Let's get on with it, then. What do you want from me?' he asked.

'First, I want to know where my husband is.'

'I have no idea. What makes you think I would know?'

'I am not stupid, Mister Dabbs, so do not treat me that way. I know that you have taken over his businesses. You have benefitted very well since he disappeared. The fingers are all pointing to you.'

'Well, those fingers need to point somewhere else. I am not responsible for his disappearance; I simply did what any businessman would do when the opportunity arose. You would have done the same.'

'Yes, Mister Dabbs, I probably would. But here's the thing, the businesses that you have taken over were not my husband's, they were mine. You have stolen those businesses from *me*. I want them back and I want my money back.'

Dabbs was surprised at this, and it showed.

'Why so shocked, Mister Dabbs, did you not think a woman capable of running a criminal empire? He did everything for me. It's simple. I sent him here to grow our businesses, and he did a wonderful job—*for me*. Now, give everything back and there will be no problems. Are we clear?'

Dabbs paused for a few seconds before responding.

'How can I make this clear without being insulting? The answer is no. Hell, no. I run those businesses now and I will continue to do so. You can threaten all you like, Mrs Qupi, and you can bring an army over if you wish, but my army will always be bigger—and we will fight for every inch. It would be a fight you couldn't win.'

She stared at him, her expression unchanged. In that few seconds, Dabbs knew that they would be going to war with this woman.

'If that is your final word, then we have nothing further to say. Good day, Mister Dabbs. I will see you in hell.'

She walked back to the SUV, her guard ready with the rear door open. Dabbs watched as they drove away. It was only when they were out of sight that he returned to his car.

'Spread the word, Ernie; we're about to go to war with the Albanians — again.'

RICK WATTS ASKED Kendra to meet him in his office again. This time, when she arrived, she saw that DI Damian Dunne, Pablo Rothwell, and Jillian Petrou were also in attendance.

'Thanks for coming, all,' Dunne said as they took their

seats. 'This is a somewhat delicate situation and I want to make sure that only those of us in this room are aware and involved in the investigation. Are we clear on that?'

'Sir, you can rely on everyone in this room. I wouldn't have involved them otherwise,' Watts said.

'Thanks, Rick. That's good enough for me,' Dunne replied. 'What I need is a discreet investigation into the serious assault on my brother-in-law, Jimmy Crawford. He was tortured and had a finger cut off, several bones broken, and received a bunch of other injuries. They threatened his life and that of his wife, my sister Marion, if he came to the police. Hence the secrecy.'

'Sir, can we be sure that the attackers won't find out he's spoken to the police? I'm just thinking maybe we can send a couple of people to their house to watch over them, in case,' Pablo suggested.

'I've already taken care of that, Pablo, thanks. To be clear, the bosses are aware of my involvement and are okay with me doing so, providing I don't veer away from proper procedure, if you follow. They've given the go-ahead for my sister and her husband to go into protective custody until this is resolved. They're currently safely ensconced somewhere in the Lake District with a close protection officer looking after them. They're in good hands. I had to call in a favour for that.'

'That's good to know, guv,' Watts said. 'What do you want us to do moving forward?'

'I want to know the significance of the auction item, the jewelled eyepatch. I also want to know more about the beneficiaries of the sale. I understand it was a handful of youth clubs or something. Find out what you can, and we can go from there. There's no indication of who the attackers are so far, although Jimmy did give a description.'

'Can we get that, guv?' asked Kendra.

'Yes, it's pretty basic. There were two heavy bodyguard types, mid-thirties, wearing dark clothing and with cropped brown hair. The woman, though, he described very well. She's white European, slim build, mousey brown hair in a tight ponytail, wearing a long black quilted coat with white fur trim. She also had a fan with her, some kind of lace. She was clearly the boss and scared the hell out of him with her demeanour. Cold, calculating, stern, and ruthless is how he described her. Oh, and she had an accent, probably eastern European.'

'It's not great, but it's a start,' Watts said. Anything on the vehicle?'

'No, nothing. A white van was all he could remember. It was clean in the back, with two benches, one on either side, probably a hire van. Maybe we could check the CCTV in the area for the night of the attack?'

'If we can have the approximate time and date, I can get that checked, sir,' Kendra replied.

'Thanks, Kendra. I'll get that to you later.'

'Great. I appreciate your help with this. Keep me in the loop and hopefully we can find the culprits and deal with them quickly,' Dunne added. 'You're dismissed.'

The three detectives left the room, leaving Dunne alone with Rick Watts. Dunne closed the door and sat opposite the detective sergeant.

'Rick, it goes without saying that we need this investigation to be clean and professional. The bosses upstairs will be watching. Are you with me?'

'Yes, sir, of course,' said Watts, unsure why the DI felt the need to repeat himself.

'However, I won't be too upset if—when we catch the bastards—they get a good kicking when they decide to struggle. You good with that?'

Rick nodded. He was old-school and did not need to hear anything more.

'Yes, sir, I'm good with that.'

4

Kendra met with Andy and her dad that evening at Andy's house, where they enjoyed their usual pizza and bottled beers. It was a regular event and one they enjoyed. Although there was a great deal of trust in their team, the bond between the three of them, along with the trust they had in each other, was much stronger. The banter between Trevor and Andy was consistent and kept them on their toes, despite the frequent threats and the occasional slap to the back of the head. Andy and Kendra's romance had been put on hold; it was unfair for them to engage intimately while they fought against the most vicious of criminals in their quest for justice. Love would have to wait.

Their gathering that night was a more sombre affair as they discussed the implications of the past few days.

'Basically, what is happening is that the clubs will be visited by the police to ask questions about their windfall, but also to warn them of a potential threat,' Kendra said. 'What we're unsure of is whether the criminals will be visiting, but it's best not to take any chances and just *assume* they will, right?'

'Right,' said Trevor. 'I've warned the guys and gals to be aware and they'll be taking extra precautions.'

'Additionally,' she said, 'the police will be investigating the van that was used to kidnap the auctioneer. If we can get something going with your software, Andy, we can get a leg up on my colleagues. Maybe we can find out whose van it is and go from there.'

Andy's use of the *Cyclops* programme to gain access to local council CCTV cameras and their records had proven invaluable to date. If the security processes were poor, which council processes generally were, then he could access and control everything remotely.

'I can do that. I'll need the address, time and date, and the description of the van, though.'

'I have that. I'll send it to you later. Dad, the money from the auction. How was that going to be paid?'

'I submitted the eyepatch anonymously with instructions to pay the money into the bank accounts of the clubs. There are two different accounts, one for the boxing clubs and one for the women's. I'm the account holder on both but have given Charlie and Charmaine access as they are managing them for me.'

'They're both aware of the threat, right?'

'Yes. I've told them not to carry any banking info or cards around with them and to keep themselves safe, in case they're targeted.'

'Okay, good. And you?'

'What about me?' Trevor asked, bemused.

'What if they target you? Have you put the cards and info somewhere safe, like the others?'

Trevor paused before replying, sheepishly.

'No, I haven't.'

'Give them here,' Kendra said, her hand outstretched.

'Fine.'

He took out his wallet and removed two cards, which he handed to his daughter.

'We'll keep them here for now, until this is all over,' she added.

'Until we know who's behind this, we're gonna struggle to do much against them,' Andy said.

'I'm hoping it won't take long, Andy. Between what we can do here and my colleagues at the station, I think we should get an idea pretty soon. Then we can decide how to deal with it.'

'It goes without saying, make sure you're careful too, love, these are dangerous times for everyone involved. They've shown what they're capable of.'

'Trust me, Dad, I am aware of that. This one is going to keep me on my toes unlike anything I've ever dealt with.'

KENDRA'S WORDS WERE PROPHETIC. The following morning, she was back at her desk, sending the appropriate request forms to access the local council CCTV for the area around Christie's. The forms weren't difficult, but getting the permission took longer that it should have, which in this case was beneficial for her and her secretive team.

What she was concerned about was one of her team connecting the clubs to her dad and asking awkward questions. She needed a plan for that, just in case. She went over to Pablo Rothwell's desk and sat down to talk to him.

'How's it going, K?' he asked.

'Good, thanks, Pablo. When do you think you'll be going out to speak to those clubs?'

'Me and Jill will be popping out this afternoon, all being well. Looking forward to getting out and about with her again.'

Kendra smiled knowingly.

'You have a bit of a crush on her, don't you, Mister Rothwell?'

He looked around, alarmed that someone might overhear.

'Steady on, Kendra! It's not something I want to make public, you know?'

'Yes, I do, you sly weasel, you!'

She giggled when he blushed.

'It's that obvious, is it?'

'Well, I don't blame you. She's a hottie, and she takes no shit from anyone. She's just your type.'

'I'd appreciate it if you kept it quiet. I don't want to ruin it before I've had a chance to do something about it.'

'My advice is that you don't wait around too long, Pablo, otherwise someone else will come along and sweep her off her feet.'

'Why are you here again?' he asked, blushing again. Kendra laughed.

'Sorry, I couldn't resist it. I just want to find out when you're going so that we can have a catch-up after. There's not a lot to go on at the moment, is there?'

'No. You needn't worry; we'll report back if we find anything.'

'Great, I'll see you later,' she said, leaving him alone. He looked around again, hoping that their conversation hadn't been overheard.

Kendra went downstairs to get some fresh air, where she was able to phone Andy.

'Just so you know, the forms have gone in for the CCTV request, so we have maybe a couple of days before the access comes back. Over to you, Mister Genius.'

'Ah, that's so kind of you, Detective March. I will do my utmost to please you.'

'I won't lie, Andy. This one has me worried. I'm worried for my dad, just keep reminding him of the seriousness, will you?'

'Of course, K, don't worry about him. He's a tough nut to crack and also cleverer than we sometimes give him credit for.'

'Yep, that's my dad,' she said. 'I'll see you later.'

Walking back to the office, Kendra couldn't help but think of the strengthening of the relationship with her dad these past few months. She didn't want anything to endanger that.

~

ANDY DIDN'T TAKE LONG to access the Westminster Council CCTV unit. Surprisingly, there were no cameras in King Street itself, or at the top end of St James's Street, so Andy had to widen the search. The closest cameras were in Piccadilly, at the junction with Berkeley Street, and it was this camera that had a white Ford Transit turning left onto Piccadilly on the evening of the abduction, just a few minutes after Jimmy Crawford was grabbed from the street.

Andy zoomed in and was able to record the registration number. He was also able to obtain a somewhat fuzzy image of the driver, a large man with short, dark hair. He messaged Kendra with the registration number, as she would be able to check it on the police national computer, where all vehicle registrations were held, along with owner information.

He smiled when she replied with '*Thanks, Andy x*'.

Switching computers, he checked the CCTV live feed for the three boxing clubs in London, along with the one for the single mums. He was happy that all were working well, and the resolution was clear for identification purposes, in the event that something were to happen.

He then went onto the dark web and discreetly started asking his contacts if they had heard anything about the abduction. Nobody he knew had heard anything, so he asked them to get in touch if they did in the near future, with promises of rewards. That always did the trick, and he was rewarded with many thumbs-up.

'I guess we just have to wait and see what happens next, don't we?' he said out loud.

~

PABLO AND JILL arrived at the first club that afternoon, keen to start the furtive investigation and help their well-liked boss.

The door was answered by Charlie, who—thanks to a call from Trevor—had been expecting them.

'Can I help you?' he asked.

'Hello, sir. I'm Detective Constable Pablo Rothwell and my colleague here is Detective Jillian Petrou,' Pablo said. He showed his warrant card, as did Jill.

'What can I do for you, detectives?'

'We're hoping you can spare a few minutes to answer

some questions, is there somewhere we can sit and talk in private?' asked Jill.

'Of course, please come in,' Charlie said, opening the door fully.

The club was quiet. Charlie had told the youngsters to stay away for a few days. He allowed one or two of the older, more capable fighters to stay and keep him company. Today was Danny Baptiste's turn. He was busy at the speed ball, his arms a blur as he pummelled it mercilessly. He looked over at the guests and was still able to keep the momentum going despite averting his eyes from the ball.

'That kid looks like he knows his stuff,' Pablo said, a keen fan of the sport.

'He's a future champ, that one,' Charlie replied, 'make no mistake, in a couple of years, everyone will be talking about Danny Baptiste.'

'I'll remember that name, sir, for sure.'

Charlie led them to his office. He stepped out for a few seconds to grab an extra chair.

'Apologies for the lack of comfort, but, as you can see, it's not a priority here. My name is Charles Fenway, you can call me Charlie. I run this place.'

'Thanks, Charlie. This is a somewhat unusual case we're working on, and it may be that you can't help us much, but we have to ask. Someone recently donated an item to Christie's auction house and asked that the proceeds be split between a number of boxing clubs and a women's club. Were you aware of this?'

'I was, yes. Someone from Christie's actually called us, something to do with the Fraud Act or something. I had to confirm we were a genuine business and that the item wasn't being laundered.'

'Oh, good, so you were aware. Do you know how much was raised from the sale?'

'I don't, no. The guy, Mister Crawford, I think his name was, he didn't get back to me. I assumed it hadn't sold.'

'It was sold for a pretty penny. Half a million pounds, to be exact.'

'Bloody hell!' exclaimed Charlie. It was a genuine surprise for him.

'Yeah, that's a lot of money. A good quarter of that is coming your way, apparently.'

'Wow, that will help tremendously. This place, as you can see, could do with a lick of paint and some new equipment. That's fabulous news. When do you think they will pay?'

'That, we can't answer,' Jill said. 'We came more to warn you of a potential threat as a result of an incident relating to that item.'

'Oh, okay. What threat?'

'The auctioneer who was responsible for the item was abducted and seriously injured. The attackers were intent on finding out who had submitted the item for auction and also who was benefitting from it,' Jill continued. 'As the item was donated anonymously, they were given the names of the beneficiaries, namely your club and the others. We're concerned that they will be attempting to make a grab for that money.'

'Right, that is awkward, isn't it? Can't Christie's hold on to the funds until the investigation has been concluded?'

'We've spoken to them, and they can,' said Pablo. 'But the attackers won't know this. We have every reason to believe that you'll be visited as a result. Other than to find out if you knew anything more, we really just wanted to warn you of the potential threat. We're hoping you give us permission to put an alarm in the club so that you can get an instant response. You okay with that?'

'Yes, that's good of you, thank you.'

'Mister Fenway, Charlie, do you know who was likely to have donated the item? If we can find out, it would help our investigation tremendously,' Jill asked.

'Honestly, I don't have a clue. Maybe an ex-trainee who has succeeded in life, I have no idea. Whoever it was, if you find them, please do thank them. Their generosity is incredible.'

Pablo and Jill stood. They shook hands with Charlie.

'Thank you for your time, Charlie. If anything comes up in the meantime, please give us a ring on this number,' Pablo said, handing him a business card. 'We'll be in touch regarding the alarm.'

'I will, for sure, and thank you for keeping us informed. I'll be sure to warn everyone to be more cautious.'

Pablo and Jill left, having gained no further intelligence to assist with the investigation. They returned to their car and set off for the next club.

'I'm guessing that's pretty much the same response we'll get from the others,' Jill suggested. 'These people don't know anything and yet they're at risk of serious injury, if not worse.'

'Yeah, but at least we're giving them the heads-up. They know of the threat now so we may get a call. You don't know,' Pablo replied.

'Okay, on to the next one, driver,' Jill said.

∼

KENDRA WAS at her desk the following morning, armed with the registration number of the van. She carried on with her usual duties, waiting for the right time to log in to the PNC in a colleague's name in case of any future investigation.

When lunch time came, Gerrardo called over to her.

'Coming to the canteen, Kendra?'

'I'll be there in a few minutes, just finishing up a report,' she replied.

A few seconds after they had left, she logged onto the computer as Gerrardo, having noted the passwords of several colleagues in recent months. She quickly accessed the PNC and entered the registration number of the van.

Thought as much. The van came back as belonging to Allied Van Hire, a company based in Slough. She wrote down the information and quickly logged out. Before joining her colleagues for lunch, she messaged Andy with the information.

'Over to you x.'

Andy replied immediately with a thumbs-up and a wave. The hire company was all that Kendra could have supplied at this time. It was now down to him to find out who had hired the van, when, and for how long. *Cyclops* was useful for accessing CCTV systems, which he would attempt in this instance for the chance of getting better images of the driver and passengers. *Hades* was the system he used to find out more on the dark web, but until there was more intelligence, it wasn't particularly useful.

'Okay, Cyclops, let's see what you can do for us this time,' he murmured.

The hire company was based in a retail park on a main road, so the CCTV coverage for that area was excellent. He guessed that the van used for the abduction had probably been hired on the same day as the offence, so he went straight into the archives and started his search from 8.30 in the morning. As he fast-forwarded through, he'd stop when a van would leave the car park, check the number plate, and continue his search if it wasn't the one he was looking for.

At 3.27pm, his perseverance paid off when the Ford Transit slowly pulled out of the car park. He paused the feed and zoomed in to see the occupants. The camera feed was excellent, so he was able to get a good image of the driver, much clearer than the one from Westminster Council. He saved the image for Kendra and Trevor to view later. When he resumed the feed, he noticed that there was a car following closely behind, a silver Volvo SUV. Pausing the feed again, when he zoomed in he saw there were two occupants. The driver, a heavy-set man with short dark hair, a full beard, and wearing a dark jacket; and a woman in the passenger seat. She had lighter hair, which she wore in a ponytail, and was wearing a dark coat with a white fur-trimmed hood. Andy saved these images and made a record of the time, place, and vehicle details.

Not a lot else we can do for now, he thought, as he sent Kendra a message to come and see the images later, after work. He sent the same message to Trevor.

They were getting some information and intelligence, just not enough to do anything useful with at this time. It was a waiting game now, waiting to see what else came up and hoping that nothing bad would happen in the meantime.

His phone pinged.

'*I know who it is*,' said the message from Trevor. '*Will see you both later.*'

5

The three met at Andy's house in the early evening. Kendra had received the message and driven straight there from work, eager to hear the update. They sat in Andy's lounge, much tidier now than it had been months earlier, before Kendra had recruited him to their cause.

'Can you put us out of our misery, please, Dad?' Kendra said.

'Yeah, the suspense is killing me!' Andy added.

'I needed to tell you in person, as things are likely to get very nasty around here, very soon,' Trevor replied.

'We're here. Carry on,' Kendra said impatiently.

'This morning, I received a call from our old gangster friend, Brodie Dabbs. We've kept loosely in touch since the adventures we had with Qupi, remember? He was very happy with our help in taking over Qupi's operations.'

'How could we possibly forget?' said Andy.

'Anyway, one of his brothels was visited a couple of nights ago and later set on fire. The madam was tortured and had several fingers broken when questioned about the owner of the business. Well, she told them it was Brodie, and they called him to set up a meeting.'

'Who called him?' Kendra asked.

'You'll never believe this, but it was a lovely woman by the name of Leandra Qupi – Guran's wife.'

'What? Seriously?' said Andy, incredulous.

'Yep. She came over to find him and was on a mission. She told Brodie that the businesses he had taken over were in fact hers and not her husband's, and that her husband had been working for her all along. She wants them back, and Brodie naturally refused. She made all sorts of threats to burn him to the ground.'

'Wait, are you saying that the nasty, evil, vicious bastard that we sent to an African mine for the rest of his life was actually just a minion? And that his boss is even worse?' Kendra was stunned.

'That's exactly what I'm saying. We need to prepare for all sorts of shit to come flying our way.'

'Why? Do you think she'll find out about us and come after us?' asked Andy.

'Listen, we've covered our tracks brilliantly. You know that better than most. But do you want to take any chances? Knowing what these gangsters are like? We need to double down and be very careful until this eventually blows over.'

'I agree with you, Dad, no good can come from this; we can't take a ruthless gang on in an even fight. We have to pull back and think really carefully about how we move forward.'

'I think we need to call the team to the factory and give them the news, make sure they're cautious and on full alert. Any other suggestions?' said Trevor.

'I know you won't approve, but at some point, we may

need to take them on, albeit on our terms. I say we order some extra supplies, just in case that happens,' Andy said, 'and we should be creative about it.'

'Good call, Andy,' Kendra said. 'I think the police are going to be getting involved very soon. Maybe I can help from that angle and keep you informed. It may come to them taking the gang on. What do you think?'

'Yeah, I see no problem with that. Okay, let's start calling people and getting them in tomorrow afternoon,' Trevor said. 'Andy, start making a list, but hold off until after the meeting so we can add stuff.'

'I'll go to work tomorrow; I was supposed to be off but can work overtime because of the auctioneer case. If there are any updates, I'll be in touch,' Kendra said.

They started making the calls for the team to meet with them in a couple of hours. Within seconds, their phones started pinging in acknowledgement.

'Okay,' said Trevor, 'let's go and tell them the good news.'

∼

THE FACTORY HAD BEEN TRANSFORMED since Trevor had renovated the property with Qupi's money. Once a tired old commercial building with no prospects of a new tenant, Trevor had seen its potential immediately, primarily due to its location near Tilbury Docks, but also due to its remoteness. It was difficult to approach without being spotted. His decision to buy it was nothing short of genius, coming at a time when the owners were struggling during a financial downturn and needed funds urgently to survive.

Andy had installed cameras covering every approach and every angle of the building, inside and out. The building had been made as secure as modern technology would allow. It was now registered as a legitimate business, *Sherwood Solutions*, a security services company. Funds for the company were provided by the accounts Andy had set up in the Cayman Islands, where more than fifteen million pounds had been deposited after being appropriated from Qupi. It was this money that allowed the team to fund the initiative to dispense summary justice.

The front end of the building, affectionately called *the factory*, had been kitted out for the *Sherwood Solutions* business, with a reception area, meeting rooms, a lounge for clients and staff to relax, and several rooms set aside for the display of security products and solutions. Trevor had instigated a plan to recruit apprentices from the boxing clubs as a way of teaching them a trade and to earn a wage as they learned the trade. The business had started to grow and already had many clients, making it profitable and self-sustaining. Trevor's decision had been vindicated very quickly.

Behind the scenes, though, things were very different. There were now multiple secure rooms where their criminal 'guests' could be detained until a decision was made as to where to send them. There were storage rooms stocked with modern equipment and technology, most of which was designed to keep the team safe but also to give them an edge against the gangs. Andy had built an operations room where CCTV footage could be monitored and from which their operations could be managed. The factory was very well-equipped for current and future operations, which, however unpredictable, were challenging and dangerous. They even had a mooring within the grounds, giving them access to the river Thames and beyond. It was here that Andy had safely moored *Soggy Bottom* until it was required.

The team gathered in the loading bay a couple of hours later. Along with Trevor, Kendra, and Andy were the twins, Mo and Amir; Charmaine; Zoe; Greg; Charlie; and several trusted men and women from the boxing clubs.

'Thanks for coming at such short notice, guys and gals,' Trevor started. 'I've also left word with Darren and his mob from Walsall, who will be joining us in the next day or two. They were very happy to hear from us—*again*, nothing like an adventure in east London to tickle their fancy, eh?'

'What's going on, Trevor? You sounded pretty worried, and that isn't like you,' Charmaine pointed out.

'You're quite right about that, Charmaine. We find ourselves in a somewhat different situation than we have been used to. Most of you will remember the Qupis and what we had to do to get rid of them, right? Well, you'll be pleased to know that his wife has come looking for him. It turns out she is also his boss and is much nastier than he was.'

'Uh-oh, we did a good number on her old man. She's gonna be pissed with us, right?' Amir added.

'Yes, she is, Amir, if she finds out about us,' Kendra said. 'She's currently going after Brodie Dabbs and claiming her businesses back. He's not having that, so there's likely to be a war between them, which may drag us in due to our connections with Brodie.'

'We need you all to be prepared for the worst. Please be careful with whatever you're doing and report back anything out of the ordinary. When Darren and the guys turn up, we'll start planning ahead,' said Trevor.

'In the meantime, if any of you want to stay here while

this is going on, there's plenty of room, but we'll need to stock up on provisions,' Kendra added.

'Okay, I want you all to think of potential scenarios and how we can deal with them. Remember, she's going to have a small army at her disposal. Let's work on them having twenty to thirty-plus with them.

There were lots of nods as the seriousness hit home. There was no fear shown, only a determination not to let the bad guys win—ever.

∽

KENDRA LEFT them to it the following morning as she went to work. The development with Leandra Qupi had left her nervous about the immediate future. There were many unknowns, and it meant that too much was based on assumption rather than fact. Other than the fire at the brothel and the abduction and torture of the auctioneer, there was very little to go on. It was important to find out as much as possible and help her team, along with Brodie Dabbs, who had proven a useful ally.

Once she had logged onto the police systems, she was surprised to see an email from Westminster Council regarding the CCTV request, giving approval for examination. They had sent a link to the cameras covering a small area around the auction house, including the one that covered the junction with Piccadilly, showing the van turning left.

Thinking ahead, she noted the information from the footage and went to see Rick Watts.

'How's it going, Kendra?' he asked as she closed the door behind her.

'Regarding the DI's brother-in-law, I have a registration number of the van that was used to abduct him. I just wanted you to know in advance of me carrying out the relevant searches.'

'Oh, that's good work. Go for it, but keep it quiet. I don't want anyone outside of our small group knowing about it, okay?'

'Okay. I'll check the PNC first to see who it belongs to and then see about paying them a visit.'

'It's a green light from me. If you carry out the visit today, take someone with you: Pablo or Jillian. I don't want you going alone.'

'Understood. I'll update you later,' she said, leaving the office.

Back at her desk, she went through the motions of checking the PNC, noting the name and address of the hire company, and checking the company online for any red flags. When she had exhausted all the checks expected of her, she went and spoke to Jillian Petrou.

'Jill, I need to pay someone a visit and was hoping you could come with?'

'Sure. Where are we going?'

'Slough,' Kendra said. 'It's a van hire company.'

'Say no more,' Jill said, winking.

The drive took a little over an hour but was incident-free. As they parked up, Kendra saw that although the hire company was a small operation, they kept their offices and vehicles in great shape. They walked to the reception, where they were greeted by a young man.

'Good morning, ladies. My name is Sean. Welcome to Allied. How can I help this morning?'

'Good morning, Sean,' Kendra said, showing her police

badge. Jill did the same. 'I am DC March, and this is DC Petrou. We've come to ask for some information on a van that you hired a few days ago that was involved in a serious crime.'

Sean's smile disappeared. He switched to professional mode, which impressed Kendra.

'Happy to help, ma'am, what do you need?'

Jill placed a sheet of paper on the counter in front of him, showing the image of the van in Piccadilly, with the date and time stamped in the top corner.

'Can you please tell me who hired this van on this date and give me whatever information you have on record about them?'

'Let me check the system. It won't be a problem,' Sean said, typing away.

It didn't take long.

'Here we go. The van was hired five days ago by a Mister Mateo Ionescu. He used his passport and driver's license as identification and paid for one week in advance by visa credit card, along with a deposit of six hundred pounds.'

'Can you print out all that information, please?' Kendra asked.

'Yes, ma'am.' Sean typed again, and the printer under the counter whirred into action. A few seconds later, he handed the sheets over.

'Thank you, that is very useful. Can you remember anything else about this man or anyone who might have been with him?' Kendra asked.

'I can do better than that. I can show you the CCTV footage of him and his companions. I remember there was one other man and a woman waiting for him in another vehicle. They looked pretty serious, which is why I remember.'

'That would be fab, thanks, Sean,' she replied.

'Just give me a sec. I need to copy them to a disc in the back.'

He started typing again before going into the office behind him to retrieve the disc. It was a couple of minutes before he returned with it.

'Here you go. I took the liberty of marking the times on it to help speed things up for you.'

'Is the van back with you?' Jill asked.

'Yes, they dropped it off a couple of days ago. There was no problem with it at all and I returned his deposit.'

'Sean, you are a star, thank you. If you can think of anything else, or if you see them again, please call us on this number,' Jill said, handing him a business card.

'I will. Always happy to help the police.'

Back in the car, they looked at each other and smiled.

'He was helpful, wasn't he?' Jill said. 'I wish everyone was like that. We'd solve a ton more crimes.'

'Let's get back to the office and see what we can find out about Mister Ionescu, shall we?' Kendra said.

Her mind was a whir as she considered how to expedite getting the police involved. Knowing who was involved, she needed to find a way to link Leandra Qupi to this investigation, which would likely prompt another, separate investigation into the damage and chaos that she was likely to cause.

∽

ONCE THEY WERE BACK, it took just over an hour for Kendra to find the connection she needed. Interpol had records of Ionescu going back many years. It also had a list of associates and the name of his boss. She printed the information off and went straight to Rick.

'You'll like this,' she told him as she handed over the paper.

He read for a few seconds before responding.

'Hell's teeth!' he shouted, almost spilling his coffee. 'He works for Qupi? The bastard that disappeared without a trace?'

'Yes, well, not quite, he works for *Mrs* Qupi. Her name is Leandra Qupi, and she is the actual boss of the entire operation. It gets better.' She handed him a screenshot that she had printed off from the CCTV footage at Allied.

'So, we have Ionescu hiring the van, and these two are…?'

Kendra handed him another printout, this time from Interpol, showing the records for Leandra Qupi, including a mug shot from three years earlier.

'Shit, that's her! She's in the UK?'

'Yep, she is here, and apparently, if you check her record, a much nastier piece of work than her missing husband. It wouldn't surprise me if she's responsible for his disappearance. He's probably propping up a bridge support on a motorway somewhere.'

'I doubt that. This lot are as nasty as they get, but if she's behind the abduction and torture to locate the person who sold his precious eyepatch, then she's probably looking for him.'

'You're probably right, but this is a major development, isn't it?'

'Absolutely it is. I need to speak to the DI and see how he wants to proceed, it's more than my job's worth to start making decisions on subjects of this calibre.'

'In the meantime,' said Kendra, 'they're out there somewhere and we have no idea, so what do we do now?'

'I imagine the DI will have us put the word out. Give me some time to speak with him and I'll let you know, okay?'

'Okay. I'll speak to you in a couple of days when I'm back,' she said, 'but if things take a nasty turn, call me and I'll come sooner.'

'I will, thanks. And good work, Kendra,' Rick said as she left.

She said her goodbyes and left shortly afterwards, still trying to think ahead and plan for all eventualities. The Albanians were known for being ruthless but also unpredictable, so it would be an arduous task to stay one step ahead of them.

Hopefully they'll calm down for a few days while we take stock, she thought.

∼

DI DUNNE HAD DECIDED it was time to spread the word about Leandra Qupi and made sure all local police divisions were aware of her presence in London and of the crimes she had committed. They were informed that intelligence suggested more was to come, and for officers to approach with utmost caution, with back-up, if she was located. The registration number of the silver Volvo SUV was given out.

Unfortunately, that information was misheard by police constable Edwin Fisher, who was driving his panda car in the Chigwell area when the Volvo was spotted ahead of him. He was accompanied by PC Lina Redfern, a probationary officer with less than one year's service.

'There's that Volvo they put up a short while ago,' Fisher said, turning his blue lights on.

'Shouldn't we wait for back-up?' Lina said, having heard the full announcement over the radio.

'Nah, it's fine, nothing we can't manage.'

The Volvo pulled over at the side of the road, coincidentally near the Chigwell Police Sports Club.

'Can you call the station and get a PNC check confirmed, please?' Fisher asked, putting his cap on as he exited the vehicle.

As he approached the car, he saw three occupants: two men in the front, and a woman in the back. He approached the driver's side as the driver opened the window.

'What is it, officer?' he said in a thick accent.

Fisher looked at the passengers and decided there was a minor threat.

'Please step out of the vehicle, sir, and bring any identification documents with you.'

'What for, officer? I wasn't speeding or doing anything wrong, so why stop me?'

'This car was involved in an assault, sir, so I'd like to speak with you about it. Please step out of the car and—'

The knife thrust was so quick that Fisher didn't see it coming. He felt the blade enter his throat and slice sideways in one swift move. He collapsed to the ground, unable to breathe, drowning in his own blood as the SUV calmly drove away. There were no witnesses, not even his colleague, whose attention was on the radio rather than on her partner, who was dying on the ground twenty feet in front of her.

By the time she noticed his body, the Volvo was nowhere to be seen. She screamed for assistance on the radio before going to his aid, trying to stem the flow of blood from his throat. It did not help.

Kendra was woken at 11pm by Rick Watts.

'Sorry, Kendra, but I need you to come in early in the morning, if that's still okay with you? It's all kicked off and we need to focus on this case as a priority.'

'What's happened?'

'The silver Volvo was stopped by a unit out near Chigwell and instead of waiting for back-up, the officer decided to deal with it himself. They killed the poor bastard, Kendra, stabbed him in the bloody throat. He bled to death in the street with his probationer partner holding him. Bloody awful.'

'Oh, fuck, they really don't give a shit about anything or anyone, do they? They know what we're like with cop killers, but they were still happy to go ahead with it.'

'That's not all, K. Half an hour later, Jimmy Crawford's house was burned to the ground. They went straight there after killing the PC, so they must have realised the information about them had come from Crawford and decided to make good on Leandra Qupi's threat if he blabbed. They probably set it on fire thinking he was inside with his wife. Luckily, they're safe.'

'That's a blessing. It was good thinking by the boss. I'll be in first thing, Rick. I'll see you then.'

Well, that didn't take long, did it? she thought.

6

The station was abuzz with activity the following morning when Kendra arrived. The atmosphere was charged, as it always was when one of their own was killed, and most resources available—and some that weren't—were now being briefed throughout the station on PC Fisher's death and the suspects involved.

The *Serious Crime Unit* was no different, as she found out when she went to the third floor. The entire team had been called in early for their briefing and the room was busier than she had seen it for a while.

'Settle down, everyone. Let's get this briefing started. The DI wants a quick word before we go on to our taskings,' Rick Watts said, and the room fell quiet as everyone took their places.

'Thanks, Rick. Good morning to you all, thanks for coming in so early this morning. Most of you are unaware of some background information that is linked to this case, hence this briefing to bring you up to speed. The people that we are now hunting recently abducted and tortured an auctioneer from Christie's in London. That auctioneer is my brother-in-law, Jimmy Crawford,' DI Dunne said. There was a buzz of surprise from the room as a result.

'It's important that you know this,' he continued, 'as we managed to identify the culprits, and we were in the process of tracking them down. As a result of this, the poor PC in Chigwell was killed when he conducted a routine stop on them and ignored instructions to wait for back-up.'

There was more murmuring.

Watts stepped in. 'Okay, settle down, everyone, there's more.'

'The bosses upstairs are fully aware of my links to the first victim. After killing the PC, these bastards then went and torched Jimmy's house, reduced it to ashes.'

'Shit, is he okay, sir?' asked Wilf Baker.

'Yes, he and his wife are safe and well, thank you. We suspect that it was retribution for talking to the police, as he was warned against that when they released him. Unfortunately for them, my sister wouldn't have any of it and made sure I was informed immediately.'

'Who are these people, guv?' asked Nick McGuinness.

'You're all familiar with the infamous Qupi gang of a few months ago?'

There were more murmurs and plenty of nodding.

'They disappeared, didn't they?' McGuinness asked.

'They did. The entire gang just vanished, resulting in an investigation of their whereabouts, which, as you know, proved fruitless,' Dunne replied.

'And introduced us to the biggest wanker in the NCA,' added Pablo Rothwell, eliciting a number of laughs.

'That's right—all of it,' Dunne said. 'Well, you'll be happy to know that they haven't made a miraculous comeback, but his horrid, evil wife has come looking for him. For your information, it turns out that she's the *real* boss and is even nastier than her husband.'

'So how are they connected to all this, boss?' asked Norm Clarke.

'It turns out that it's all down to an item that was auctioned at Christie's, a bejewelled eyepatch. Apparently, it belonged to her husband, and she came looking for the person responsible for putting it up for auction, thinking it would help her find her husband. It was donated anonymously to benefit some charities in east London, hence Jimmy's abduction and torture, to gain information.'

'Make no mistake, this woman and her people are vicious killers. They didn't hesitate to kill PC Fisher and they won't stop until they have what they want,' Rick Watts added.

'We think she is looking for her husband, and it appears that she will leave no stone unturned in her efforts to find him. We're expecting a lot worse to come,' Dunne said.

'Guv, we've asked for panic alarms to be installed at the clubs and warned them that they may get visitors,' Jill said, suddenly concerned about their welfare.

'That's a good start. I think it may be prudent to go back and visit them all again, explain the seriousness and see if they want any further assistance. As much as I'd love to put a couple of people at each venue, we just don't have the manpower to do that, but also it may give them the idea that we're protecting something. I don't want to give them a target they don't already have.'

'Right then, as of this morning, unless otherwise instructed, you are all assigned to work on this case. I want to find as much intelligence as we can on this woman, and anyone associated with her. I want names and addresses of associates her husband had. I want all cases involving her husband checked for anything we may have missed, including his business interests, where he and his team lived, everything,' Watts said.

The team waited, pens at the ready, to see what they'd be assigned with.

'Pablo and Norm, you two go back and check all crime reports relating to Qupi and make a note of anything you think may help us,' Watts said.

'All received, Sarge,' Pablo replied.

'Wilf and Nick, you two liaise with other forces and agencies nationally who may have intel we've missed. That includes the NCA, okay?'

'Yep, we're on it,' said Nick.

'Jill and Kendra, I want you to start researching and contacting overseas agencies that are likely to have had dealings with Leandra Qupi and her gang. Try to get names, addresses, businesses, associates, the more the better.'

'Consider it done, Sarge,' Jill said, nodding at Kendra. Kendra was pleased to be working with her on this. She trusted her implicitly, and they had always worked well together.

'Rula, I want you to contact all ports and see if we can find their port of entry, airline used, or any other transport they may have used to come here, including Eurostar.'

'Will do, Rick.'

'Me and the boss will try to visit the clubs again, to reassure them that we're not far away. The intel unit downstairs are at your disposal, so don't be afraid to liaise with them if you need to. They may have useful contacts you can use, okay?'

The team all nodded, and the buzz returned as the briefing appeared to come to an end.

'Listen up, people,' Rick said. 'Before you go, the boss wants to say something more.'

'Whatever you do out there, do it carefully and with a partner. Do not underestimate these arseholes. Just be careful with everything that you do, okay?' DI Dunne told the hushed room.

His words hit home, and the buzz dissipated as everyone nodded solemnly, before going to their desks to start on their tasks.

They were all very aware of the dangers involved, and equally determined to see the culprits caught as soon as possible before anybody else died.

∼

'I JUST SPOKE WITH KENDRA AGAIN,' Trevor told Andy as they met in the canteen for a coffee. She had called them immediately after her phone conversation with Rick the previous night.

'How's it going? I imagine it's mental at work,' Andy replied.

'Yeah, they've mobilised pretty much everyone to look for the bastards.'

'Is there anything new to report?'

'Not really,' Trevor said. 'I think it's one of those where we just stay in the background and help out where we can.'

'Agreed. I guess she'll be busy there for a while, at least until they find them. What are you thinking about, moving forward? How can we help them?' Andy asked.

'Is there any way you can grab any CCTV from the area

around Jimmy Crawford's house? It's a long shot, but if we can get a direction of travel or anything like that, it may help.'

'Yeah, I can do that. I'll go back to the dark side and ask some folks if they've heard anything. Not sure it will help; the Albanians tend not to interact much, but I'll give it a go.'

'Okay, in the meantime, I'm going to send the team out to the clubs to keep them company in case anything happens. At least they'll have some back-up if the bastards turn up.'

'Okay, I'll catch up with you later. Oh, by the way, I know you said to hold fire, but I went ahead and ordered some basics, just in case,' Andy said as he stood to leave.

'Like what?' Trevor asked.

'If we're going to have a run-in with this lot, then we need more protection, so I ordered half a dozen more protective vests, some tactical helmets and goggles, masks, that sort of thing. I've also ordered a stash of highly illegal CS gas from the dark web and some retractable batons. I'm going to look into getting some more night-vision goggles too, amongst other things. As this develops, we can be flexible and stock up on more stuff. It will always come in handy.'

'Can't argue with that. You may want to get a few fire extinguishers, too. This woman likes to burn things.'

'Good call, Trev, I will. Right, I'm off to the dock to see about kitting *Soggy Bottom* out, too. You never know, eh?'

'Well, you proved me wrong with Marge. I guess I don't think of it as being weird anymore. Have at it,' Trevor said.

Who knows what we'll need to get through this, he thought, as he went on his way to see the rest of the team.

THE DAY PASSED QUICKLY as the police conducted their investigations. Nobody complained about the workload, and nobody grumbled about the lack of intelligence available about the Qupi matriarch.

Pablo and Norm were able to locate a number of crime reports relating to Leandra's husband, but very little intelligence was gleaned from them. Most reports were quickly closed due to lack of evidence or the witnesses having changed their minds, something that Qupi had always addressed diligently back in the day through threats and violence against entire families.

Wilf and Nick fared even worse, mainly due to Guran Qupi focusing his businesses in the east London area. If people wanted to do business from outside the area, then they'd go to him, never the other way around. The only records of Qupi being away from his patch were a couple of reports from Essex Police and one from Thames Valley Police, detailing serious assaults that had been carried out on victims who had not pressed charges and who would never point the finger at Guran Qupi. The police suspected his involvement but could do nothing about it. The victims were gamblers who were unable to pay their debts to the Albanian, so the reports were quickly closed and filed away as NFA — *No Further Action*.

Kendra and Jill fared slightly better. Kendra focused on Interpol and contacted her sources there, whilst Jill contacted the Albanian State Police. They would then check with SHISH, the state intelligence service, and also the primary intelligence service of Albania.

'If we can't find anything with this lot, we never will,' Kendra told Jill as they started their tasks. Working at adjoining desks, they were quickly up and running, contacting the agencies and carrying out open-source checks whilst waiting for the replies.

'This is interesting,' Jill said, pointing to a Google entry about Leandra and her husband. Kendra leaned over for a look.

'I did not know they had kids. That could be very useful information to have,' she said, looking at the family photo. The Qupis were at a gala in Tirana, where they had donated an undisclosed amount of money to rebuild a number of orphanages. Leandra was taller than her husband, athletically built, with a stern face, even in this photograph. In front of them were two children: a boy of approximately ten years of age, and a girl, maybe a year or two younger. The girl was smiling, but the boy, not unlike his parents, was not.

'I wonder if she brought the kids with her, or whether she left them back home. Who would be looking after them?' asked Jill.

'Hopefully, we'll get some answers when the police or Interpol get back to us,' Kendra replied.

'To be honest, there's very little else about them that is any use at all, a couple of newspaper reports in Albanian which I translated. Nothing to shout home about, one was an anonymous accusation of murder against the gang, but with no body found and no other evidence of wrongdoing, and the other was of a large brawl at a wedding that Guran Qupi had single-handedly stopped by beating unconscious the first two men he came across. No further action had been taken by the police because again, there were no witnesses willing to give evidence.'

'I guess we just wait for the replies, then, and hope they have something more. Hopefully, they haven't embedded too deeply into the police out there. That's a handy way of getting rid of records,' Kendra said.

'In that case, I think it's time for tea,' Jill said, 'and it's your round.'

∽

WHEN THEY RETURNED from their tea break thirty minutes later, there were messages waiting for them. One from the Albanian State Police for Jill, and the other from Interpol for Kendra. The detectives read the contents in silence, hoping to find some answers.

'Interpol has just sent an outline of the gang and a list of known gang members. It seems pretty historical, to be honest, and includes Guran Qupi and a few lieutenants of his,' Kendra said as she kept reading. She didn't tell Jill that she knew where Guran and his lieutenants were—deep underground in a mine in Central Africa, for life.

'I suppose that's better than nothing. Having some names is better than having none. We can give the list of names to Rula and see if any of them have shown up at any of our ports,' Jill replied.

'Yeah, I suppose. Anything on your end?'

'Actually, yes. Surprisingly, they have been quite forthcoming with plenty of intelligence about the Qupis. Including a nugget about Leandra herself. Did you know she's the daughter of a murdered judge?'

'Interesting. How old was she when he was murdered?' asked Kendra.

'She was in her late teens, according to this. The suspect was a local hoodlum she was dating, of whom her father disapproved. It wasn't long before the dad was found dead in his house, slumped over his desk with a kitchen knife through his heart. Strange thing is, there was no forced entry or signs of a struggle.'

'What, you think Leandra let her boyfriend in to kill her dad?' Kendra asked.

'Either that or she killed him herself. I wouldn't put it past her, she's one nasty bitch.'

'Wow, what a family.'

'So, we have a list of associates—including our friend Mateo Ionescu — several known home addresses in Albania, businesses, known travel. This is really quite comprehensive, and relatively up to date. The last entry was just ten days or so ago, when she's listed as leaving her Tirana home with her kids and a car full of suitcases.'

'Anything about travel plans? An airport or anything like that?'

'Sadly, no,' Jill said, 'they either came over land, which many do, and came through the Eurotunnel, or they used assumed names and false passports.'

'So, there's a chance her kids are here?' Kendra was surprised.

'Yep, I guess there is. Not a lot of trust within these gangs, is there?' Jill replied.

'Okay, let's go and speak to Rick about all this, see what he wants us to do with it.'

'I have a bad feeling about this one, Kendra.'

'Me too, Jill. Me too.'

∼

7

'I found something that may help,' Andy told Trevor.

'Okay, what is it?'

'As you know, there's no CCTV around the auctioneer's house, but there is on the local main road. It's only fleeting, but I have the Volvo SUV turning left and heading towards Epping. And I have them again at a roundabout, again towards Epping and away from London. That's all I have. There's no sign of them appearing in Epping or anywhere else, so I reckon they're between the area of Abridge and Epping itself.'

'I know that area well,' said Trevor. 'There's not a lot of housing there, so although it's not a small area, it shouldn't be hard to search for a car like that.'

'I'll see what I can find online. Maybe ask Kendra to do a check on the police systems to see if anything comes up. They're pretty brazen but they can't be stupid, so it wouldn't surprise me if they've hidden it away somewhere.'

'Where was the car registered?' asked Trevor.

'To a car dealership in Slough, so whoever bought it hasn't changed the registration documentation yet.'

'I guess that's where Kendra's lot will have the advantage over us. There's not much we can do really, Andy, until we get more intelligence to work with.'

'I agree. I'll continue asking around on the dark web, but there's not much of a response so far. If anyone knew anything, they'd be happy to sell that information. They're greedy bastards on there, so we know they can't help at this time.'

'Alright, well, I'm gonna go and help the guys out with the clubs. Darren and his mob are here now, so they can help out. That makes sixteen of us, not including some of the youngsters from the club, so we should be able to look after ourselves if it kicks off.'

'We'll be fine,' Andy replied. 'Say hi to the guys and I'll catch up with you later. I'll call Kendra now and update her.'

'Alright, mate, see you soon,' Trevor said, waving goodbye.

That is, I hope *we'll be fine*, Andy thought as he picked up the phone.

∽

MINUTES AFTER RECEIVING the information from Andy, Kendra went to the intelligence unit to get the results on checks done on the silver Volvo.

'Anything back yet?' she asked Sam Razey. Waving to the rest of the team, she sat down next to him.

'Nothing yet, Kendra. We sent a local unit to the car dealership that it's registered to, but they told us it had been sold for cash a week or so ago. They filled out the necessary documentation, but it looks like the buyers used false particulars.'

'Do me a favour, will you? Can you check with Essex police and ask them if they've had any reports about it? I reckon they may have dumped it after killing the PC, and leaving the area and going further out into Essex is what I'd do,' she said.

'I'll do more than that,' said Sam. 'My mate Derek works in the operations room. I'll get him to send some units to take a look. You never know.'

'Thanks, Sam. Give me a shout when you hear back.'

It would be some time before the Volvo would be tracked down.

∼

THEYDON BOIS WAS the second-to-last station at the eastern end of the Central Line, the last being Epping. It was a quaint village, conveniently placed for commuters in Central London who wanted to live somewhere much quieter, closer to the countryside. With a population of less than 4,000, it was easy to keep a low profile, with mostly expensive houses that were well-kept by their affluent owners.

One such house, located in a cul-de-sac near the green, hosted some of those affluent residents and many outsiders on a regular basis—secretly. Its location allowed for just enough privacy to keep the neighbours from shaking their heads in disapproval too often. The madam that ran the house also made a point of contributing regularly to village causes, ensured the house was well-maintained, and insisted on discretion from the clients.

It had been a favourite of Guran Qupi's before his disappearance and before Brodie Dabbs had taken over its management. As such, Leandra was aware of it and had made a beeline for the place just minutes after setting fire to Jimmy Crawford's house.

'I hope he and his wife are both in their beds when the fire reaches them,' she told Esad as they left the scene.

They drove straight onto the drive of the house in Theydon Bois and into the unlocked garage, hiding the Volvo from the world. Within minutes, the house was under their control. There were no clients at that time; just Elise, the madam; and one resident sex worker who was comfortably paying for her tuition at the Royal College of Art as a result.

Both women were strangled within minutes of the Albanians' arrival, their bodies unceremoniously dumped in the boot of the SUV. It would be days before the smell attracted anyone, by which time the gangsters would be long gone. Leandra took the key fob from Elise's body before it was taken to the garage, and pointed it at the car parked directly outside, a grey Volkswagen Golf. The lights flashed once, reassuring her that they were not without transport.

'We'll rest here a few hours and then go back to Palmers Green,' she told Mateo and Esad.

The North London safe house they were staying at was large enough to keep Leandra, her two children, and the nanny comfortable during their stay. The granny annexe, with its two rooms, was saved for Esad and Mateo, who rarely left her side. As her cousins, they were fiercely protective of her, and she had looked after them very well in return. The rest of the gang she had brought over were staying at three houses in the Wood Green area, a short five-minute drive from her luxurious safe house. The three houses were temporary homes to ten men, more than enough—in her eyes—to take on any opponents. They were armed to the teeth, thanks to the connections her husband had maintained, so it was unlikely they'd come across any opponents who would be as well equipped.

Leandra Qupi wanted three things. She wanted to know the whereabouts of her husband, and she wanted her business interests restored. After that, she wanted someone to pay—heavily.

'Brodie Dabbs will find out very quickly that I am not to be trifled with,' she told her men. 'Before we leave, prepare another message for him. We shall not stop until he gives everything back—and more.'

∼

'So, what we have at this time is a list of associates, businesses, addresses and previous history going back to her teens?' Rick Watts asked.

'Yes, said Kendra. 'We're working on the associates now. Rula is checking all ports for any sign of entry and we're starting to put a map together of any businesses here in the UK. Most of it is too historical to be of use, but we'll give it a shot.'

'Early indications are that another gang took over Qupi's businesses when he disappeared, but it's gonna be tough to get much out of them,' Jill added.

'We have little else to work with,' said Watts, 'so at some point, we may have to go and speak with them.'

'Will do. Is there anything from the others that's of any use?' Kendra asked.

'Not really. Now we have this list from the Albanians, we can try to match them to what Pablo and Norm have managed to find on the systems here. We may get lucky, you never know. Nothing much yet from the others. We just need a break, otherwise we'll never catch the bastards.'

'Alright, Sarge, we'll keep working on it and get back to you if we find anything new,' Jill said, before they left his office.

'If we can't find anything amongst this lot of associates, then we won't find diddly squat,' Jill said as they sat at their desks.

'Some of them must be up to date. I mean, Mateo Ionescu is one of them, right? I think we might be on the right track here. Let's just keep looking, one at a time,' Kendra said enthusiastically.

She was hoping to find as much as possible here so that the Metropolitan Police would do the dirty work and take this lot out of circulation quickly. At the moment, there was little that she or her secret team could do. This was too big and too dangerous, with little hope of success without the manpower and equipment that specialist units in the Met could bring to the party. Her role was simply to gather any useful intelligence to feed back to Andy and Trevor and make sure they were ready to spring into action if an opportunity arose for them to act.

'Bingo!' Jill exclaimed triumphantly, holding up a sheet of paper.

'What is it?'

'I'm pretty sure this is the other guy from the CCTV footage at the van hire,' she said, handing over a printout detailing another Albanian national.

'Esad Abazi, thirty-two years old, known for assault, firearms, drugs, prostitution. Is there anything he hasn't done?' Kendra asked.

'Look at the list of associates at the bottom,' Jill said, smugly.

'Mateo Ionescu is his brother? Cousins of Leandra Begu... wait, could it be the same Leandra?'

'Not a fan of coincidences, K, you know that.' Jill handed over another printout.

'It is the same Leandra! They all lived on the outskirts of Tirana, in the same house.' Kendra read on. 'And there was a third brother, Gjon Ionescu, who came to the UK and went to Leeds University to study engineering. He met fellow student Wendy Taylor there and they married two years later, allowing him to stay in the country. We know this because he was a person of interest when he arrived due to his family, so they made a point of updating his files.'

'This could be the key to finding her. Find the brother and it may lead us to her,' Jill said.

'It's much better than what we had, isn't it?'

'Unfortunately,' said Jill, 'there's no address, but I'm sure it won't take long to find them. I'll start with Wendy Taylor, aka Ionescu. You go with the brother.'

They both started searching feverishly on open source and police databases. After what seemed like an age, they sat back in their chairs and looked at each other, disappointed.

'Nothing's ever easy, is it?' Jill said.

'They can't just have disappeared, surely,' Kendra replied. 'We need to think about this differently.'

'How?'

'Well, for one, how many Albanians do so well as to come to the UK and study engineering at a prestigious university?'

'True, most of them come here illegally and never get that chance.'

'He then meets a local woman and falls in love, marries

her, and decides to settle in the UK. Knowing what he does about his criminal family, would he want to be associated with them?'

'What are you getting at, Kendra?'

'Does it say where Wendy Taylor was living *before* she left for university?' Kendra asked.

Jill searched through her printouts.

'Here we go. Yes, she's a north London girl from the Enfield area.'

'That's as good a place to start as any. If you search the electoral register, it'll tell us who lives there now,' Kendra said.

Jill went back to her computer and started her search.

'Okay, here we go. Green Dragon Lane, N21 2LB. We have a John and Wendy Jones. Hmm, another coincidence?'

'That's them, Jill! Gjon in English translates to John, and Ionescu loosely translates to Jones!'

'Really? John Jones? Not very original, is it? Sounds more like a porn star's name,' Jill said.

'Who gives a shit? That's a big breakthrough for us. Let's go and see Rick.'

'Lead the way, girl,' Jill said, bowing theatrically to the younger detective.

'Not you as well,' Kendra joked. 'Can't a girl just get a pat on the back nowadays instead of all this fawning and arse-licking?'

'Ooh, pardon me, Miss Fancy Pants who can't take a teeny tiny joke. Tell you what, I'll be all stern and moody with you from now on, shall I?'

'Now who can't take a joke?' Kendra laughed, giving her friend a hug. 'You're like the older sister that I always wanted,' she added.

'Luckily for you, I have a great sense of humour, so I won't take any offence at you taking offence,' Jill replied.

'Touché! And by the way, how do you know so much about porn star names?'

∼

'That's great work, ladies. Are you okay to follow up with a visit? By the time you get there, they should be home from work. Just add a couple of hours of overtime and I'll square it with duties,' Rick said.

'I can't do tonight, Rick. I have other plans,' Kendra said. 'Is there anyone else who can do it?'

'Yeah, no problem. I'll ask Pablo to tag along, if that's okay with you, Jill?'

'That works for me,' she said, blushing just enough for Kendra to notice.

'Okay, go and find him and get yourselves over to sunny Enfield.'

As they walked back to their desks, Kendra decided to be a little mischievous.

'You're still single, aren't you?'

'Yes, why do you ask?' Jill replied. 'Wait, you're not asking me out, are you?'

'You should be so lucky!' Kendra smiled. 'No, the reason I ask is that I think Pablo's got the hots for you.'

Jill looked around, horrified that someone had overheard them.

'What? Keep your voice down, will you?'

Kendra laughed.

'You like him too!' she whispered accusingly, stifling a laugh.

'Not funny, Kendra March, please keep your opinions to yourself, otherwise I'll use some of that Aikido I know so well.'

'Look at your face. I've never seen it so red. Detective Constable Jillian Petrou, as I live and breathe, you have the proper hots for Pablo Rothwell!'

'Seriously, I can do some proper damage to you if you don't keep your voice down,' Jill said, again looking around in case anyone overheard.

'Tell you what. I promise to keep my mouth shut if you promise you'll do something about Pablo. You know how shy he is. You two should get together. You'd be great for each other.'

Jill stopped and stared at her, serious and ready to pounce with some martial arts moves. She suddenly relaxed and looked around once more.

'Do you think so?' she whispered.

Kendra stifled another laugh and gave her friend a hug.

'Yes, Jill, I do,' she whispered back.

'Well, that's alright, then, I won't do any martial arts nastiness to you. I'll have a word with him and see where it goes, but I make no promises, okay? Just don't say anything to anyone else.'

Kendra mimicked zipping her mouth and crossing her heart, before turning and walking back to her desk. When she sat, she could see Jill pause, before straightening her posture and walking determinedly towards Pablo's desk.

'Go get him, girl,' Kendra whispered to herself.

Inside, she was slightly envious. This was what she had sacrificed when making the promise to Andy to stay friends. They both had strong feelings, but had acted with their heads instead of their hearts. Only time would tell whether they had made the right decision, and at least they had time on their hands. Or so she hoped. The situation with Leandra Qupi made her very nervous, more so than when they were dealing with her vicious husband.

She picked up her phone and dialled Andy's number.

'Fancy a pizza and beer night?'

'Count me in,' he replied. 'Shall I call your dad?'

'No, he can miss out tonight. We'll call him later. There's a lot going on and he needs to focus on keeping those clubs safe.'

'Alright, that works for me. I'll see you later.'

The call ended, and Kendra sat back in her chair, mulling over the day's events. There was certainly a lot going on, but was it enough for the police to make an impact?

∼

TREVOR WAS MAKING THE ROUNDS. He had visited three boxing clubs and the club he'd set up for vulnerable single women who he was hoping to later integrate with the other clubs. It had proven a roaring success, especially with Charmaine and Zoe's assistance.

He had asked Darren and the twins to assist with checking the premises and sticking around for extra support. It was all they could do at the moment while the police were investigating. Trevor was in no doubt that the Albanians would visit, he just had no idea when. Although he was preparing for the worst, it didn't feel like it was ever going to be enough.

'Seriously, Trev, stop worrying about us. Everyone in the clubs knows how to fight,' Mo had told him.

'Yeah, I get that, but knowing how to fight is one thing;

knowing how to deal with guns is another–and this lot may be coming with guns,' he had replied.

'Well, we'll just keep the doors locked and won't let anyone in unless we know them. Easy, isn't it?'

Having seen the best-laid plans go down the toilet, Trevor was sceptical about that tactic, but happy that the clubs were listening and being careful.

When he had finished his rounds, he called Kendra.

'I'm at Andy's giving him an update, Dad. We've found some names and addresses for associates that the Met will follow up on, otherwise there's not a lot to report. Are you staying at the flat tonight?'

'Yeah, I'm heading there now,' he said. 'Be about an hour.'

'Okay, I'll see you there later.'

Staying with Kendra was becoming a regular occurrence and one that he enjoyed, like a comfort blanket during these hectic months. He had considered buying a larger place for them to share but decided against it, considering her feelings towards Andy. He smiled, reassured that she was in safe hands if anything were to happen to him. The knot in his stomach was still holding strong.

∼

8

Having not heard from his Theydon Bois operation, Brodie Dabbs had feared the worst and sent a car to check on it the next day. The grey Land Rover pulled up onto the drive and parked. The driver and his passenger got out and had a cursory look around. It was, as expected, quiet, with nobody around. Tall hedges on either side of the house kept it well screened from its immediate neighbours, and there was no movement in any of the windows opposite. They had tried calling Elise several times with no luck, hence the visit.

The driver rang the doorbell, which chimed melodically within. There was no reply after several attempts. He looked through the letterbox and saw that the place had been trashed inside.

'Something's happened in there, Jim. We need to get inside,' the driver said.

'Let me have a go,' Jim replied. His partner moved to one side.

Jim had a last look around in case anyone was watching,

before he charged the wooden front door with his hefty bulk. The door frame gave way and splintered as he fell forward to the floor, eliciting a grunt. As he turned to his companion, his expression changed from one of hilarity at his fall, to one of horror as the trap that Leandra's henchmen had set was activated. The flame that he saw now spurted from the top of the door frame where it had ignited when he sprung the trap, along the thin, petrol-soaked rope towards the kitchen and its destination–the gas cooker. At the same instant he smelled the gas, which just a couple of seconds later ignited in a ferocious fireball, giving him no chance of escape. A moment later he was dead, his skin burned to a crisp, his arm outstretched in one last futile attempt for assistance from his friend.

His friend was much luckier. Having stood to one side to allow him to charge for the door had saved his life. The explosion had sent him flying into the front garden, where he had landed in an unconscious heap, singed but very much alive.

When he woke, a few minutes later, the house was in flames, the heat so ferocious that he had to back off onto the road, where several neighbours stood; some on their phones, calling the emergency services.

The fire took several hours to put out. It had engulfed the entire house and the garage, just as Leandra had demanded, thanks to the petrol that her guards had liberally spread throughout. Jim's remains were taken away, his identity and information given to the police and the fire brigade by his surviving friend. It would be another day before the fire investigator would discover the burned remains of the two women in the boot of the charred Volvo SUV.

It was a message that Brodie Dabbs would never forget, especially as Jim was his younger brother.

∼

'How do you want to do this, Jill?' Pablo asked, as they arrived at their destination. Green Dragon Lane in Enfield, north London, was an affluent area, with huge, detached houses at one end, where they now knew Leandra Qupi's brother lived with his wife.

'I'm happy to take the lead, if you're okay with that?' she said.

'Sure, let's go.'

Pablo locked the car, and they walked up the long front drive to the door. Jill rang the doorbell. The door was quickly answered by a slim blonde in her mid-thirties who was in a blue dress and was somewhat tired looking.

'Mrs Jones?' asked Jill.

'Yes, how can I help you?'

'I'm DC Jillian Petrou and my partner here is DC Pablo Rothwell.' They both showed their warrant cards. 'We'd like to ask you a few questions, if we may?'

'What about?' came the reply, as Wendy Jones closed the door slightly, clearly defensive.

'Can we come in?' Pablo asked.

'Wait here while I get my husband,' Jones said, closing the door before they had a chance to respond.

'Well, that was a bit weird,' said Pablo.

The door was opened again, this time by a well-built, grey-haired man who wore jeans and a patterned cardigan over a white polo shirt.

'Can I help you, officers?' the tall man said, in a slight accent.

'Mister Jones, I presume?' said Jill.

'That's right.'

'Mister Jones, is it alright if we come inside and talk with you? We have a few questions regarding an investigation I believe you can assist us with.'

'If it's alright with you, I'd rather just talk here,' he replied, also defensively.

'Sir, we're not here to cause any problems and you are not under investigation,' Pablo reassured him.

'Then why are you here?'

There was a commotion inside the house as two young children ran into the hallway and up the stairs, shouting loudly at each other as they played their game of chase.

'Children, come here at once,' shouted Wendy Jones, out of their line of sight.

The young girl replied in a foreign language, clearly upset that their game had been curtailed. The boy then added his displeasure.

John Jones turned and spoke to the children harshly in the same language, and their dissent ceased immediately.

'Sorry about that,' he said, turning back to Jill, 'we are looking after a friend's children, and they are a little too excitable for us.'

'That's okay, sir, I understand. I often babysit my brother's kids and they're a nightmare. I just leave them to it sometimes,' Jill replied.

Jones smiled understandingly.

'Do they play well with your kids?' asked Pablo.

'We don't have any, so we do what we can to keep them

amused. It's a relief that we have so many television channels and tablets to keep them busy nowadays, isn't it?'

'Yes, sir, it absolutely is,' Pablo said.

'Sir,' said Jill, 'we're here to ask if you've heard anything about a recent assault on one of your neighbours.'

Taken by surprise, John Jones shook his head, confused.

'No, I haven't heard a thing. I didn't even know anyone had been assaulted, to be honest. We keep ourselves to ourselves.'

'That's fine, sir,' said Jill. 'That's all we wanted to know. Thank you for your help.'

'And good luck with the kids,' Pablo added. 'I hope they don't wear you out too much.'

'Me too! They'll be gone next week, so I'm sure we can handle them until then. Thank you, officers, good evening.'

They walked back down the path as Jones closed the door behind them.

'I'm a little confused, Jill. Why did you lie about the reason we were here?'

'Because, Detective Rothwell, the children we just saw are almost certainly Leandra Qupi's kids and I don't want him to know we're looking for her. That way, we can keep an eye on the house and wait for her to come here. Let me call Rick and let him know.'

She made the call.

'Sarge, we think that Leandra's kids are being looked after by her brother while she's out turning east London into a warzone. We didn't let on that we were there for her, so maybe we should sort something out to keep an eye on the house?'

'That's great work, Jill,' Rick said. 'I'll start the paperwork at this end and get a surveillance team up there tonight.

Hopefully, we can get an eyeball on the house and see if our friend Leandra decides to visit.'

'Thanks, Rick. We're heading back now and will catch up with you tomorrow,' she replied.

Pablo remained silent for a few seconds before nodding in appreciation.

'You're not just a pretty face, detective Petrou,' he said, before he realised what he'd said and started to blush.

'I... I mean... I... sorry, I didn't mean...'

'You don't think I'm a pretty face?' Jill asked innocently, teasing him.

'Yes, yes, I do! I mean... sorry, I... oh hell, I'm useless at this.' They reached the car, opening the doors.

As they sat in silence, Jill turned to him as he stared ahead, his shoulders slumped, wondering what to do next.

'It's alright, Pablo. I forgive you. And yes, I will,' she said.

'Thanks, Jill. Sorry about that, sometimes I don't... yes you will *what*?' he asked, his brow furrowed.

'I will go out for a coffee with you after work,' she said, turning to face the front.

'What? I mean, really? Like as on a date?'

'Yes, Pablo, as on a date. It will be our first, and if you say anything to anyone, I'll not be pleased,' she said, turning back to him and smiling. She grinned as he blushed, all in a fluster. The grin then turned into a laugh.

'Stop being so embarrassed, Pablo, it's just a coffee! You may not even like me and that will be the end of it, okay? So don't make such a big deal out of it.'

'I doubt that very much, Jill,' he replied confidently, his face returning to its normal shade. It was his turn to smile.

~

WHEN BRODIE DABBS found out about the death of his younger brother, he was initially distraught, lashing out and smashing a defenceless computer monitor to pieces. Hours later, when he had calmed down enough to engage with his men, he rose from his office chair and called in his most trusted.

'That Albanian bitch has made it clear that she'll be coming after everything her husband ran. I want you to call all the businesses and let them know there may be problems ahead. If they want some back-up, then we'll send it. We must protect our assets,' he told them.

'Do you want us to arm them, boss?' asked one.

Dabbs stared at him, his resolve growing alongside his fury.

'Damn right I want them armed. Now get to it.'

When the men had left, he sat back down in his chair and slumped forward, his head in his hands, sobbing quietly. It didn't last long. The fury returned, and he stood up, holding a picture of the two of them together.

'I promise you this, Jim. I will not rest until those bastards are dead and buried, all of them.'

The second he had made his vow, his phone rang.

'What is it?' he asked Brad, one of his confidants who had left earlier.

'They've attacked the Hornchurch and Romford operations, boss. We're too late. Both houses are on fire. A couple of our people have been beaten up but are still alive, and they were given a message to send you, boss.'

'Go on, then, spit it out!'

'When we have burnt down your operations, we will start burning your homes and your families' homes. Give everything back that belongs to me or face the consequences.'

Brodie ended the call and paced around his office, trying hard to think of the next step before his entire empire was burned to the ground. He unlocked his phone and called someone who he knew could help.

'Trev, the Albanians are burning us to the ground. They killed young Jimmy and are destroying everything. I need your help, mate.'

∼

TREVOR MET with Kendra and Andy at ten in the morning, a couple of hours before Kendra was due to start her next shift.

'This situation is escalating at a rate of knots,' he told them. 'Qupi's wife is going around and burning all the brothels that Brodie Dabbs runs, mainly the ones her husband used to operate. She's killed several people doing it, too, and clearly doesn't give a shit. She's threatened Brodie with the total destruction of his businesses and then said she'd be going after their families, too.'

'What's he planning to do?' Kendra asked.

'He's mobilising his people, but he's not sure how many Albanians he'll be facing, so he's asked for our help.'

'Dad, we're only a small operation, if we abandon the clubs to help Brodie it'll leave our people defenceless.'

'I know that, K, but we have to help him. We wouldn't have lasted an hour without his help against Qupi, remember? We have to take a chance and hope she's concentrating on Brodie's operations.'

'Still, we're less than twenty people, Trev. How can we help him? No doubt he'll be armed by now, taking fewer chances, so how is he expecting us to help?' asked Andy.

'He's asked us to send people to his other businesses, the

gambling clubs and a couple of cash businesses that he's worried about. At the moment, they've only targeted the brothels, so he's worried they'll escalate even further to the rest of them.'

'And if they turn up, what is he expecting our people to do against armed gangsters?' Kendra asked.

'He wants us to *do our thing*,' he said, doing air quotes.

'Well, that's clear,' Andy said.

'Look,' said Trevor, 'we were clever against the husband when we started this, and just as smart against the Russians in Hackney. We took on a much larger biker gang, too, and on each occasion, we were outnumbered. But we managed to beat them, didn't we? Let's put our heads together and come up with something cunning for this lot. What do you think?'

'The problem is, Trev, that this time we are on the defensive, trying to protect people. The successes we had before were offensive each time, we had the momentum and the time to do things on our terms. This is a very different situation, and not on our terms in any way,' Andy replied.

'Agreed, but we have to be flexible, and we must help Brodie. If this woman gets her way, there'll be chaos in London and our jobs will be so much tougher than they are now. We have to look at ways of changing it to be on our terms.'

'Alright, Dad, we'll have a think and come up with something,' Kendra said, 'but don't be surprised if you don't like it.'

∼

KENDRA MADE her way to work, her mind working overtime as she tried to come up with ideas on how to protect Brodie Dabbs' businesses and people–along with her own. It was a tough one, but she was determined to come up with options that she'd later run by Andy and Trevor.

There was a message for her to go and see Rick Watts as soon as she arrived at work. Jill and Pablo were already there when she reached his office.

'Come in, K,' Watts said. 'Please, close the door behind you.'

'How's everyone doing?' Kendra asked. She could see from their expressions that something was wrong. 'What have I missed?'

'If you recall, we found out that another gang had taken over the Qupi operations when they vanished,' Watts started.

'We now know it was Brodie Dabbs who took over,' Pablo said. 'We were going to speak with him in a day or two on the off chance he knew something about Leandra Qupi being here.'

'Okay, so how does that affect what we're doing?' she asked, confused.

'For one, Dabbs contacted New Scotland Yard and asked to speak to the commissioner, which had a few people laughing—at first. When he was eventually put through to a senior officer, he explained that Leandra Qupi has started systematically burning his operations to the ground, killing some people in the process.'

'What? A gangster called the police for help?' she asked, astounded, especially knowing Dabbs had asked for their help as well. 'He must be desperate.'

'One of those killed was his younger brother. He was a nasty piece of work, don't get me wrong, but it was very close to home and enraged Dabbs. They also murdered a couple of sex workers just outside London, in Theydon Bois, where his brother was killed. And he told the senior officer that she has since burned another two premises.'

'Why?' asked Jill. 'Does she think Dabbs knows where her husband is?'

'According to the call, he said she's after her husband's operations. She wants them back and she will stop at nothing until she succeeds, whilst destroying them one at a time just to take them out of Dabbs' hands. She doesn't care that she's also losing them, as long as he doesn't have them.'

'So, what are we supposed to do about it?' Kendra asked.

Watts smiled before speaking. 'He insisted on his taxpayer rights and ordered that the Met take care of her.'

'You can't fault him for trying,' Pablo said, also grinning.

'Honestly, I can't see this situation ending up well for anyone,' Watts added. 'And before you ask, I suspect that he's cut a deal with Scotland Yard that will undermine some competitor operations in London in exchange for our helping him now.'

'Wow, I suppose we shouldn't be surprised that we're cutting deals with gangsters nowadays. I suppose it's better the devil you know and all that,' Pablo said.

'Rather him than the Albanians,' Watts replied.

'So, what do we do now?' Kendra asked. She was pleased that the Met's position had escalated so much, it meant the onus would be on the organisation to respond appropriately very soon.

'He's asked for protection of his operations. We initially said no because it would be ridiculous for the police to be seen to protect operational brothels, but eventually, they agreed to covertly protect them if they were closed for business. Until it blows over, at least.'

'How many are there? And where will the staff come from to watch over them?' asked Jill.

'Apparently,' said Watts, 'there is a number that haven't been destroyed. Dabbs took over Qupi's, of which there were seven, and he had four of his own, for a total of eleven.'

'So, we're looking at fourteen people per shift, minimum?' Kendra asked. Fortunately, only the brothels were mentioned so she needn't have worried about any overlap with what they were doing with the other businesses.

'That's right, and unfortunately, some of that is going to come to us. There will be overtime, but it will be a tough way of earning it on top of everything else we're doing,' he said.

'What do we do in the meantime regarding the maniac wife?' Jill asked. 'It's all well and good protecting gangsters, but we're still investigating a cop killer and murderer, aren't we?'

'Absolutely, Jill, which brings me to my next point. Yes, we may have to help with protection, but in the meantime, we will intensify our investigation; if we can catch them before they kill anybody else then we've done our job, right?'

'Sarge, can I make a suggestion?' Kendra asked.

'Sure.'

'I know this may sound unethical, but if we know where her kids are, can we take them into protective custody?'

'I wish it were that easy, K. Sadly, while they are under the protection of family there isn't a lot we can do. The kids seemed happy enough when Jill and Pablo saw them, so there's no reason to pull them out of there. Not now, anyway. We keep the surveillance operation going and hope that when Leandra eventually turns up, we can grab her without too much fallout.'

'So, what can we investigate in the meantime?' she asked.

'Look deeper into the other associates and addresses for a start. Also, there's a car missing from the crime scene in Theydon Bois. It's likely they took it when they hid the Volvo there. Check all the ANPR records and see if we can get an idea of where they could be. Any clue is welcome at this time.'

'I'll check the ANPR, Sarge,' Pablo said. 'I have a mate at the traffic ops room who may be able to help out.'

Automatic Number Plate Recognition cameras were installed at strategic locations covering major routes in and out of London. They were installed to facilitate the swift detection and recognition of vehicles, allowing for mobile units to intercept if crimes had been or were being committed. They were a fantastic asset in the fight against crime and used regularly in all types of investigations.

'That Volvo was reported stolen, by the way. We're unable to trace the person who hired it. He reported it to the hire company and told them he couldn't speak good English and asked if they could do it. Somewhat suspicious; maybe they're looking for potential alibis in case they're caught later?'

'Maybe, who knows? I'll leave you to find out what you can. Let me know if anything comes up,' Watts added as they stood to leave. 'It goes without saying, whatever you do, do it safely.'

'I'll catch up with you guys later,' Kendra said. 'I've got a call to make that can't wait.'

'See you in a bit, K,' Jill replied.

Kendra went out to the back yard and called Andy to update him.

'Make sure you pass it on to Dad, I need to go back inside now. I know you can't access ANPR but maybe you can get a direction of travel again like you did before? It all helps, and I can feed it in here for them to deal with.'

'No problem. Leave it with me,' Andy replied. 'See you later, maybe?'

'Not sure, Andy, it's pretty manic here. They're giving everyone as much overtime as they want. It's been a while since that happened.'

'Well, it's a murderous, cop-killing gangster going on a rampage in London. If they can't find overtime for that, then we should all pack our cases and move abroad.'

Kendra laughed.

'I'll try to call later when I know more. Don't forget to call my dad and let him know,' she said, ending the call.

∽

PABLO'S CONTACT at the ANPR unit proved fruitful. The car was spotted passing several points along the A406 North Circular Road, a notoriously busy road. The ANPR unit's last record of the vehicle was as it passed its cameras just before the junction with the A10 Great Cambridge Road, now noted and passed on to all units as the last known location.

It would help narrow down the search to an area where officers could be better deployed, so although there was plenty of work still to do, it was a positive contact.

∽

9

In the main office, the Serious Crimes Unit checked every possible lead to determine the whereabouts of the murderers. Associates' photos and information were put on the whiteboard and marked with all known addresses, business interests, or family members in the London area and suburbs. Every possible location, however remote, was marked on the large map with different-coloured pins marking the type of contact, whether family, business, or address. It soon became clear that a pattern was developing.

'Almost every pin is in the Tottenham, Wood Green, Enfield, or Barnet areas,' Wilf Baker said as he added a new pin.

'So, we're looking at north London as a possible hideout, which narrows it down—not,' added Nick McGuinness.

'Stop being so negative, Nick,' said Wilf. 'We'll narrow it down even more, don't you worry. If we can find out where that VW Golf is, then we're golden.'

'Mate, I love your enthusiasm, but if we're going to find a

car—which, by the way, is like looking for a needle in a haystack—then we're gonna need help.'

'Really? You thought we were going to go out and look for it ourselves?'

'Don't be daft. You know that's not what I meant. The uniforms will have to do their bit, but I think we need even more help. Maybe get the Neighbourhood Watch schemes to chip in?'

Wilf whistled and shook his head.

'Mate, knowing how dangerous the Albanians are, do you think it's a good idea to ask Joe Bloggs to go out looking for a car they've been using? I don't think so. That's asking for trouble.'

'Yeah, fair enough. Can you think of anyone else?' Nick asked.

'Perhaps. I'll ask the training unit. Maybe they'd be willing to send the recruits out for a few hours. I know, I know, they'd likely be just as impulsive as Joe Bloggs, but the trainers can give very strict instructions, from what I remember.'

'Yeah, that sounds fair. I'll run it by Rick and pop to the training unit if he green lights it,'

'Good man. Oh, on the way back, stop off and get some doughnuts, will you?'

~

THE SEARCH for the Volkswagen Golf started in earnest within the hour. Strict instructions were given to all officers involved in the search. Under no circumstances were they to approach it, but simply call for assistance and wait. Kendra went with Rick to brief the uniformed officers starting the next shift, whilst Nick and Wilf briefed the training unit and the recruits who were on their probationary training.

Rick and Kendra also contacted satellite stations and local boroughs to make them aware and to give the same instructions if the car was seen in neighbouring areas.

When the briefings had concluded and all officers given their patrol sectors, Kendra found a few minutes to call Andy.

'Is it still manic there?' he asked.

'Yep. We've briefed pretty much everyone in the northeast of London, so a lot of officers will be looking for the car whilst on their routine patrols. Hopefully, we'll get lucky.'

'Since they're confident of the likely area that the car will be, I can have a look at local CCTV and see if we can narrow it down,' Andy said.

'Thanks, my lot need all the help they can get at the moment. I'll pass it on as an anonymous call or something. Is Dad up to speed with everything?'

'Yeah, he's been driving people to the clubs and popping from one to the other to make sure everyone is alright.'

'Okay, great, I'll be in touch if I hear anything else.'

Andy logged onto Cyclops and proceeded to hack into the Haringey Council's new state-of-the-art CCTV control room. The council had recently spent millions on it and on increasing and upgrading their cameras throughout the borough, so Andy expected it to be more difficult than he was used to. He was not wrong.

Cyclops was a very useful programme that utilised 'out of the box' methods to hack into CCTV systems and control rooms. It was very effective and was regularly updated and improved by Andy's dark web associates, who charged a lot of money for the software and all updates. It was worth it, though, and had proven invaluable in the past few months alone.

'Finally, a worthy adversary,' Andy muttered, as his attempts to gain access were rebuffed.

'Let's see if this works,' he said, typing in an unusual command that he had retrieved just a couple of days earlier when the last system update had taken place. Although the council had greatly improved the camera infrastructure, it was only as strong as its weakest point. In the case of Haringey Council, the weakest point was a pair of cameras covering a busy junction, which had not yet been upgraded. Because they were traffic cameras, installed only to monitor traffic flow, they were not considered high enough priority at the time of the upgrades, and the council instead chose to focus on crime. This included anti-social behaviour, illegal waste dumping, and parking offences which generated revenue.

Andy was able to gain access via one of the cameras, which gave backdoor entry into the new and sophisticated CCTV system.

'Bingo!' he exclaimed.

Within minutes, he was in the system and searching for the Volkswagen Golf. The intuitive software that utilised artificial intelligence to conduct its searches was easily able to search historic entries. It didn't take long for the vehicle to be 'pinged' in Green Lanes, heading northbound towards Enfield. This necessitated access to the Enfield Council control room, which was marginally easier to get into. Several snapshots then followed, all within a relatively small area north of the A406, the North Circular Road, the vehicle highlighted in an orange box where it had been captured by a camera along Green Lanes. The vehicle was last sighted turning left onto Aldermans Hill, towards Broomfield Park.

He called Kendra immediately.

'The vehicle was last seen turning onto Aldermans Hill towards Southgate, K. There's a camera at the other end which it didn't reach, so I'm guessing it's somewhere in that area around Broomfield Park. That's the Palmer's Green area, which is Enfield and not Haringey.'

'Great, thanks, Andy. Pablo got a hit on the A406 near there, so that shows us the direction of travel from Essex to the park. It must be in that area, so I'll make sure units are sent there.'

'Let me know if there's anything else I can do, okay?'

'I will. See you soon, Andy.'

Kendra went back to the office and inspected the map where the car had last been seen. She noted that many of the roads off Aldermans Hill were blocked at the other end with Fox Lane, so there was every chance the car was still in the area, as it hadn't been pinged anywhere else.

'We're closing in, you evil witch,' she muttered, before leaving to find Rick Watts.

~

'Rick, can we send a couple of units to Palmers Green? We just received information that a car matching the description had been seen near a park there.'

'Sure, ask Nick or Wilf to send the training unit. It'll give them some good experience,' he replied.

Minutes later, Wilf made the call, and the six probationary officers, along with their instructor, were diverted to Aldermans Hill in Palmers Green.

'I want you to remind them that if they see anyone with the vehicle, they are not to approach it under any circumstances. Do you understand?' Wilf told their instructor.

'No problem,' came the reply. 'We'll call it in immediately and leave the scene.'

After a relatively short drive along the A406, the minibus turned left onto Aldermans Hill and parked up at the first available opportunity, alongside Broomfield Park.

'Listen up, people,' the instructor said, before they left, 'remember what I told you. If you see the car and there's anyone with it, or even close to it, then you walk away and call me immediately, understand?'

'Yes, Sarge,' came the collective reply.

'Good. Okay, Paul and Eileen, you two cover the east side of the park. Bryn and Tyrone, you cover the north, and Stacey and Petra, you go east. Anything you want to ask before we leave?'

Nobody responded.

'Good. Get out there and stay safe, whatever happens,' the sergeant said. 'I'll be close by with the minibus, in case you need anything.'

They disembarked and went off in their pairs, walking proudly in their pristine uniforms and polished boots. This was an exciting situation for them to deal with so early in their careers, and they felt special as a result. They also felt nervous, not wanting to screw up, but also a little fearful of what to do if they encountered the vicious killers.

Over the next thirty minutes, they assumed their positions and started searching the side roads as well as the perimeter of the park. The radio message that the sergeant had waited for came after forty-five minutes from Paul and Eileen, who had been covering the east side.

'Sarge, we've found the car,' said Eileen. 'It's in Derwent Road, facing north, almost at the junction with Fox Lane. There is nobody with it.'

'Good work, Eileen. Don't pay any attention to it and continue walking to the end of the road. When you get there, stay close by and cover that junction in case it leaves while we're waiting for units to attend. I'll cover the other end from the van. The rest of you, come back to the van. I'm in Aldermans Hill at the junction with Ulleswater Road.'

They were soon in position, covering both exits to Derwent Road. The instructor called the Serious Crime Unit and spoke with Nick to let them know they had located the car.

'Great work, guys. We'll send our lot over there shortly; we should be with you in about half an hour. If you can cover it until we get there, that would be fab,' Nick told him.

The team quickly mobilised, three cars leaving within minutes to investigate the parked car. It was likely the Albanians wouldn't be too far away, so they wanted feet on the ground to maximise their chances of finding them quickly. Wilf and Nick arrived first and relieved Eileen and Paul at the Fox Lane End, whilst Pablo and Jill covered the park end. Kendra and Norm drove along Derwent Road to get a view of the car for potential surveillance opportunities later.

'Not being funny, but if you had just killed a cop and a couple of civilians and then nicked one of their cars, would you park it on the road you were living in?' asked Norm.

'Of course not, but I bet they didn't walk far from it. Would you? I reckon they're within a few hundred metres of it,' Kendra replied.

'Fox Lane is quite a busy road. We should have a drive along it to see if there're any cameras around,' Norm said.

'Yeah, that's a good call, Norm,' Kendra said, thinking it was something that Andy could check a lot quicker.

As they drove along Fox Lane, they could see that most of the roads had restricted access towards Aldermans Hill. It had been a rat run before to avoid traffic and so they had made many of them *no entry* as a result. They had also installed CCTV cameras to catch those who thought they'd try their luck.

'They look like new cameras, too,' Norm said, as they spotted them along the route.

'I reckon we'll be lucky to get anything, but it's better than nothing,' Kendra said, hoping that Andy could work his magic with Cyclops and give them the lucky break they needed.

'What do you reckon?' asked Norm, 'shall we go for a walk along Derwent Road, see if there's anything we missed?'

'Absolutely,' she quickly replied.

They updated the rest of the team and parked up near the middle of the road and walked north towards the Golf.

As they got close, they saw an elderly couple trimming their hedge, the husband clipping a little at a time with his old-fashioned hedge shears while his wife picked up the clippings as they dropped to the ground. It was slow, but it was efficient. They'd stop every time to chat as she did her thing, and he would wait patiently until she was ready for them to go again.

'That's a big old hedge. I reckon they've been at it for days,' Kendra said as they approached the elderly couple.

'Hello there. Sorry to trouble you, I'm DC March and this is DC Clark.' Kendra showed her warrant card and Norm did the same.

'How can we help you, detectives?' asked the man.

'We're here to ask if you have seen anything suspicious within the last couple of days,' Kendra said.

The couple looked at each other and shrugged.

'I don't recall seeing anything weird, do you love?' the man asked his wife.

'No, darling, I can't say that I have.'

'Maybe it wasn't unusual. We're trying to locate the people that drove here in that car,' Norm said, pointing to the Volkswagen that was parked less than twenty feet away.

'Oh, that,' the man said. 'Yes, that got here a couple of days ago and we haven't seen the driver since. Big fella, he was, walked towards Fox Lane. We've never seen him before; I only remember because he was such a big unit getting out of such a small car.'

'So, it was just one person you saw?' Norm asked.

'No, there was another big fella and a woman with him.'

'That's very helpful, thank you,' Kendra said.

As they walked back to their car, she dialled Wilf's number.

'Wilf, we've just spoken to a couple of witnesses who saw the three occupants walk towards Fox Lane after dumping the car.'

'Thanks, Kendra. I'll let the others know, including Rick. He'll want that car sealed off for forensics.'

'Yeah, I think we'll park here until someone can relieve us,' she said.

'I'll move us closer,' Norm said as they got in the car. He parked a couple of car lengths behind it and turned the engine off while they waited to be relieved.

'I'm just gonna call my dad, quickly,' Kendra said. 'I'll be back in a minute.'

Kendra was excited about the breakthrough, but

concerned, again, that it would take forever to get the permissions required. Instead of calling her dad, she got out of the car and called Andy.

'Andy, we've found the car on Derwent Road near the junction with Fox Lane. Witnesses saw three occupants walking towards Fox Lane, two large men and a woman. Do you reckon you can access the cameras covering the no entries in Fox Lane?'

'Almost certainly, thanks for the heads-up. I'll have a look now,' he said.

'Even if we got a direction, it would help, Andy.'

'No worries, K. I'll message you if I find anything.'

She was soon back in the car with Norm.

'I spoke with Rick,' he said, 'and the Murder Investigations Team are sending a couple of units to relieve us, along with the Crime Scene Manager and Exhibits Officer to check the car over before it's removed.'

'That's good. Hopefully, we won't be here long,' Kendra replied.

'I miss just dealing with SOCOs,' Norm suddenly announced, referring to the Scenes of Crime Officers. 'They'd turn up, we'd have a cup of tea whilst discussing the scene, they'd do their thing, and then we'd have more tea and a chat.'

'You miss it because everything was easier back then, that's all,' she said, smiling at his reminiscing. 'Just because there's more people involved now doesn't make it more complicated, it's more efficient and mistakes are easier to spot and rectify.'

'There's nothing wrong with simpler times, Kendra. Don't you think things were better back then?'

'Of course I do, but not because of the way things were

named. Things were better back then because the job was much better managed. Nowadays, most managers are just thinking of the next rank, and they don't care about the mess they leave behind when they get promoted. Back in the day, if you made a mess, you had to clean it up before you passed it on to anyone else.'

'Yeah, I guess so. Still, it's nice to think back to those days.' He sighed.

'Those days are long gone, Norm,' she said wistfully.

10

'Well, would you look at that?' Andy exclaimed as his search bore fruit. He immediately picked up his phone and called Kendra.

'Hi, Andy, what's up?'

'We are so very blessed to have the most densely concentrated CCTV camera systems in the world, that's what's up,' he said.

'You got a hit?'

'Yes, I did, indeed!'

'Out with it!' she demanded.

'So, after they parked the stolen car, they turned left onto Fox Lane, which I picked up on the council cameras monitoring the junctions. I then lost them when they went out of view of the camera, so I checked at the next camera along, at the junction with Conway Road, and they never reached it.'

'So, what are you saying, that they're holed up somewhere in between?'

'It suggested they were either in that small stretch of Fox

Lane or in Crothall Close, the only other road they could have gone onto,' he replied.

'Okay, I suppose that's better than nothing,' she said. 'Maybe we can get a camera van down there to monitor the close.'

'I haven't finished, K, there's more.'

'Honestly, you can be infuriating at times,' Kendra replied.

'I can hear your anger, but I bet you're smiling, aren't you? You still think I'm cute, right?'

'Cute wasn't what I was thinking, but it was very close.'

'See, I knew th... wait, what?'

'Will you spit it out, man!'

'Okay, okay. What I was trying to say, before you so rudely interrupted, is that at the junction with Crothall Close, on both sides of the junction, are two very posh and expensive blocks of luxury flats.'

'So?'

'So, the owners, being very protective of their swanky properties, decided to install some expensive state-of-the-art CCTV, which is monitored from the concierge's office in one of the blocks. I was able to find a phone number and some other information online that allowed Cyclops to gain access. That's how I saw them.'

'Saw them? The Albanians? What did they do?'

'They turned onto Crothall Close, is what they did. It's a dead end, so they must be shacked up in there somewhere. I can eliminate the first hundred yards or so, all past the bend in the road and out of camera view.'

'How many houses does that leave?' she asked.

'Well, it's a weird sort of close, as it is cactus-shaped with five arms, so it isn't going to be easy to pinpoint their exact location in there. I reckon there's about thirty houses, give or take. It'll be difficult to conduct much surveillance in there as they are so security conscious.'

'That's great work, Andy, thank you. I'll have a look and see what we can do there. In the meantime, is there any news your end?'

'Nothing. It's deadly quiet with everyone out protecting clubs and businesses. I thought I'd come home and work from here.'

'Alright, give me a shout if anything else comes up and I'll do the same my end.'

'Will do,' he said. 'So, do you really not think that anymore?'

Kendra smiled knowingly and decided not to tease for much longer.

'Think what?' she asked innocently.

'You know... that I'm cute,' he whispered.

She laughed.

'Seriously, did you just whisper, when you're alone and in the basement of your house?'

'Yes... well... it's a sensitive subject, okay?'

She laughed again.

'I'm not mocking, by the way,' she said. 'I'm laughing at your cuteness. Anyway, I have to go and find a way to get Rick to sort some surveillance out before anything else happens.'

She ended the call, having put Andy out of his misery.

Damn that good-looking scoundrel, she thought.

∽

'Anything unusual happened yet, Charlie?' Trevor asked his old friend.

'Nothing, Trev, it's all very quiet here. I've restricted the number of youngsters coming here, and just let the older lot train.'

'That's a good idea. I keep thinking we've missed something, you know? It's like an itch I can't get rid of,' Trevor replied.

'That's your parental senses kicking in, that's all. You're just concerned about the kids. I wouldn't worry about it. There's not much more you can do that you haven't already done.'

'Thanks, but until those bastards are off the scene, I think I'm going to be like a cat on a hot tin roof.'

'Well, you could do with losing a couple of pounds, so it may do you good,' Charlie said, patting his boss on the stomach.

'I walked right into that one, didn't I?' Trevor laughed. 'Alright, I know where I'm not wanted. I'll move on to the next one. Take it easy and call me if anything changes.'

'Will do, boss. Try to jog to the car. Every calorie burned helps,' he said, giving Trevor a big hug.

'Everyone thinks they're a comedian nowadays.'

'Well, you ask for it sometimes. This isn't like the old days, you know, when we were left to our own devices to come up with mischief.'

'The less we talk about those days, the better.' Trevor laughed. 'We'd probably be in prison if we did those things now.'

'Maybe, but we'd be laughing a lot more, wouldn't we?'

'Like I said, me old mate, those days are gone. Catch you later, okay?'

He drove off and aimed for the next club, wanting to check them all before they closed for the night.

So far, so good, he thought, *and long may that continue.*

~

ALTHOUGH ANDY HAD NARROWED the search down to the one multi-limbed dead-end road, there were limitations to the footage from the cameras that did not allow him to see the occupants of any vehicles going into and coming out of the close, especially in the dark. It was why he was unable to see that the silver Fiat Ducato van was being driven by Esad Abazi, with Leandra Qupi in the central seat and Mateo Ionescu in the window seat.

Having narrowed down the road where the Albanians were staying meant nothing if there wasn't surveillance being conducted to spot them, which is what Kendra would be hoping to organise very soon. Until then, especially at night, there was every chance they'd be able to come and go without being seen.

Leandra Qupi had decided that they'd be changing tactics tonight, having sent a very clear message and causing Brodie Dabbs significant losses. Tonight, they were heading back to east London. It was time to spread the message, shake a few more trees, scare a few more people, and cause as much damage and pain as possible.

'Tell me again what Burim said,' Leandra asked Mateo. Burin was the team leader of their back-up crew, who she had tasked to stake out a number of other business premises that her husband had interests in, including the remaining brothels, a currency exchange bureau, a minicab firm, and a mini mart.

'Burim thinks the police are watching the brothels in unmarked cars and may have private security watching the other businesses. It will be difficult to do anything unless we attack with more men,' Mateo replied.

'It is as I thought. We were lucky to get away with destroying what we have. It has taken those fools that long to realise we are a serious threat,' Leandra said. 'No matter, let them spend their time waiting for us to attack. We will look elsewhere for information, no?'

She leaned over and stroked Mateo's cheek affectionately.

'It is a shame that we are related, my handsome cousin. All this destruction and adventure is making me very affectionate,' she said, smiling provocatively.

Esad tried to stop himself from laughing at his brother's discomfort and failed miserably, pretending to choke and cough to cover his amusement.

Leandra turned to him. 'You are not handsome, not at all, you ugly baboon.'

It was Mateo's turn to laugh, which he did without trying to disguise it. Leandra quickly joined in as she saw Esad's face brighten with embarrassment.

'I am only joking, foolish boy,' she said, ruffling his hair. 'I love you both like brothers, but you have to learn to take a joke, okay?'

The three laughed again, but the brothers both knew that one false move, one mistake, would lead to the matriarch disposing of them as quickly as she had the dozens of other gang members who had thought her a soft touch. Her brutality was not lost on them at all.

'Now, enough jokes. Let us get to this stupid boys' club before they close for the night,' she said.

∼

'SEE YOU GUYS LATER,' Charlie told the last trio of trainees leaving the club. It was late, and he'd likely miss last orders at the pub, but he didn't mind as it kept the young men busy, and fit and healthy. He didn't mind missing a beer or three, not tonight.

'Almost done, Charlie,' Greg Petrucci said as he mopped the floor. 'I've just got the dressing room to do, and we can go.'

'No rush, Greg. I'm not going anywhere, son.' He would be giving Greg a lift home, the least he could do for the young man who had regularly been volunteering at the club.

He sat down in his office and picked up the local paper while he waited for Greg. As an ex-military man, Charlie's instinct for danger had never left him, even though he had left the services many years ago. The hair on the back of his neck was a reliable early warning system, and it was telling him that something was wrong, more so because of the lack of any noise than anything else—the sloshing of the mop had stopped. He put the paper down and walked out into the gym to see if Greg was okay. He froze in place.

Greg was being held by a huge brute of a man who had him in a choke-hold from behind, one arm held against the small of his back and the other trying frantically to free the giant arm around his neck. The hold around his neck was so tight that Greg couldn't speak and struggled for breath. Another giant stood next to his compatriot, staring at Charlie, before indicating for the trainer to come forward and join them. A tall, stern-looking woman in a long black coat walked slowly from behind the three men, her eyes fixed on Charlie, her hands in her coat pockets and her shoes making the only noise that Charlie could now hear, other than Greg's faint struggles.

'Please, let him go, he's only a kid,' Charlie said, his arms outstretched.

'Is he your son?' Leandra asked.

'No, ma'am,' Charlie replied.

'Then why do you care for him, old man?'

'I am responsible for him while he is in the club,' Charlie replied.

'How very noble of you! What will his parents think when they find out what has happened to him?' Her voice was icy and harsh.

'What do you want? Why are you here?' he asked.

'Ah, that's better. Now we are getting somewhere, no?'

Charlie did not respond and stood still, staring at the woman he knew would kill on a whim.

'Very well, I will tell you. I want to know who sold the eyepatch from which you are to benefit.'

'I don't know what you mean,' Charlie said, hoping he sounded convincing.

'I think you do,' she said, continuing to pace slowly back and forth like a lion stalking its prey.

'No.'

'I was told by a nasty little man that your club was going to make a lot of money from the sale, which means you must know about it, no?'

'I know that someone made a charitable pledge a few months ago, but they didn't say how, or how much, or when we were to receive it, or anything like that. I had completely forgotten about it.'

'Well, I'm glad you remember it because you can tell me now, can't you?'

Charlie remained silent.

Leandra could see that the man before her was going to

be a tough nut to crack. She would need to try a different tactic. She turned to Mateo, and in Albanian, instructed him to grab the old man.

Mateo stepped forward towards Charlie, who could sense what was about to happen. He raised his arms and said, 'Please, I don't know anything.'

She nodded to her other cousin, who swiftly pulled Greg's arms behind his back. Holding both wrists together, which was easy to do as Greg wasn't struggling, he took out a zip tie and expertly bound the young man's wrists tightly together. Esad then stood by his side and held him firmly by the arm.

'Let's try something different, shall we?' Leandra said, smiling. She nodded at Mateo, who forced Charlie to his knees, holding both his arms behind him. He then pushed him down to the floor, so he lay on his front, arms outstretched. Mateo stepped on Charlie's left arm to stop it moving whilst simultaneously lifting his right arm up and holding his hand in a tight hold. He then stepped on Charlie's back with his other foot to stop him from moving completely. He turned to Leandra, who nodded again.

Mateo grabbed Charlie's index finger and pulled viciously downwards, breaking it instantly. It happened so quickly that it took a second for it to register with Charlie and Greg. Charlie screamed in pain, his finger now at an obscene angle to the rest of his hand.

'No!' Greg shouted, trying to move to help his mentor. Esad yanked him back.

'No, what?' Leandra said, before turning and nodding to Mateo again.

Mateo instantly broke another finger, eliciting the same loud crack and scream as before.

'He is very good at that, you know,' she told Charlie, who was breathing hard, trying to control the excruciating pain.

'Leave him alone, you bastard!' Greg shouted, desperate to help but unable to do so.

Leandra looked at the young man and saw an opportunity.

'Let us see how much you really care for this old man,' she said, walking towards him.

'Where is your knife?' she asked Mateo, speaking in English to prime the young captive as to what she was about to do. Mateo spoke in Albanian and indicated with his chin to his inside jacket pocket.

Leandra reached in and pulled out a black-handled folding pocket knife that had killed the police officer a few days earlier. She released the four-inch blade that was serrated along the top edge and regularly sharpened by its owner. Walking slowly to Charlie's exposed side where Mateo still held his arm up, she looked towards Greg and, without taking her eyes from him, quickly stabbed down into Charlie's lower back, withdrawing the knife almost immediately. Charlie screamed in pain as she glared at Greg.

'Nooo... please stop!' he shouted, struggling in vain against Esad's powerful hold.

'No, what?' she repeated, readying the knife for another thrust.

'P-please, don't hurt him,' Greg stammered, 'please.'

Leandra thrust the knife in again, close to the original wound, which was now dripping blood. This time she lingered with the blade in Charlie's back, before removing it slowly. Charlie screamed again and passed out from the intense pain. At no point did she remove her eyes from Greg, knowing that her only hope for information was him and not the old man.

'God, no,' Greg whispered, tears now streaming down his face, 'please, don't do this.'

'The next time will be the last time; do you understand me?' I will kill him and then I will kill you. It is very simple. Tell me what I need to know, and I will leave you both alive.'

'I don't know anything, I swear! I just help here every now and again.'

Leandra walked slowly over to where Esad held the young man captive and stopped inches from his face. She held the knife up so he could see the blood dripping from it.

'I will not ask again. If you don't tell me, I will kill him.'

Greg continued to cry, not knowing what they were after, as he hadn't been privy to the sale in any way.

'I don't know!' he shouted defiantly.

'Very well,' she replied, turning back towards Charlie.

She assumed the same position and looked back towards Greg, ensuring that he would witness the next move. Again, without taking her eyes away from him, she thrust the blade down violently, this time higher up Charlie's back, the razor-sharp knife grazing his ribs as it entered, and no doubt hitting his vital organs. Charlie, already unconscious, did not move as his attacker left the knife in situ for Greg to stare at.

'Remember, that was your fault,' she said, walking back towards him.

Greg tried to be defiant, but the tears streamed down his face. Leandra could see him fighting to remain strong and decided to change tack.

'I will not kill you. Instead, I will make you watch as I kill everyone else. I will not stop until you tell me who is responsible. Do you understand?'

'Go to hell!' Greg screamed.

Before he could say another word, Esad elbowed him violently in the face and he dropped like a brick to the ground.

'Bring him,' she told her men. 'He will tell us what we need to know.'

11

'Rick, we have a possible street location of the suspects, but will struggle to find an exact address. Can we spare any more surveillance units to take a closer look?' Kendra asked her boss.

'How did you manage that?' he asked.

'We checked CCTV footage from the road where they abandoned the car, and it shows them turning left onto Fox Lane. They don't appear again in any of the camera footage further down, so they can only have gone to ground within a small section of Fox Lane or a close that has around thirty houses in it.'

'Good work. Let me call the ops room and see if they can arrange something. What do you think they'll need, a van?'

'A van, definitely, but it might also be worth sending someone on foot to have a closer look. We may get a lucky break.'

'Okay, leave it with me,' he replied.

'Any other news from the rest of the team?'

'Nothing, K. The units are all in place and rotating when

required, so the businesses are all well protected. I doubt we'll have any problems, and if we do, we'll have warning and hopefully enough time to get help to them quickly.'

'Great. I'll head off home, then, and will see you tomorrow,' she said.

'See ya.'

Kendra was keen to get to Andy's to find out if there had been any developments on his end. She wanted to make sure there was no overlap with the police protection and didn't trust Brodie Dabbs enough to hope that he hadn't messed things up. She called Andy.

'I'm on my way over to you, give or take twenty minutes. Do you want me to pick anything up en route?' she asked him.

'I'm good, thanks, K. Listen, call your dad. He thinks something is wrong with one of the clubs, as he can't get an answer from Charlie. He's on his way over to check for himself, so go and see if he needs any help.'

'Will do. See you later,' she said, hanging up. She immediately called Trevor.

'You alright, love? I'm just heading over to see Charlie. He isn't answering his phone and I'm a bit worried.'

'When did you last speak with him?' she asked.

'Earlier this afternoon, before I went to check on all the others. I called to see if he had gone home yet, because he normally messages me when he's closing up for the night. I'll be there in about five minutes.'

'I've just left work, so I'll meet you there shortly,' Kendra said, diverting to the club. It was on the way, so she'd be there soon after Trevor.

As she arrived, she saw her father's car parked up near

the entrance, the door to the club ajar, and the lights on inside. She quickly parked up and went to join him.

As she entered, a scene of carnage unfolded ahead of her. Trevor was kneeling on the floor, cradling Charlie's head in his lap, gently slapping his face to keep him awake. There was a big pool of blood under his body.

'Hang in there, brother, just hang in there, okay?' Trevor said gently, as Charlie opened his eyes fleetingly.

Trevor turned to see Kendra come in.

'Call an ambulance, K, quickly,' he shouted. Kendra ran to Charlie's office and called 999 from the phone there, using an assumed name so as not to connect her to the scene.

Charlie reached up slowly and grabbed Trevor's collar, pulling him closer to his face.

'Th... they... they have... G-Greg,' he whispered.

'Who has him, Charlie?'

'Wo... wom... woman. Alb... Albanians. Thr... thr... three of them.'

'Qupi's wife?' Trevor asked, stunned.

Charlie nodded slowly, struggling to speak.

Kendra came over and knelt alongside him.

'They're on the way,' she said, placing her hand gently on her father's. Charlie was unconscious again, his breathing shallow and laboured.

'They stabbed him in the back, K, the bastards stabbed him in the back,' he whispered. 'He's lost a lot of blood.'

'Try to keep him awake. The ambulance should be here very soon. I'll go and wait for them, she said, standing. He nodded and turned back to his old friend.

When she got outside, she called Andy immediately.

'They stabbed Charlie, Andy, and have taken Greg,' she

sobbed, letting her emotions out now that she was away from her father. She had wanted to stay strong for him inside.

'Shit, is Charlie okay?'

'No, he's in a really bad way, keeps blacking out. He's struggling to breathe. An ambulance is on the way. Is there any way you can track Greg? I'm worried for him, too,' she said.

'I'll have a look. If he has his GPS tracker on him, then we'll find him. Otherwise, no chance.'

'See what you can do, okay? I'll call when I know more.'

'Kendra, wait. Before you hang up, you both need to think about what you're doing next. Can you afford to be linked to this? Leave it with Trevor, it's bad enough he'll be linked, but you most certainly can't be.'

'Yeah, that's a good point. I'll speak with Dad about it when the ambulance comes,' she said. 'I'll call you later,' she added, hanging up.

She took several deep breaths to compose herself. She could hear the siren getting closer and was grateful for their swift response. Within a couple of minutes, the ambulance was parked and the paramedics unloading their kit.

'The victim is inside with several knife wounds to his back. He's lost a lot of blood,' she told them.

'Thank you, we'll take it from here,' one of the paramedics replied.

They rushed inside and placed a blanket underneath Charlie's head so that Trevor could gently lay him down. The paramedics then immediately attended to the prone man, still unconscious, his breathing becoming shallower and his skin turning pale and waxy.

'No visible wounds to the abdomen or chest,' the female paramedic said. 'We need to turn him over.'

They gently placed him on his side in the recovery position and quickly saw the holes in his t-shirt where the knife had entered. They cut the shirt away so they could attend to the wounds, which were still bleeding profusely.

'We need to apply pressure to the wounds and slow the blood loss,' her colleague added.

They applied three dressings quickly and then bandaged them tightly. The blood flow eased but still seeped through the dressings, causing them to apply more pressure.

'I'll go and get the stretcher; you keep the pressure on. We need to get him to the hospital urgently,' the male paramedic said, trotting towards the door.

His colleague kept applying pressure. She looked up and spoke to Trevor.

'Is he a friend, or family?' she asked.

'Both,' Trevor replied. He was emotionally charged, flitting between deep concern for his friend and anger towards the perpetrators. His fists were clenched, and the paramedic sensed he was struggling.

'What's his name, sir?' she asked.

'Charlie. Charlie Fenway.'

'We'll do what we can for Charlie, okay?' she told him.

'Thank you.'

'What's your name, sir?' she asked. 'Mine is Emily.'

'Trevor,' he replied.

'Trevor, do you want to come with him to the hospital?' she asked.

'Yes. Please.'

'Is there anyone we should call to let them know?'

Trevor shook his head. Charlie was divorced and had no children of his own.

Emily continued to apply pressure as they wheeled the

patient to the ambulance on a stretcher. He was soon safely inside with Trevor sitting on a bench opposite, watching as his friend slowly faded.

'Call me later,' Kendra whispered from the back door. She saw him nod just before the door was closed. Within seconds, the ambulance was on the move, its blue light on but no siren, making its way to the nearest hospital.

Kendra watched it leave and then went back to the club. She knew that Andy had installed cameras there and called him.

'Dad is in the ambulance with Charlie, and they've just left. Did you have any cameras set up here?'

'I did, but only at the front door. I'll check and see what it shows. What are you going to do now?'

'Nothing. I'm going to close up here and leave before the police get involved. They'll probably go to the hospital and start their enquiries there,' she said, 'but I don't want to take any chances that they'll come here early, it depends on their response times to 999 calls tonight—if they're busy, it'll be the hospital; if they're quiet, they may come here too.'

'Okay, double-check and make sure there's nothing to link you there before you leave, okay? They'll see the cameras on the door and will probably want to grab that footage straight away. Once they view it, they'll soon link the attack to the cop killers. Hopefully, they'll ramp up the investigation even more.'

'It will also show me going in and helping. Can you do anything about that?' she asked.

'I'm not sure, K. I'll have a look, but it may mean deleting it all to save you from being identified.'

'Okay, do what you can and let me know.'

'I'll call the others and let them know what happened so they can be more vigilant,' he said.

'Good idea, thanks.'

'You okay, Kendra?'

'Not really. Can I still come over? I don't want to be alone tonight, Andy.'

'Of course. I'll see you soon.'

It didn't take long to check inside and then lock the door behind her. She was soon on her way, tearful and concerned for her dad, Charlie, and also Greg, who was missing.

Please don't hurt him too, was all she could think.

∼

TREVOR PACED the hospital waiting room as he waited for an update on Charlie's condition. They had rushed him to theatre immediately. His vital signs were faint, and surgery plus a blood transfusion were imperative in order to save him. The wait seemed like an eternity to Trevor. He had recently lost one close friend and did not want to lose another.

Eventually, he was joined by a senior theatre nurse.

'How is he?'

'He's alive, Mister Giddings. Surgery went well and we've managed to stabilise him, but he is still in critical condition. The next twenty-four hours are very important, so we'll be keeping him in intensive care for close observation.'

'Thank God,' he said, breathing a sigh of relief. 'Can I see him?'

'He's still unconscious, but you can pop in for just a couple of minutes, okay?'

'Thank you,' he said, following the nurse back to the ICU.

'Remember, just a couple of minutes, okay?'

'Yes, thank you.'

The nurse pulled the curtain aside then left him alone with Charlie.

Trevor gasped at the sight of his friend lying there with tubes coming out of his mouth and his arms. The monitor next to the bed beeped every thirty seconds or so and Trevor could see that although Charlie was still alive, he was barely clinging on.

He took his hand and held it tenderly.

'I'm so sorry, Charlie. I should have been there with you,' he whispered.

He bowed his head and prayed for Charlie to recover. It was when in mid-prayer that the monitor stopped beeping and emitted the dreaded alarm, indicating that the patient's heart had stopped. A red light flashed on and off. Trevor let go of Charlie's hand and stood, pulling the curtain aside just as two nurses arrived at the cubicle.

'Sir, please wait in the waiting room,' said one, closing the curtain behind her.

Trevor left the cubicle but ignored the request and stayed close by, continuing to pray for his friend.

The two nurses were joined by a doctor, and they frantically attempted to save Charlie's life. The alarm continued to sound, indicating that they were failing.

'Nurse, the defib, please. Now.'

'Ready, doctor.'

'Okay,' the doctor replied, and a couple of seconds later said, 'analysing now. Stand clear!'

There was a thump as the defibrillator delivered the first electric shock. The alarm still sounded.

'Again. Clear!'

Another thump followed, and the alarm was relentless. Trevor brought his hands to his face and bowed, helpless.

'Once more,' the doctor said.

There was another thump. The alarm did not stop.

Trevor could hear the sounds of chest compressions and occasional breaths as the team battled valiantly to save Charlie using CPR. After a few minutes, the activity in the cubicle became noticeably different and the alarm was finally turned off.

'He's gone. Time of death, ten fifty-seven pm. Thank you, nurses,' the doctor said. He came out to see Trevor standing there before him, tears streaming down his face. Realising that he was connected to the deceased, the doctor ushered him into ICU to say goodbye.

'I'm very sorry for your loss, sir. We tried everything, but he just lost too much blood. The police are on the way and will want to speak to you,' the doctor said.

Trevor had no words and could only nod.

'Please, take as long as you need. We'll come and get you in a few minutes, we have a family room you can wait in until they arrive, okay? Can I get you something to drink?'

Trevor shook his head.

'Okay, I'll leave you to it. Again, sir, I'm sorry for your loss,' the doctor said, turning to walk away.

'Doctor,' Trevor called after him.

'Yes?'

'Thank you for trying.'

The doctor nodded and walked away.

Trevor slumped forward in his chair, head in hands.

∼

12

'Dad, is everything okay? How's Charlie?' Kendra had been waiting for the call and was with Andy in his living room when it came.

'He's gone, Kendra. They tried everything they could, but he didn't make it,' Trevor whispered.

'Oh no,' Kendra said, quickly covering her mouth to stifle a sob.

Andy put his arm around her.

'Dad, I'm so sorry,' she whimpered. 'I can't believe he's gone.'

'Me neither, darling. He was a special man,' Trevor said. 'The police are waiting to speak to me. I just wanted to make sure you know they'll be looking at the CCTV and that we're both on it.'

'We know. Andy has made some changes. It will show them coming in and leaving, but he's cut the shots that I'm in. He's made it look like a glitch. It's enough that they're shown.'

'That's good. I'll keep it brief with them. I'll call when I'm done, okay?'

'Bye, Dad,' she said, hanging up. She burst into tears and rested her head on Andy's shoulder.

'I can't believe it. He's gone. Dad is in bits,' she said between sobs.

'Sorry, K, I'm not sure what to say.'

'Poor Charlie,' she cried, 'and poor Greg, God knows what that poor boy is going through right now.'

'I've been meaning to tell you, K, he didn't have his GPS tracker with him, so I have no idea where he is or how to find him. Sorry,' Andy said.

It was some time before the crying stopped.

~

AFTER THE POLICE had questioned Trevor at the hospital, a unit was quickly dispatched to the club to secure it as a crime scene. The murder detectives arrived the following morning to inspect the scene for themselves and to secure any additional evidence that hadn't already been seized, such as the CCTV footage in Charlie's office. The night duty CID officer had gone through it already and had seen the three Albanians enter the club and then—after a glitch in the system—leave, taking with them a young man whose hands were tied behind his back. The officer had quickly called the operations room at New Scotland Yard and informed them of the situation, linking the murderers to another fatality and now an abduction. All units were made aware, including the Murder Investigations Team that was working on the linked murders.

The investigation, already ramped up because of the police officer's murder, was escalated in an effort to trace the whereabouts of the trio in order to find Greg Petrucci, presumed alive but with major concerns for his welfare.

Kendra had arrived at work early, having slept very little during the night. She had waited for her father to call and had insisted on seeing him when he'd left the hospital. He arrived at Andy's house in the early hours to be greeted by the longest, tightest hug he'd ever received from his sobbing daughter. They had talked for an hour before attempting sleep, which came fleetingly.

Now, as she sat in the briefing room, her mind was filled with images of Charlie and her dad laughing, the pool of blood on the gym floor, Trevor's face in the ambulance. It was hard to concentrate.

Get a grip, Kendra March, she told herself. *You're no good to Greg or your dad like this.*

'Listen up, everyone,' Rick Watts said, addressing the room, 'the guvnor wants to say a few words.'

'Thanks, Rick,' said DI Dunne. 'Morning, everyone. I know some of you are already aware, but there have been a few developments overnight in the murder investigations that we're assisting with. Last night, a boxing gym was visited by the Albanians, where they murdered the coach and abducted one of the trainees there.'

'Why attack a boxing club, guv?' asked Rula.

'We know for sure that it's connected to the eyepatch from the auction, as the club was to be one of the beneficiaries of the sale. We can only assume, at this time, they went there to find out if the club knew who was responsible for selling it,' Dunne replied.

'Why take the boy, though?' asked Wilf.

'That, we can only guess. Maybe they'll use him to get the information they want, or as bait to draw out the person they're after? What we do know is that there is no trace of them or the boy at all. All we have is the CCTV footage showing them entering and then leaving the club. No vehicle, no direction, no clues.'

'What's the plan then, guv?' asked Watts.

'To start with, the surveillance unit is now in place in Fox Lane, covering the stretch where the suspects were last seen. They have footies in place to move quickly and hopefully identify the house. Until then, we'll keep trawling through business associates and addresses and hope we get a hit. These bastards are ruthless, and they don't give a shit that we know who they are. That suggests they have an exit planned, so I want some of you to work on that. Check all ports for private charters to Albania or crossings to France and make sure their photos are sent over, along with all other information we have. They must not get away.'

After the briefing, Kendra went to her desk to work. Jill joined her shortly afterwards, noticing that she was quieter than usual.

'You okay, Kendra?'

'Yeah, sorry, Jill, just knackered. I didn't get much sleep last night,' she replied, yawning.

'You don't just look tired, girl, you look upset, too. Anything you want to talk about?'

Kendra hesitated before replying. She really did want to offload but couldn't afford to do it here.

'No, honestly, I'm good. I appreciate it, though.'

'Well, you know I'm here if you change your mind,' said Jill.

'Thanks.'

She went about her duties as usual, keeping busy enough to distract herself from the previous night's events. Each passing hour helped ease those chilling memories, making them slightly more acceptable, as though she was desensitising. She performed her duties in an efficient, almost robotic manner, stopping only for lunch and a bathroom break, checking every possible lead that she had been expected to check and recording her non-findings in the live worksheet the team used for their investigations.

Just before the end of her shift, Kendra unexpectedly stumbled across a strong possibility for the Albanians' exit strategy. She printed off the information and went to see Rick Watts.

'Find anything?' he asked, as she closed the door behind her.

'Actually, I think I may have,' she said. 'I was checking ports for any groups leaving for Albania on private planes when I came across a jet that was booked a few days ago for Tirana, leaving from Norwich airport in one week.'

'That's an unusual airport to fly from to Albania, isn't it?' he asked.

'It is. They have very few private charters flying to Tirana from there, maybe one or two a year. There is one issue, though,' she said.

'What's that?'

'I don't have a complete manifest or passenger list. It isn't unusual, as the flight is still a week away, but they do mention that it will be for up to fourteen passengers. They booked all the seats.'

'You don't think it's a coincidence?' he asked.

'No, I think they're planning to cause as much damage as they can in the time they're here and then make a quiet exit. Going via a small airport makes it easier for them to elude the authorities. I imagine they'll have fake passports, too.'

'Okay, well, the least we can do is put a marker on it and alert Special Branch. They can conduct all the necessary searches closer to the time and stop the plane from taking off, as well as arrange for armed back-up to take the passengers off,' Rick added.

'Can I leave that with you then, Rick? I'll start helping with the other searches tomorrow if that's okay?'

'Sure. Good work, K, I'll pass this on to everyone that needs to know. We'll catch those bastards, don't you worry.'

∼

KENDRA LEFT SHORTLY AFTERWARDS and drove to her flat, where Trevor was waiting. As soon as she walked in, he smiled at her from the sofa where he'd been sitting looking out of the window. He looked tired. She could see that he was still struggling with the loss of his friend and hadn't slept much. The bags under his eyes were evidence of that.

After another long hug, they sat down, holding hands.

'How are you feeling?' she asked.

'Not great, love, I haven't slept much at all. I found a number for his sister who lives in France, so I called to let her know of his passing. She was upset but can't make it out here for a few days yet and asked if I could help with the coroner and the funeral.'

'Are you okay with that? I don't know what they do in the instance there's no immediate family,' she said.

'Of course I'm alright with that, it's the least I can do. He was my best friend, Kendra,' he whispered, 'and family.'

'If I can help in any way, please let me know, okay?'

'Of course. Now, tell me what's going on,' he said, sitting up straight.

'Well, we can't track Greg because he hasn't got his tracker with him. We have no idea where the Albanians are now but have set up surveillance in the area where we think they're staying. And we may have found how they're trying to leave the country, using a private jet. That's about it,' she said.

'It's better than what we had before, love. We need to prioritise finding Greg and getting him back safely. If they wanted to kill him, they would have done it at the club, so they must want him to squeeze information out of him. What is the Met doing?'

'They've got a lot more people on the investigation now, but other than what I've told you, there isn't much more to report, Dad.'

'What, we sit and twiddle our thumbs until something comes up? It may be too late by then. There must be something we can do,' he said.

'Honestly, I don't know, Dad. I have a horrible feeling that they have Greg to try to find out who sent the eyepatch to the auction house. I know he doesn't know it was you personally, or anything about its history, but he may give us up if he's being tortured. We shouldn't rule that out.'

'You're right, love, it's what I'd do if I were a vicious bastard. If he gives us up, she'll probably contact us, or worse, try to exchange him for the money or even for her husband's whereabouts. Shit, we should have figured that out sooner. We need to get ready.'

'Ready for what?' Kendra asked.

'They're gonna come after us, love, so we need to be ready for them.'

～

'Burim called to confirm they are on the way here,' Esad told his boss.

'Good, now we have secured the warehouse. It will give us some breathing room, we can all be in one place. The police will be looking all over for us, and I was not comfortable in that fancy house with its stupid, nosy, posh neighbours,' Leandra replied.

She had quickly confirmed that the warehouse on the Sterling Industrial Estate in Dagenham, which had been acquired and used by her husband, trading as *Tirana Import & Export Ltd*, still had six months left on the existing lease. It hadn't been difficult to see that nobody was using it in his absence, so they had quickly gained entry and secured it for their own use.

'He is bringing supplies with him, including bedding and food, so we shall be comfortable here,' said Esad.

'We are not here to be comfortable, cousin, remember we have only one week to find Guran and the money, and to secure our businesses here again. We must work fast and we must work quietly so nobody notices us here. Make that clear to Burim and his men, okay?'

'Yes, of course,' the bodyguard replied.

'Now, has our young guest been more forthcoming?' she asked, rubbing her hands together.

'No, but he is weakening, so it is only a matter of time.'

'Again, we do not have that luxury. We need information now!' she exclaimed, storming off towards their captive.

Greg was tied to a metal stanchion near one corner of the warehouse. He was slumped forward, exhausted, unable to even sit due to the way they had secured him. Although awake, he tried not to move and expend any more energy until he needed to, clinging on to the hope of escaping from his friend's murderers. He heard the footsteps of his tormentors before he saw them, staying slumped forward. His head was painfully pulled up by his hair, his vision slightly blurred by the lack of light in his corner. He saw the monstress standing in front of him while her minion held his head up.

'I will not ask twice,' she said, leaning forward menacingly. 'You remember what I did to the old man, so you will know that I enjoy using knives very much.'

'I don't know anything,' he replied hoarsely.

'You are a brave boy. I respect that. It is now time for you to respect the knife.'

She held out her hand, and Esad handed her his knife, similar to his brother's. She held it in front of her, twelve inches from his head, moving it slowly from side to side.

'My question is this, boy,' she whispered, right up to his face. 'Where can I find the person responsible for sending the eyepatch to the auction house? Remember, I will not ask again,'

Greg knew that if he denied any knowledge, it would mean big trouble for him, as she would not accept anything but an answer to her question. He did the only thing he could think of to give him a chance—and said nothing.

After a minute or so, Leandra nodded respectfully at the young man, understanding his predicament.

'Clever boy,' she said, 'but not clever enough. Let me ask you another question. Do you remember The Joker?'

'Mm-hmm.'

'Good, good,' she said. 'Then you will know that he has a messed-up mouth, yes?'

Greg nodded.

'Good, good. So, I will ask you my question again, but first I must do something.' Moving to one side, she took the sharp knife and slowly pierced Greg's cheek with the tip of the blade. The young man screamed as the blade entered his mouth and continued through to the other cheek, where it came out the other side. The pain was intense, but any sudden movement meant he could lose his tongue or cause worse damage, so he tried to remain still, difficult while he was shaking from fear.

'That's better,' she said, smiling, 'now you understand pain a little better, no?'

Greg, tears falling down his bloodied cheeks, nodded slowly and carefully.

'Good, good. Now, when I ask my question again, I want you to nod if you have something to tell me, okay? If you refuse to answer again, then I will pull the knife towards me and cut your face open. Understand?'

He nodded slowly again.

'Good. Now, where can I find the person responsible for sending the eyepatch to the auction house? Nod if you can tell me something.'

Greg closed his eyes momentarily, tears still flowing, as he finally surrendered and nodded.

'That's much better, no?' she said. 'Now, this may hurt a little.'

The matriarch grabbed the hilt and slowly pulled out the knife, giggling at the pained animal-like noises that her victim made as he tried to keep still.

'You are a brave boy,' she said, leaning over. 'Maybe I will not kill you... yet.'

Greg closed his eyes momentarily, thanking God. When he opened them, she was still standing there, holding the knife.

'Tell me,' she said.

13

After discussing with Kendra and agreeing on the best course of action, Trevor and Kendra went to meet with Andy at his house the following morning.

'I am so sorry for your loss, Trevor,' Andy said, giving him a brief hug. 'I only knew him for a few months, but he was a great guy.'

'Thanks, Andy. And yes, he was,' Trevor said as they adjourned to the living room.

'Andy, we had a long chat last night about what we should do next,' Kendra started. 'We don't want to lose any more people, including poor Greg, so we made some decisions that I hope you're okay with.'

'I understand. What are we doing?'

'First off,' said Trevor, 'we're going to call everyone now and keep all the clubs shut until the danger has passed. We're also going to pull back from Brodie Dabbs' businesses and bring all our team together to the factory.'

'That's a great idea,' said Andy. 'Brodie won't be happy, but we can't take any chances.'

'We're pretty confident that Greg was taken to squeeze information from him, poor boy. He'll only be able to hold out for so long, so we need to start preparing for the Albanians to come after us,' Trevor continued.

'Makes sense.'

'We'll make the calls now to bring everyone in and then meet them at the factory,' Kendra said.

'Andy, this is likely to be a serious attack on us, so we'll need a heads-up that they're approaching while we prepare. Are you okay with taking Marge and monitoring the factory from somewhere close by? We may need the drones to help out. I was going to ask Mo to go with you, if that's okay?' Trevor asked.

'Yeah, I'm good with that. Mo can fly the drones too, so it's a good call. Marge is prepped and ready to go, so as soon as we get to the factory, I can take her out.'

'Thanks, Andy,' said Kendra. 'I think we have all the kit we need there, unless you can think of anything else?'.

'No, we stocked up well, remember?'

'Right, I suggest we make a move, then,' Trevor said. 'Kendra, you drive, I'll make the calls en route.'

They were on their way within minutes, heading towards the factory, a safe haven that was likely to become a battlefield very soon.

∼

THE ALBANIANS, now all gathered at the warehouse, quietened down as their boss prepared to brief them.

'We have an address from the boy. Whoever these people

are may know where my Guran is and what happened to our money and our people. When we go there later, I want you to show no mercy. None,' Leandra Qupi told her men.

The dozen heavies standing in front of her were all imposing and deadly, specially chosen for this trip. They nodded and murmured in approval.

'We have less than a week to get back what is rightfully ours. I anticipated more from Brodie Dabbs, but he fears us. Now we shall show him and his allies why. As long as we stay away from the police, we shall succeed with our mission and be on the plane home in a few days.'

'I will go alone to check this place the boy told us about, nobody will be bothered about one man on his own,' Mateo said. 'The rest of you, wait here and prepare for later.'

'What about the boy?' Esad said, nodding towards Greg. 'Do you want me to get rid of him?'

'Not yet. The fewer of us people see outside, the better. We stay here until we are done, then you can do what you like with him.'

Esad grinned in anticipation. The boy had proven stubborn and obstructive for too long. His lesson was far from over and would be a very harsh one.

'Okay, go and prepare your equipment and then get some rest. We will leave at four to get there before they close,' Mateo told the men.

The Albanians dispersed to do as he had asked. Mateo approached his boss.

'I will leave now, and will call if there are any concerns,' he said.

'Very well. Remember, Mateo, quiet as a mouse,' she said, teasingly stroking his face again.

Mateo could see his brother trying not to laugh and nodded sombrely.

'Nobody shall see me, cousin,' he replied confidently.

~

THE TEAM, with the exception of Andy and Mo, who had left earlier with Marge, stood quietly and respectfully as they waited for the briefing to begin. Marge was Andy's camper van and his pride and joy. The van was kitted out as a mobile operations room so she was perfect for the role. Trevor had asked they leave immediately and start monitoring the site surrounding the factory and the roads leading to it.

'First of all, I am grateful to you all for being here today. It has been a difficult couple of days, and you have shown courage and loyalty that I shan't ever forget,' Trevor said. 'Losing Charlie, one of the closest friends I have ever had in my life, was a bitter blow so soon after losing Jacob. My loss has been painful. They also have young Greg. God knows what they are doing to him, and we have no clue where he is. Because of these circumstances, I cannot ask any of you to put yourself in the sort of danger that we are expecting here very soon.'

He looked at the young men and women standing in front of him. His intention was to ask the younger members of the team to go home and stay safe and ask the older members to volunteer. Before he could say anything, Amir stepped in.

'There's more chance of us holding you down and stripping you naked,' Amir said, to laughter from the rest of the team, who were nodding in agreement.

'Listen, as much as I appreciate it, this is no place for some of our younger colleagues here. I reckon we could hold this place with four or five of us, so there's no need to risk anyone else,' Trevor replied.

'Well, if it's gonna be that easy for you to hold them off, then there won't be a problem with the rest of us staying, will there?' Charmaine added.

'I think you've backed yourself into a bit of a corner there, Dad.' Kendra laughed.

'Alright, alright. But I want you all to make sure you are fully kitted up, with GPS tags safely tucked away, and be ready to run if I tell you to, okay?'

'That's more like it!' Charmaine said. 'Except for the running bit, there won't be any of that.'

The team laughed, garnering a smile from Trevor as he shrugged his shoulders in acquiescence.

'Right, then. If that's the case, let's get started. We have a lot of work to do. Andy and Mo are out there now and will give us the nod if anything or anyone suspicious comes close. Kendra is leaving us to go to work, so we'll have some feedback from there if anything changes. Any questions?'

'Yeah, I have one,' Amir said, raising his arm. 'Can I be the first to use the pepper spray?'

~

'Okay, we have good vision covering the road leading to the factory, and all external cameras are working perfectly,' Andy told Mo.

'Great, so what now?'

'Now, we wait. I'll monitor the cameras and you make sure to keep an eye on anyone or any vehicle heading towards the team. We have nothing scheduled for delivery today, so traffic will be very minimal.'

The factory was ideally situated. It was far enough away from the other industrial buildings that it wasn't overlooked, and only one road led to it, making it difficult to approach without being seen. Andy had installed cameras to cover every inch of the exterior of the building, and many along its perimeter to monitor potential intruders. The cameras also had infra-red capability, which detected body heat and made it difficult to approach without being noticed. With his police intelligence and tech capability, Andy had been careful to conceal many of the cameras, knowing that top-end professionals would find a way of detecting regular cameras.

'Righty-ho,' Mo said, stretching his arms, 'have no fear, Mister Pike, nobody shall pass without being seen.'

'I like your style!' Andy laughed as he watched the cameras. 'If we spot anything approaching, we can also use the drones to get a bird's-eye view, which will help.'

'You mean Mabel and Tim?' Mo asked, grinning. He found Andy's choice of names for equipment funny. 'How did you come by those names, by the way? Been meaning to ask you for a while now.'

'Well, Tim is the size of a thumb, so he's named after Tiny Tim. I thought Mabel was a cute name that was popular about fifty years ago. Marge is named after Marge Simpson, who I used to fancy when I was a kid.'

'Seriously? You fancied a cartoon?' Mo laughed.

'Dude, have you never seen Who Framed Roger Rabbit? You're telling me you didn't have the hots for Jessica Rabbit?'

Mo almost fell off his seat.

'You fancied a rabbit, too?'

Andy laughed.

'Jessica was no rabbit, my friend. Roger was, but she was human. A cartoon human, but human.'

'Man, you oldies like the strangest things.' Mo laughed again. 'Fancying cartoons and rabbits.' He shook his head.

∼

'I'M WORRIED, Dad. I should be here with you lot, not hiding away in an office,' Kendra said.

'Darling, you know I'm right on this one. There's a chance the police could get involved if it kicks off, so you can't be here. Plus, we need your eyes and ears at work in case you hear anything. So please don't worry and just get yourself away from here,' Trevor replied.

'Alright, but check in with me every few hours, okay?'

'I will, I promise. Now leave, I have traps to set and Albanians to catch!'

∼

TREVOR WATCHED as Kendra drove out of the yard and away from the factory to safety. He was relieved to know she would be safe from the likely encounter with the Albanians, but also keen to find out if the police had made any breakthroughs.

He went back inside to check on progress so far, which had been swift—and very creative! All windows and doors to the factory had been reinforced with plywood from the inside. The previous owners had left an outbuilding full of timber and other supplies, which came in useful for making it difficult for attackers to gain entry. The downside was that visibility outside was restricted, so Trevor had told the team to drill holes before securing the wood to the frames. They would also have the upstairs windows as a vantage point.

More creative traps were being laid in the loading bay at the rear and also in the main reception area at the front. The areas in between were made more secure, some doors locked and then screwed securely shut so they couldn't be smashed open, thus forcing attackers along to their traps.

Amir had joked about pepper spray but had been serious about showing several team members how to use the canisters he had acquired, which were now strategically placed both on the ground floor and upstairs.

Each team member now wore body armour and had a gas mask, night-vision goggles, and a taser to hand. As soon as the factory was breached, they would all don their gas masks and release CS gas to incapacitate and stall the intruders.

Trevor had also insisted that great effort be made to contain a 'safe area' upstairs, to which they could retreat as a last resort. They would be able to barricade themselves into a large room and exit from a window using the rope ladders they had put in place for such an eventuality. He had vowed that if it were to get to that stage, the police would be called to get them out of trouble. Two vans were parked under the window for a swift retreat, the keys hidden under the seats. More offensive equipment was placed in the back to give them a fighting chance. Trevor had no idea how many people would be attacking them, so he had erred on the side of caution.

There were other, more subtle traps laid throughout the factory, which would handicap anyone trying to gain entry.

'Remember this,' he told the team. 'We're not just digging in to fight them off, we need to take some of them captive so we can get Greg back, okay?'

Hang in there, kid, he thought, *we'll come and get you soon.*

Mateo followed the sat-nav route until he was a couple of minutes away. He zoomed in on his phone to better see the road leading to the industrial building which, he had been told, was where they would find their answers. It seemed isolated, so he was keeping his wits about him.

He had seen the building, home to Sherwood Solutions, on the internet, but the image was years old, and his approach would be cautious, expecting changes. He had passed the busy Tilbury Docks area and was surprised to see how quickly it had become more rural, with the landscape scarred from what appeared to be a small quarry that was now abandoned. Having seen that there was only one way to approach it by road, he decided to abandon the car and strike out on foot. It was risky, but he decided it was quiet enough that traffic would be minimal.

He saw the occasional vehicle parked on the side of the road: builders' vans, one or two camper vans, nothing that concerned him. He followed the single-track road leading to his destination, sticking closely to the verges in case of traffic. When he arrived at the perimeter, he saw that changes had indeed been made. The fencing that surrounded the compound had recently been renovated, with the dense foliage allowed to grow wild, giving the business privacy and also hindering any potential illegal entry.

Mateo walked along part of the perimeter, looking for cameras. He spotted several, halting and making sure to avoid their line of sight, before turning back. There was no point in taking chances now, before the team arrived, thus ruining the element of surprise. This was good intelligence for his team, which he could now pass on. He retraced his steps and cautiously approached the entrance, which he reckoned was the only one. The heavy iron gates stood open, allowing him to look inside towards the vast two-storey building some hundred metres away.

Taking his phone out, he took a video as he passed by, attempting to look covert in case anyone was watching, which he thought was unlikely. He saw several cars parked near the main entrance, and lights on inside, indicating the presence of staff. Another good sign, suggesting there were only a few people inside. He turned back and retraced his steps again, this time back to his car. He smiled confidently.

It shouldn't take long at all, he thought.

∽

14

Andy and Mo were surprised when they saw a powerfully built man get out of his car and walk towards the factory. It was so brazen and unlikely that initially they stood there, looking at each other.

'Surely not?' Mo said, slightly bemused by what he was watching.

'I'd rather not take a chance. Call it in and I'll check the feeds,' Andy replied.

Mo called Trevor.

'Trev, there's a big dude making his way on foot towards you. Looks like he's checking the factory out. Just him at the moment.'

'Thanks, Mo. It's actually a good sign, as it gives us time to prepare better,' Trevor said. 'Call if anything else happens and stay safe, okay?'

'Will do,' Mo replied, hanging up. He turned to Andy and said, 'Where is he now?'

'He's walking along the perimeter, probably checking for cameras. When he saw the overt ones, he stopped and turned back, but I have him on the hidden feeds and he's about to reach the gate.'

'He's probably thinking that it's ideal to attack because it isn't overlooked, so no witnesses,' Mo said.

'He's in for a shock, isn't he?' Andy laughed. 'He's taking photos or video now as he passes the open gate, thinking nobody is watching.'

Mateo had no idea that he was being monitored on camera, but also by Trevor and several of the team, who saw him walk past the gate and then back again.

'Wow, this is great,' Charmaine said, 'he's thinking this will be a doddle. How long do you reckon we have?'

'I'd say an hour or so,' Trevor replied. 'Gives us plenty of time to finish up here.'

'Okay, I'd better get back to it,' she said.

'Can you ask Zoe to man the fuse box when the bad guys get here? If they breach, I don't want them turning the lights on. We'll be using our night vision and gas masks throughout, okay?'

'No problem.'

~

'I'M ON MY WAY BACK,' Mateo told Leandra as he followed the sat-nav out of the area again.

'Will there be any problems?' she asked.

'Maybe. It is a solid old building, so we'll need a way to break down the door or get through the windows. Ask Esad to gather some kit in case. Other than that, it should not be a problem. Get the men ready. I will brief them on my return.'

'Yes, of course. Good work, Mateo.'

'WHAT HAVE I MISSED?' Kendra asked Jill when she was back at her desk.

'The surveillance team has been in place for a while now but there's been no movement. It all seems to have gone very quiet.'

'I'm guessing that's the calm before the storm,' Kendra said. 'The bastards aren't stupid; they know we're after them now and they're being more careful. They still have a lot to do, I think.'

'Yeah, you're probably right. Anyway, I've been looking at their previous business interests and associates again to see if there was something we missed.'

'Find anything?'

'Not really. I mean, there are a couple of weird things that aren't easy to explain. For example, we know that Brodie Dabbs basically took over all the brothels, he just swooped in and took over seamlessly, as if he knew it was happening—otherwise he has perfect timing and a shit-ton of luck. Did you know that the rentals on the houses were still in the Albanian's business names?'

'Does that matter?' said Kendra. 'I'm guessing they kept it that way in case the landlord raised the rent for the newcomer.'

'That's a fair assumption, I suppose. And there are the warehouses that we searched. They're not being used, but the leases are still valid as they paid a year in advance.'

'I guess the owners are happy to have had their rent, and no wear and tear on their premises,' Kendra added.

'I just think it's weird. They disappear and leave everything behind as if they were still around. It smacks of something very strange indeed, as if they were abducted by aliens or something.' Jill laughed.

'Now you're just being daft,' Kendra said, with a giggle.

'Yeah, that's what happens when you reach a dead end, you start making things up. Remember the famous Sherlock Holmes quote?'

'Which one?'

'When you have eliminated the impossible, whatever remains, however improbable, must be the truth—that one!'

'Well, he wasn't a real person, was he? He didn't have to report the theft of milk bottles or common burglaries, or any of the shit the modern police end up dealing with. It isn't a book or a TV show, Jill,' Kendra replied.

'Yeah, I know that Miss Snarky Pants. I'm just saying, reaching a dead end when you're a detective is bloody frustrating.'

'Of course, it is. Otherwise, everyone would want to be a detective, right?'

'I hate that you're always right,' Jill said, smiling as she threw a balled-up sheet of paper at her colleague. Kendra caught it mid-air and threw it back, laughing.

If only you knew, she thought.

∽

MATEO ARRIVED at the warehouse to see his men lined up and ready for action. They were all armed with Sig Sauer P320 handguns that they'd smuggled into the country from their homeland. One man was carrying a sledgehammer, and there was another with bolt cutters. They also now wore protective vests underneath their jackets, enhancing their already large frames and making them seem like a troupe of bodybuilders going for a lads' night out.

'Listen up, men,' Mateo said, calling them to order. 'The building we will be attacking is remote from the other industrial premises, so it gives us cover from witnesses. There are a handful of cars there, suggesting only a few members of staff inside.'

'Are they likely to be armed?' asked Burim.

Mateo and Leandra laughed.

'Burim, this is the UK. They don't like guns, remember?' he replied.

The men all laughed.

'We will drive through the gate which they have kindly left open for us and then make a swift entry into the building. Remember, we must leave some alive. The chances are that their boss won't be there, and it is that person we need to find.'

'Keep one or two alive, do what you wish to the others. No mercy, remember?' Leandra added.

The men each raised a fist in the air and acknowledged their leader.

'We will take three cars and the van,' Esad added. 'Burim, divide your men accordingly.'

The men gathered in their groups, raring to go.

'Let's go!' Mateo shouted, before opening the door to the front car park.

Within seconds, they were all in place and the convoy left for its thirty-minute journey.

None of the gangsters noticed the Land Rover that had passed them going the opposite way, heading for a familiar garage in the industrial estate.

~

'STAV, this is not a good time, mate. Can we talk tomorrow?' Trevor said, after answering the call from his mechanic friend. Stav also disposed of criminals' vehicles and often provided transport for Trevor and his team. He was a great ally in their quest to dispense justice.

'How many?' Trevor suddenly asked. 'What cars are they using? Just now?'

The call lasted just thirty seconds, but it was the news Trevor had been hoping for. He was expecting company but had no idea from where. Now that he knew, he would have to reconsider the plan.

'Listen up, everyone. Gather round, quickly,' he shouted.

The team duly obliged.

'Okay, I've just heard that the Albanians are on the way. They'll be with us in half an hour or so. I also think I know where they're holding Greg, so I'm going to send Andy and Mo to see if they can grab him safely.'

'Should any of us go with them?' Darren asked, concerned by the sudden change of plan.

'I don't think they'll need help, Darren. I'd think they're sending all their men here. They're coming in three cars and a van, probably a dozen or so all together.'

'That's pretty even, then,' Darren said, smiling as he looked at his Walsall buddies and nodded.

'That may be,' Trevor said, 'but they have something we don't — guns. These guys are coming to kill us, remember? Please do not take their numbers lightly. These are vicious bastards in every sense of the word.'

'We understand, Trevor. I figured the boys here just

needed a pep talk to gee them up a bit, you know? They're way too cocky sometimes,' Darren said.

There was laughter, and the tense atmosphere eased a little.

'Don't worry, Trevor, we know how dangerous they are. We'll be careful,' Izzy added. The six men from Walsall had been terrific allies in recent months and had helped turn the tide in their favour on several occasions now. They had almost been Trevor's first call each time, and had never let him down.

'That's good, Izzy, glad to hear it. Right, first thing, I want one of you to go and shut the gates. The padlock is heavy duty, so will hold them off and slow them down. That's our new plan. We slow them down as much as we can to give Andy and Mo a chance of recovering Greg.'

'I'll go and lock the gate,' Rory, another of the Walsall team, said.

'Next, I want all the upstairs windows checked to make sure they're locked, and I want you all to be aware of an attack from there. If they can't get in on the ground floor, they will climb. Got it?'

'The window we have set aside as our last resort exit has been left alone but the others all have surprises waiting for anyone breaching,' Charmaine said.

'Like what?' Trevor asked, surprised.

'Do you remember the film *Home Alone*?' she asked.

'Yes, of course. What about it?'

'Well, let's just say we copied a few of the boy's techniques when setting up the traps,' Charmaine hinted.

'Alright, well, you can tell me later, when it's all over and we're all safe and well,' Trevor laughed.

'We've also prepared the rooms to keep them in,' Amir

added, 'we just need to figure out what we're gonna do with them after.'

'Let's cross that bridge when we come to it,' Trevor said. 'It'll be a nice problem to have, won't it?'

'So, I guess we're ready for them, aren't we?' said Charmaine.

'I guess we are. Listen, I can't keep asking you to put yourselves in danger for us, so this is probably your last chance to leave safely,' he told the team.

'Seriously, if you ask again, we'll throw you out of the window,' Amir said, laughing.

'Alright, alright. Thank you, all of you. Now, get to your places. Zoe, please wait by the fuse box and turn it off when I shout, okay?'

'I'll be there,' she replied.

Rory returned and gave the thumbs-up. The gate was now locked. Darren, Rory, Izzy and young Danny Baptiste were positioned on the ground floor. They had placed a number of metal lockers strategically as barriers, having filled them with timber scraps and anything else that could protect them from bullets. They were tasked with slowing the attackers down once they had breached the reception area, the least secure and most likely way into the building.

Zoe, Martin, and Jimmy were placed at the rear of the building, covering the loading bay and gym area. It was also where the fuse box was located for Zoe. They had placed cars in front of the loading bay and inside it to prevent a vehicle ramming its way through. Trevor, Charmaine, Amir, and Clive were positioned upstairs to cover their colleagues' retreat if needed, but also to shower the attackers with a few surprises from above. They were joined by two other young boxers, friends of Danny, who had insisted on staying to help.

They covered the large stairwell for this purpose and also the first floor, where they would create obstacles for the attackers as they themselves retreated to safety.

Trevor went over and over the plan in his mind to make sure he hadn't left anything out. He was anxious about losing any of the team and wanted to be sure of his plan.

When he was satisfied that they were ready, he called Mo.

'Mo, listen carefully. I need you and Andy to go to the warehouse in Dagenham where the Qupis were operating from before, remember? We think they're keeping Greg there. The Albanians are on the way now, so be careful and do what you can to get in and out quickly and safely, okay?'

'Shouldn't we be here with you to fight these guys?' Mo asked, surprised at the change.

'No, we'll be fine. The building is secure, and we have an exit strategy. It's important that we get Greg back, so we'll try to keep them here for as long as possible to give you time.'

'Do you think they have left anyone behind to watch over Greg?'

'I doubt it. Stav told me they're on the way in three cars and a van, so they're coming mob-handed.'

'Alright, we'll set off now and call when we have an update.'

'Thanks, Mo, and remember—stay safe, both of you.'

'You too, Trev,' Mo replied, before hanging up.

He turned to Andy and said, 'Best we get a move on. We have a friend to rescue.'

~

15

'Hi, Dad, how's it going? Any news?'

'They're on the way, love. Stav saw them leaving the Dagenham warehouse that her husband was using before, which is where they could be holding Greg. I've sent Andy and Mo to see if they can grab him while we keep the Albanians busy here.'

'Oh, okay, that's a good development. Did he see how many are on the way?'

'Three cars and a van, so hopefully no more than fifteen or sixteen,' he said.

'Dad, please be careful. They'll all be armed, and you know how nasty they can be.'

'I know, darling. Don't worry, we have prepared as best as we could, and have lots of surprises in store for them.'

'What are you going to do when the attack is done with? Have you thought of that?' she asked.

'We've prepped the rooms to keep them until we decide what we want to do. It's not as simple as just sending them off in a container like before. The police are after them for killing a colleague and for a bunch of other murders too, including Charlie's. This lot needs something more... official.'

'Let me know if I can help in any way. I'm a bit worried about Andy and Mo being on their own. What if they've kept people behind?'

'I'm banking on the fact they haven't, love,' he said.

'Alright, keep me in the loop and I'll speak with you later. Love you, Dad,' she whispered.

'Love you too, darling.'

Kendra sat at her desk staring at her monitor but thinking of Andy and Mo putting themselves in potential danger at the warehouse, and worried for her Dad and the rest of the team, who were about to face a potentially lethal foe. It didn't take long for her to decide what to do. She went to speak with Rick.

'Anything to report?' he asked.

'Nothing, Rick, sorry, it's very frustrating for us all. Jill made a good point about the missing husband and the businesses he ran, that they were still in his company's name. I'm thinking it's worth a drive-by to see if there's any activity. It's a long shot, but we don't have anything else. I can leave now and check a few of them on the way home, if you're okay with that?'

'It'll have to wait until later, K. I need you to help Jill with a lead she's had. Should only take a couple of hours,' he said.

'There's nobody else who can help her with that?' she asked, more in hope than anything.

'Sorry, no. Go see Jill and she'll explain,' said Rick.

'Okay, will do,' she said, leaving. She was already aware of Jill's lead and knew it would amount to nothing, but she had to comply and keep the subterfuge going. She had no choice.

Don't do anything stupid, Andy, she thought, her mind spinning with the things that could go wrong.

~

Leandra and her cohort arrived in the vicinity of the factory and parked their cars where Mateo had earlier. It was a short walk, which they would make once they were happy there were no witnesses.

'I will go and take a look before we go in,' Mateo said.

'Very well,' Leandra said.

Mateo left his team and went on foot once more to check the venue. As he approached, he noticed immediately that things had changed when he saw the gate was locked. As he walked past, he could see it was padlocked, but also that there were still lights on in the building with several cars still parked.

He retraced his steps back to the team where he was met by Leandra, Esad, and Burin.

'They have locked the gate, but there are still staff on the premises. That is unusual,' he said.

'They are a security company,' said Esad. Maybe the gate was open because they had a delivery just before you arrived earlier.'

'Maybe, but we should be cautious. Bring the bolt cropper for the padlock and tell the men to be cautious. Things may not be as easy as they seem.'

'Very well,' his brother said, leaving to brief the men.

'I will wait for your signal to join you,' Leandra said, getting back into the car. She opened the window and added, 'Do not take too long.'

'We have done this before. We shall be quick,' Mateo replied, before joining the rest of the team.

'Esad, switch the jammer on, please,' he told his brother. The power phone jamming unit they had brought with them prevented mobile phones from working within a hundred-metre radius.

'It is on, but what about the land lines?' Esad asked.

'The phone lines go in near the gate. We shall cut them there,' Mateo replied.

Esad nodded. 'Then we are ready.'

'Burim, when the gate is open, I want you to take four men to the back and see if you can gain entry there,' Mateo said. 'The rest of us will try the same from the front. Use whatever means possible but make it quick. We do not want to take any chances. They can call for help.'

'Are we leaving anyone with Leandra?' Esad asked.

'She can take care of herself, brother. You know that better than most,' Mateo said, before turning to the rest. 'Let's go, men.'

He led them to the gate and nodded to the man with the bolt croppers.

'The phone line first, then the padlock,' he said, pointing to the junction box with the phone line coming from it.

Seconds later, the line was cut before the man moved to the gate. He raised the thirty-six-inch professional croppers to the sturdy padlock. It took several attempts and all his strength, but the man was finally able to cut through it. Another man pushed one side of the gate open to allow them all in, before closing it behind them.

'Go, go,' Mateo told his men as they stormed forward, handguns pointing to their target. Burim led his men to the rear and Mateo to the front, as planned. Mateo could see lights on upstairs, but strangely, nothing much downstairs. It was then that he noticed the ground-floor windows had been boarded up.

Strange, he thought, *are they closing down the business?*

At no point did he consider there was anyone inside that was expecting company. He approached the main door and tried pulling it open. It was locked. He indicated to two of his men to check either side while he considered what to do with the door.

'Bring the sledgehammer,' he told one of the men, who duly obliged and brought the fourteen-pounder with him.

'Give him room,' Esad told the men as they stood back and waited.

The man wasted no time and immediately started pounding on the door, aiming at the hinges rather than the obvious lock. The door was old but robust, and it took many attempts before the wood started to splinter by the bottom hinge. The man changed his stance and attacked the upper hinge, with the same result after half a dozen solid strikes. The middle hinge gave the most resistance, taking a dozen blows before it gave way. The man stepped back for one of his cohorts to move forward and aim a powerful kick to send the door flying inwards. As it was still locked, it didn't go very far, but there was enough room for them to squeeze through.

Esad went first, gun facing forward, as they approached another internal door, this time with glass panelling and metal frames. It, too, was locked. Two of the men started kicking it with their steel toe-capped boots, smashing several panes in the process, before that too gave way and flew open.

The reception area that they entered was eerily quiet. Nobody was manning the desk, and there were no lights on. Mateo nudged his brother and indicated to cameras that were facing in from the opposite corners of the spacious room. He saw a door behind the desk that he presumed led to the receptionist's office, and another wooden door to the side that led to the rest of the building.

'See if the CCTV controls are in the office and destroy them,' he told a man, who made his way behind the desk and into the small office behind. He was there for a few seconds before returning, shaking his head.

'There must be a control room somewhere,' Esad said, as they cautiously made their way to the wooden door.

'They must know we are here now and are trying to call for help. From here on it will be dangerous. Expect them to respond as they know they are trapped,' Mateo said.

His men nodded in acknowledgement as they reached the door. As expected, it was locked and seemed just as sturdy as the front door.

Mateo turned to the man with the sledgehammer again and moved out of his way.

The man did the same again, aiming for the hinges, taking a similar number of blows to splinter the wood. When he was done, he moved aside for his colleague with the powerful kick, who nonchalantly kicked at the same place as before—with no effect. The door did not move an inch. He tried kicking it again, harder. There was no movement whatsoever. Even with the damage to the hinges, the door would not budge.

'They have put something against the door,' Esad said, looking around for something to use as a battering ram.

'You men, get that sofa and bring it,' he said, pointing to the vintage dark green Chesterfield. The men dragged it over and lifted it, one side aimed squarely at the door.

'Hard as you can,' Mateo said, making sure they had room

for a small run-up. The settee smashed into the door, which moved slightly but did not open.

'Again!' Esad called.

Their run-up was slightly longer this time, and the door buckled slightly as they struck, but not enough to open.

'You two, help them,' Mateo told the watching men, 'get this bloody door open!'

'The extra strength did the trick. The door burst open, but only by a few inches. They had broken the lock and pushed whatever it was that was blocking it back slightly. There was still work to do. Mateo could see that it was dark in the room behind.

'You, bring the torch.'

When he shone the torch through the gap, he could see that it was, in fact, a short corridor, leading to another wooden door. He had no doubt they'd meet the same resistance there.

'What is blocking the door?' Esad asked.

'There is a wooden post across the door. They must have screwed it in place. It seems they were ready for intruders, men, so be cautious. This lot are not the walkover we thought they would be,' Mateo said.

'Bring the axe,' Esad shouted, prompting another man forward. The heavy, long-handled axe was similar to those used by firefighters, so it was ideal for this situation. It would take longer than he wanted, but they'd get through. As two of his comrades pushed the door inwards, the few inches that were available, the man struck with precision at the gap and the wooden obstruction behind the door.

The three-by-three-inch post was used for erecting garden fences, so it was solid and made an effective door stop. Trevor's team had secured the door by screwing several brackets to the post and then tightly to the door frame, which had prevented much movement when the hinges were damaged. The weight of the settee and four men wielding it as a battering ram did enough to dislodge one of the brackets and allow the small gap for him to aim for.

The powerful swings chipped away at the post and eventually, after several minutes, it was pummelled out of the way. Esad pushed the door forward cautiously as they moved slowly along the narrow corridor to the next door. There was one door to the right that led to the receptionist's office and one to the left that was unlocked. The sign showed it was the lavatories for staff. Mateo sent one man to check. The man returned quickly, having taken a cursory look in both toilets for anyone hiding, and shook his head. They moved forward and soon reached the second locked door.

'Expect much of the same here,' Mateo told his men as he moved out of the way for the sledgehammer.

Using the same technique as before, the door was pounded on the hinges. When the surrounding wood had splintered, more fruitless attempts were made to kick the door open, with the same predicable result.

'We can get the settee down here, but there's not a lot of room,' Esad said.

'It worked before, so it can work again. Everybody, get back,' he told the men, retreating to the reception area.

There wasn't enough room for four men to carry it, so one man had the side and another the end as they approached the second door slowly, the rest of the men behind them. They charged the door and struck it hard, but it didn't budge. They tried several times, without any buckling at all. This door was not giving way like the last one. Mateo swapped the tired men around and tried again, several times, with the same result.

'Shit,' he exclaimed. 'Esad!'

'Yes, brother?'

'Bring the grinder. This is not working. You two, take that out of here,' he said, indicating to the settee.

The Chesterfield was removed whilst Esad retrieved the eighteen-volt cordless grinder from a team member's backpack and returned to the door.

'Cut around the lock first, see if that does anything,' Mateo ordered.

The grinder made short work of the wood, but it took precious time. Esad cut around it and then, when satisfied, he kicked at the lock, which sent it spinning inwards into the room beyond. He looked briefly through the hole and asked for the torch.

'It is a large, open-plan room; I see tables and chairs and lots of lockers on their sides. They must have pushed them over to try to obstruct us,' Esad said.

'Never mind that. What is blocking the door?' Mateo demanded.

Esad put his arm through the hole and reached down to feel for any obstruction.

'I think it's one of the lockers. They must have screwed it in place, too, otherwise it would have moved.'

'Shit!' Mateo exclaimed again, 'we cannot afford these delays. Start cutting into the door. It is our only way in.'

It would take them some time.

~

'I CAN'T GET THROUGH, ANDY,' Mo said, concerned.

'It doesn't surprise me. They're probably jamming signals. It's what I'd do. We just have to trust that Trevor and the gang will be able to handle them.'

Mo nodded.

'You know, it's kinda weird that you're driving the van, what with you having one eye and one foot. Are you sure it's allowed?'

Andy laughed.

'I can't tell you how many times I get asked that. Yes, it's allowed. The van is automatic, and it's my left foot that's been amputated, so there's no clutch pedal I need to operate. My vision is slightly impaired, but I've learned to deal with it. You may see me looking from side to side more frequently, but I haven't had a crash yet,' he replied, touching his head for luck.

'Good luck to you, man. It's a bigger deal than you're making it out to be, so big respect to you.'

'We're here, Mo, so I'll park a bit further down and we can go the rest of the way on foot,' Andy said, suddenly serious.

'Roger that.'

With Marge safely parked, they walked towards the warehouse.

'There are no cars out the front, but that doesn't mean there's nobody been left behind,' Andy said.

'I've been here before, so I'll have a quick look around the back, if you want to check the front?' Mo replied.

Andy nodded. They split as they arrived, both watching for signs of activity as they went about their task. Mo had been several times with his brother, Amir, when they had taken on the Qupi gang run by Leandra's husband. He remembered the way into the warehouse, via a first-floor window that Amir had climbed through to let them in.

Although not as adept at parkour as his brother, Mo was confident he could climb the drainpipe and reach the window. The rear was obscured and there was no way of being seen, so he immediately started the climb.

Damn that talented brother of mine, he thought as he struggled up. He eventually reached over to the window and breathed a sigh of relief to see that it was unlocked, as his breaking-in skills were not as refined. He quietly and slowly opened the window, listening for any sounds. There were none, so he slowly and silently climbed through and found himself on the first-floor landing.

So far so good.

Andy was not so fortunate. He had tried the door at the front and wasn't surprised to find it locked. He then looked through the window to see if anything was visible on the ground floor. Nothing. He looked around to see if anyone was watching and decided the only way in was to jemmy the side window open. When satisfied the coast was clear, he took out his trusty penknife and used brute force to prise the lock free from the wooden frame. It took a few attempts, but he was finally able to get it open.

This is where the fun starts, he thought, as he looked down at his prosthetic foot. He was almost pain-free now and used to it, but he wasn't quite skilled at climbing just yet. Fortunately, the window was only a few feet from the ground, so he was able to use his good right foot to help himself up once he had pulled his upper body through. After some struggling due to the prosthetic foot, he clambered into the warehouse and landed safely. He stood still for a moment, listening for any sounds or potential threats. He heard nothing and moved slowly towards the far end.

The warehouse was eerily quiet. There was just enough

light from the few windows, allowing him to see what was in the space ahead of him. There were a few tables and chairs scattered around, along with metal cabinets and lockers. It was sparse, but not empty. As he scanned the floor, he heard a sound coming from one darkened corner, which stopped him in his tracks. He walked towards the sound, wary that he couldn't see clearly.

As he got closer, he could see there were cabinets and lockers lined up against both walls towards the corner, where there was a break of about three feet on each side. It was there that he saw the faint outline of someone on a chair slumped forward, seemingly tied up. He rushed forward, knowing immediately that it had to be Greg.

'Greg!' he said, as he reached the young man. His hands had been tied behind his back with several plastic zip-ties attached to the metal chair, along with both his legs to the feet of the chair. He didn't stand a chance of escaping by himself. Whoever had secured him knew exactly what they were doing.

Greg moaned, barely conscious. He managed to lift his head slowly and looked up at Andy. His eyes widened in recognition.

'A-Andy. F-factory. Attacking it,' he whispered, his mouth dry and his wounds encrusted with dry blood. He was exhausted and in agony. The wounds on his cheeks looked dreadful, but they appeared to have stopped bleeding. Andy could see splashes of blood all over the floor in the corner, testament to the brutal torture the young man had endured.

'Don't worry about the factory, buddy, the team is waiting for them and is well prepared. Let me get you out of these,' Andy said, pulling him upright in the chair. He used his penknife to start cutting at the zip ties, first at the ankles and then the wrists. He was just cutting the last one when he noticed that Greg was slightly agitated.

'T-the g-guard?' Greg said, looking past Andy as if to check for something—or someone.

'What guard?' Andy said, just as a chair smashed against his back. The force of the blow was brutal and forced him to the ground, the breath forced out of his lungs. He turned in time to see his attacker lift the chair up above his head to smash it down upon him. Everything seemed to happen in slow motion. Strangely, he noticed the attacker was a large man who had a heavily bandaged eye, the bandage very clean and neatly applied.

Andy thought it strange that the man hadn't struck him again and even stranger that the man closed his eye and fell sideways to the floor. He sat up and shook his head to clear it. That was when he noticed Mo standing behind the prone attacker, holding a crowbar in his hand.

'I never leave home without it,' he said, smiling. 'Now let's get Greg out of here before he wakes up or his mates come back.'

'You'll get no argument from me,' Andy said, getting to his feet and stretching to ease the pain.

Together, they dragged Greg out of the warehouse, using the door instead of the window, and on to Marge and to safety. Greg was semi-conscious, his head lolling against his chest as he tried several times in vain to respond to his friends.

'We need to get him to hospital,' Andy said, 'and quickly.'

'Dude, if we do that, the police will get involved and we'll end up in the shit. Let's take him to the doctor that we took Izzy to when he was stabbed, remember?'

'I'm happy with that. Do you know how to get there?' asked Andy.

'Yes, it's towards Dagenham, so head that way and I'll direct you,' Mo replied. 'I'll try to call Trevor again.'

He tried several times but could not get through.

'They'll have to do without us for now, mate,' Andy said. 'We need to get young Greg here some help sharpish.'

'Understood. Step on it, then,' Mo said. He was smiling, and they were both relieved to have Greg again, but the concern for the welfare of their friends ran deep.

'Hang in there, guys and gals,' Andy muttered.

∼

16

After what seemed like an age, the grinder finally did its job and cut a hole in the door large enough for them to squeeze through. The room beyond was in darkness, and as Esad had explained, strewn with obstacles that seemed to have been dropped as the occupants left in a hurry. Except Mateo suspected that wasn't the case, otherwise why secure the door in such a way? Once through, he looked back and saw that the metal locker had been screwed to the frame and was also held in place by a wooden baton that had been screwed to the floor. It wasn't budging for anyone.

'Spread out, but be careful,' he told his men as they all came through. Some shone torches, and others used their mobile phones to light the way ahead. It was unnaturally quiet and the hairs on the back of his neck were standing on end. His instincts were correct.

The first man was downed by a burst from the left, and within seconds, four of his men were down, the rest taking cover wherever they could. The downed men spluttered as they got to their feet, disoriented, and two of them fired their guns blindly ahead of them, only to be downed again by the force of water that came from the industrial jet washers that Andy had ordered. Only it wasn't just water that they were being attacked with, it was water mixed with creosote, a noxious substance that they were now inhaling and which some had ingested. The men started to cough and attempted to spit out the substance. Their eyes started to sting as they had not worn any protective goggles, so they were now almost blind and a danger to themselves and their colleagues.

Mateo could see this immediately.

'Cover your mouths and do not let anything get in your eyes!' he shouted. 'Quickly, we need to get these men to ground, stop them from firing!'

The four men were dragged to the floor and kept behind the obstacles that had been placed there. Two of Mateo's men, who had not been affected, fired in the direction of the liquid jets, but it was too dark to see whether they'd had any effect. What none of the men could see was that some of the obstacles on the factory floor were also hiding the men firing the jet washers. They had used the larger metal cabinets in conjunction with the smaller lockers to create the barriers towards the rear of the floor, so they had not only protection from any wayward bullets, but also the concealment and surprise that the attackers would never expect. The lockers arrayed around the floor ahead of them were there to slow the attackers and also to give a false sense that nothing was in them. It had worked brilliantly.

'Stop firing!' Mateo shouted, raising his arm in the air.

'What the hell is that?' asked Esad. 'It stinks like chemicals.'

'I think it's paint thinner or something, the guys can't see properly now, so be careful,' Burin replied.

'Burin, take one side, and Esad, the other. We will flank them. Do not fire unless you have a confirmed sighting,' Mateo shouted. He spoke, as always, in Albanian, so there was no danger of his opponents understanding what was about to happen.

Unfortunately for him, the flanking manoeuvre was exactly what the defenders were expecting—and banking on. From the first floor, Trevor looked down at the scene unfolding downstairs. His night-vision goggles afforded him excellent views of all the attackers, especially in infra-red mode, which showed their heat patterns. He was able to see what was going on via the discreet holes that had been made to allow for just such an advantage. In the dark, the attackers would never be able to see the modifications that had been made to the ceilings and walls.

'Get ready to switch on the dragon lights,' he whispered to Charmaine and Clive, who were similarly clad in protective gear including protective vests, Nightfox night-vision goggles, and M50 protective gas masks. They each carried their trusted Axon Taser 7 and were trained to use the thirty-thousand volts that would incapacitate most men.

The Dragon T12 search lights were powerful torches used by the police and the military, with two-hundred-thousand candlepower, and were as potent as they came. Trevor was aware of their intensity and was banking on the attackers trying to flank them on the ground floor. As Burin and Esad slowly made their way to the sides and then forward, Trevor gave the signal to Charmaine and Clive.

'Now!' he whispered urgently.

The two dragon lights were placed against the holes and

turned on, immediately illuminating and temporarily blinding the two men. They both raised their arms to cover their eyes, but it was too late. Their cries were the signal for Darren and his team, still hiding in the cabinets, to be released with the jet washers again. The two men were instantly thrown off their feet by the jet closest to them, while the other two were aimed at the remaining attackers, who were easy to spot with the night-vision. They were pinned down and started to fire wildly again.

The dragon lights were turned off, and the room was back in darkness, with minimal light from torches.

'Hold your fire, idiots!' Mateo shouted, wiping the toxic liquid mix from his cheek. He was lucky. Esad and Burin were now incapacitated, as were two more of his men. A quick calculation was all he needed to determine that he was down to the last three men, including himself. He needed the rest to recover swiftly, or they would be in trouble.

'Esad, Burin, are you okay?'

'I can't see!' his brother responded, wisely keeping his head down. 'It stings like hell!'

'Burin?'

'Same here. I have some water, and it is helping. Esad, use your water bottle. It will ease the stinging,' the team leader replied.

'The same for all of you, otherwise we'll be sitting ducks!' Mateo shouted.

There were sounds of splashing as the men took the advice on board.

'It's working. It still stings, and my vision is blurry, but I can find my way around now. Anyone else?' asked Esad.

There were several responses as most of the men started to recover. One or two acknowledged that it hadn't worked;

many were still coughing and spluttering. His unit was not in great shape, but they were all still alive and mainly able to function.

'We need another plan,' Burin suggested.

'Okay, when I give the signal, I want some of us to start firing randomly towards the far wall. Burin, you, Esad, and three men make your way back out of the room and try to find another way into the building. We must split our force if we have a chance of turning this around.'

'Understood,' came the reply from both men. Burin selected the three who were to accompany him.

'Ready when you are,' he shouted.

'Okay, the rest of you, start firing ... *now!*'

The noise was deafening as seven handguns were fired towards the other end of the building. As soon as it started, the five men selected to find another way in quickly made their way back to their point of entry and left the room. Only then did Mateo signal his remaining men.

'Hold your fire,' he shouted.

He listened for any activity ahead of him, hoping to hear a whimper from a lucky hit. What he was unaware of was that when the dragon lights had been switched on, it was the signal for Darren and his men to leave their jet washers and immediately retreat upstairs to safety, while the attackers were disoriented. There was no danger to anyone on the team from the random firing. Even more so, Trevor could see everything as it played out in front of him, so he saw the five men leaving.

'Okay, they've split the team, as expected. Get ready with their surprises,' he told Amir, Danny, and two of the younger members of the team.

'I loved *Home Alone*,' he whispered to Charmaine and

Clive, who remained with him. 'They're in for some painful surprises.'

From the front end of the building, there was only one way upstairs, and that was the stairwell Darren and his three colleagues were now covering. The back end of the building, where the loading bay, gym, and storerooms were, was not accessible from the room the Albanians were currently being held in. It was one of the modifications Trevor had made, to ensure that nobody could 'accidentally' find their way into the secure areas at the rear. The easiest options were via the loading bay at the back, which was now blocked by several vehicles, or the staff access door, which was similarly barricaded. There was also access to the first floor at the far end, which in this instance would be useful for the strategic retreat they might have to make.

Trevor hoped they'd be able to give the gangsters a good hiding and ideally secure them safely, without any casualties.

I just hope this isn't for nothing, he thought, hoping that the rescue had been successful.

∽

ANDY AND MO helped carry Greg into the doctor's house via the rear entrance, reserved for instances such as this. When Doctor Lee had helped them with Izzy's injuries a few months earlier, Trevor had rewarded him, allowing for new equipment, and had agreed on a 'retainer' to assist when required. The doctor was more than happy to agree, so bringing Greg here was a good call as he would be in safe hands.

'Bring him through,' the doctor said, leading them towards a door off the kitchen that led to a cellar that had been modified for discreet use, separate from the practice on the ground floor. The stairwell and cellar were spotless and covered entirely with plastic cladding that was easy to clean. The room itself was large and decked out with modern equipment, courtesy of Trevor's generosity.

'Please, close the door behind you,' the doctor asked, and Andy obliged as Mo helped with Greg.

They laid the young man on the padded table and the doctor immediately started to examine him, first checking the wounds on his cheeks and then looking for others that might not be so evident.

'He is severely dehydrated, and these wounds are infected. I need to attach a drip and clean him up before I can attend to them. Please, help me with his clothes.'

They gently removed most of Greg's outer clothing as the doctor prepared a drip to rehydrate him.

'Poor kid,' Andy said, as Greg showed signs of semi-consciousness.

'He'll be fine, I'm sure,' said Mo. 'He'll have some nice scars, but that's better than being dead, right?'

'Absolutely.' Andy took Greg's hand. 'Hang in there, buddy, we're right here with you.'

'F-factory...' Greg said, squeezing Andy's hand.

'It's okay, mate, it's okay. Everything is fine,' Andy said.

Let's hope that's the case, he thought.

~

'Listen carefully,' Mateo told his remaining men. 'When I give the signal, we will start firing and moving towards the stairwell, do you understand?'

'Yes!'

'On my mark... *now!*'

The gangsters rose from their positions and started firing towards the far wall. When they met no resistance, they increased their pace until they reached the stairwell, where they stopped firing and took cover on either side of it. The stairwell was seven feet wide and there were fifteen steps to the right-hand turn. Mateo couldn't see the next floor to assess any potential danger, but they were committed to going up if they wanted to resume their attack.

'Erjon, Gezim, take point up the stairs, continual fire until you reach the landing. Ferid, Valon, when I signal, you will follow. Understood?'

'Yes, Mateo!'

'On my mark... *now!*'

The two men started up the stairs, firing shots as they did so. Not rapid fire, but enough to scare whoever was upstairs into taking cover.

'Ferid, Valon, go!'

Two men followed behind the lead pair, their guns raised but not firing.

The two in front reached the landing before turning to the right, side by side, continuing to lay covering fire, their colleagues a few feet behind, covering them and waiting to act.

There was no warning, just the two pace-setters tumbling back and falling onto their colleagues, dragging them down and back towards the ground floor in a heap. As they tumbled, two large weights tied to a rope swung lazily at the small landing towards the first floor where they had been launched from, swinging in triumph at the direct hit.

The two lead men lay unconscious on the floor next to Mateo, blood streaming from a broken nose and a gashed cheek. The two back-ups groaned in pain, having had their colleagues land on them as dead weights.

'What is this?' Mateo screamed. 'They are toying with us!'

He reached back and grabbed the Heckler & Koch MP5 compact sub-machine gun that was slung behind him and fired indiscriminately up the stairs, roaring in anger as he did so.

'I will gut you all!' he screamed, emptying the thirty-round magazine in seconds. Without thinking, he removed the empty magazine and replaced it.

'Get up, fools! We're not finished with our mission. We go again!' he told Ferid and Valon, now back on their feet. 'I will come behind you. The rest of you follow me.'

With two men down, that left five of them, and Mateo was determined to reach the first floor and complete his mission.

'On my mark... *now!*'

Ferid and Valon started firing, wary of the swinging weights that had rendered their colleagues unconscious. As they turned right at the landing, they slowed slightly, waiting for more weights. When that threat failed to materialise, they proceeded up, slowly, watching for other threats. Mateo was behind but not so close as to fall foul of the men landing on top of him.

As a result, when they both fell backwards, he was able to avoid them, and side-stepped their falling bodies. His instincts saved him not only from the men, but also the tree trunk that followed, having struck its prey hard. It was five feet long and a foot in diameter, tied at each end with the rope from which it was swinging.

'Damn you!' he screamed as he dodged the trap and continued up slowly, firing shorter, more sensible bursts from his MP5. He couldn't see anyone in the darkness, just occasional glimpses of the ropes from the traps, which were now behind him and swinging very slightly above the landing. The two men behind him had also stayed far back enough to avoid the traps, so were able to continue backing Mateo up.

Mateo could not see anyone but suddenly smelled something very disturbing... *petrol*. He couldn't see it, but he could hear it trickling down the stairs, past him and his men, towards the ground floor. His eyes widened in fear, his anger suddenly forgotten.

'Retreat! Now!' he screamed.

The men didn't need telling twice and quickly ran down the stairs, dragging their stunned colleagues with them. Mateo followed closely behind.

It was turning out to be a bad day at the office. His men hurt, unconscious, and humiliated by an enemy they hadn't even seen yet.

'We must get out, now, leave them!' he yelled, aiming for the hole in the door. Two of his men were still unconscious and there was no chance they could be carried out in time to avoid a fire. The five men, two of whom were still struggling from being struck by the tree trunk, managed to squeeze through without incident and made for the exit, happy to be free of danger.

Within seconds of them leaving, the two unconscious attackers were searched, zip-tied, and dragged upstairs by Darren and his men, before being taken to the rooms where they'd be locked away.

'When you've secured them, cover their hands with plastic bags and tape them tight,' Trevor said. 'And make sure you all keep your gloves on when dealing with these people, okay?'

The petrol that had been released at the top had come

from a one-litre plastic bottle. It was all that was needed to scare the life out of the attackers, the potent smell doing its job perfectly. Amir was tasked with releasing it and was now carefully mopping it up.

'They'll be trying again, won't they?' asked Charmaine.

'Oh, yes, we haven't seen the back of this lot. We need to take them out – all of them,' Trevor replied.

'I wonder how the others are getting on?' she asked.

∽

17

Burin and Esad were as confident as Mateo had been when they approached the rear of the building. There were a number of vehicles parked tightly against the wall and one or two parked randomly in the yard, but there didn't seem to be any danger from their perspective.

'There.' Esad pointed to the ground-floor windows on one side of the loading bay, which was obstructed. The two metal-framed windows were traditional 1970s throwbacks; back then, toughened glass was frequently used in commercial premises. The glass had thin wire filaments running through it and was slightly opaque as a result of the thickness. It was an effective deterrent against the burglars of that decade. What wasn't ideal was that with the right tools, you could jemmy them open and use a screwdriver to open them from the inside, which is exactly what Esad did.

The five men quietly moved towards them, handguns ready, and saw that the blinds had been closed, thus restricting any views inside.

Burim took a crowbar from the backpack of one of his

men and placed it against the frame, forcing the sharp end under the metal.

'Get the Slim Jim ready,' he told one of the men, who duly obliged with the long, thin tool.

The window was tough but no match for the brute strength of the team leader, who was able to force it open half an inch.

'Now,' he told the man.

His colleague duly obliged and put the Slim Jim through the gap and against the handle on the inside, slowly moving it upwards, unlocking the window. Burim pulled the crowbar clear as the window opened. He grinned at his man and nodded for him to go first. The man put his handgun back in its holster and lifted himself up through the window. He quietly pulled the blinds to one side, revealing a darkened loading bay. He looked back at his colleagues and nodded.

'It's clear,' he whispered.

He quietly jumped onto the ledge that was a couple of feet off the ground floor and ran across the remaining width of the loading bay. The shutters were at one end of the bay and the ledge extended into an L-shape to allow for the loading of large vehicles that didn't have tail lifts.

He went over and opened the other window, speeding up the process of getting his colleagues all inside. Within seconds, all five men were inside the loading bay. There was enough light now to see the layout, and they quickly saw that a vehicle was parked tight against the shutters of the bay. They could see nothing else.

Burim turned to two of his men and indicated for them to go to the far end, whilst the remaining three would progress from their entry point. When they were in place, he gave the signal to move forward, which they all did slowly. The ledge extended only ten feet, so when they got to the edge, they all jumped quietly to the ground. That was when the screaming started, as two of his men jumped straight onto the wooden boards with six-inch nails sticking up out of the bottoms. Both men landed directly on them, the nails going straight through and out the top of their boots. When one of them dropped to the floor in agony, he landed straight onto more nails, two of which went into his backside, increasing the screams.

'Stop!' Burim shouted, wary of doing the same. He moved his foot around the floor and quickly felt more traps, waiting for them all. 'We need light. Shine the torches on the floor and be ready to fire.'

Esad and the remaining uninjured man obliged and shone the torches ahead of them. The ground was littered with the boards, the nails gleaming in the torchlight. Burim shone his own torch around the room to see if there were any more threats but could see none. He turned to his fallen men, seeing them in agony, bleeding.

'Get yourselves to safety. We have to move on, understand?'

The two men acknowledged with a thumbs-up, pain seared on their faces.

'Let's move,' Burim said, handgun raised, as he slowly led them toward the far end of the bay and the door leading to their targets.

As he reached out cautiously to open the wooden double doors, Burim realised that there was a mezzanine level at that end of the bay, something he had not noticed before. As he looked up to inspect it, he was struck on the head, first by a gallon of white gloss paint, and then by the tin it had been poured from. His men were simultaneously attacked in the same way, one of them falling to the ground unconscious from the can striking his forehead. The paint covered their heads and dropped down, making the now slippery floor treacherous for their boots.

'Back! Back!' Burim screamed to Esad, both spluttering as the paint got into their mouths and noses.

Esad panicked and fired his handgun blindly towards the area he thought was the mezzanine. His vision was impaired and the oily gloss paint neither tasted nor smelled pleasant. He spat some out and shook his head to help clear his vision, making it worse in the process and showering Burim with more paint.

Burim was in no better shape, falling over several times as he tried to retreat to the ledge. He too fired several shots up into the area he thought the attack had come from, also blindly and ineffectively. It was then that he heard his opponents for the first time, via a shout from the mezzanine area.

'Now!'

The back doors of the van that blocked the loading bay shutters flew open and Jimmy and Martin ran out, fully kitted up, each holding the corner of a tarpaulin, which they pulled over the two men, pulling them down to the floor. Zoe, also fully kitted, ran to the injured men and sprayed them with CS gas as they struggled with their injuries. At the same instant, Darren and his three men stormed into the loading bay from the double doors, each holding a metal pipe. As the two attackers were forced to the ground under the tarpaulin and before they had a chance to properly react, Darren and Rory struck them both several times on the head, knocking them out instantly, whilst Clive and Izzy attended to the two injured men who were now blindly—thanks to Zoe—trying to both clear their vision and extricate themselves from the boards, while in excruciating pain. They were quickly subdued and restrained.

As Esad collapsed to the floor, he pulled the trigger blindly, the bullet striking Martin in the thigh. The Walsall boxer fell to one knee, gasping in pain, as his colleagues quickly disarmed and secured the two attackers with zip ties. All the captives were searched and deprived of their weapons and belongings. They were then quickly removed to the rooms that were waiting for them.

Darren retrieved a first-aid kit and tended to Martin's wound. He slathered it in antiseptic cream and then bandaged it securely.

'The bullet went straight through,' Martin told his friend. 'You can see both holes in my jeans.'

'You're a lucky boy,' Darren said. 'Now you have a story to match Izzy's brush with death by stabbing!'

They both laughed, with Martin wincing as Darren tightened the bandage.

'It was worth it just for that,' he said.

'What next?' Zoe asked.

'We prep the area again, just in case the others get through. I'll go and see if Trevor has any ideas,' Darren replied. 'Martin, we need to get you upstairs, mate, where you can wait until we can get you to the doctor.'

'Thanks, mate.'

'Zoe, see if you can get that window shut again, will you? Let's not make it easy for them again, eh?'

'You think that was easy?' she said. 'We spent ages arguing about how that was going to pan out. I think we did a damn fine job, don't you?'

Darren laughed.

'As a matter of fact, I do, Zoe. And I bet most of it was your idea, wasn't it? No way did Jimmy or Martin think of the tarpaulin or even hiding in the van.'

'Yeah, well, they needed a little push, but they got there in the end,' she said, laughing. 'I'll go and sort the window out.'

Darren helped Martin upstairs, where he met with Trevor.

'We have five more locked up, Trev; seven in total, which leaves the five from downstairs. Any sign of them?'

'No, so get Martin to the office and get everyone back to their places. I don't trust these bastards one little bit. They're up to something. I know they are. We need to be careful.'

∼

TREVOR WAS right to fear the remaining Albanians. As Mateo had taken them back out, he had decided to follow Burim and Esad's idea of gaining entry from the back of the property. After exiting at the front and tending briefly to wounds and eye washes, he had led his men to the rear. He immediately saw one of the windows was open and smiled, confident that Burim and his brother would quickly dispatch anyone inside. As they approached the window to follow them inside, he heard the screams and quickly brought his men to a halt. It was clear that his associates had met some resistance. Mateo retreated with his men to the corner of the building, thinking on his feet and realising they needed another way in. He looked up and pointed to the first-floor windows.

'We go up,' he told his men.

∼

KENDRA HAD to wait an hour or so before she was able to leave work and was flustered as she got to her car and started towards the warehouse in Dagenham. She had sent Andy several messages without any response and had tried calling, again with no response. She'd had the same results when trying to call her father, which deeply concerned her. Her choice of going to the warehouse first was based on the hope that Trevor had plenty of people with him and had a better chance of success than Andy and Mo did if they were confronted.

She messaged Trevor and Andy again. *'I haven't heard back from anyone, so I'm going to the warehouse to see if I can help.'*

Hopefully, before she got there, they would respond to say everyone was safe, but until then, she had to check.

'Why isn't anyone answering?' she shouted as she sped through the streets of east London.

∼

MATEO and his men climbed the rickety stack they had put together using pallets and timber from the pile in the yard. It got them to within six feet of the window, which was close enough for them to reach up and pull themselves into the small, darkened room. There was a drop of around eight feet to the floor of what appeared to be a large storeroom. When all five men were safely inside, Mateo used his torch to take a closer look. He could see an empty floor-to-ceiling industrial shelving system on one side, metal cabinets along the other, and nothing in between. The floor appeared to be covered with large glossy tiles, unusual for the setting. It was only when he turned towards the window that he realised they were in what had once been a wet room. The shower heads had been removed, but the pipes were still there, against the back wall. It had since been converted to a storeroom.

The door at the far end was another of the sturdy wooden ones, like those they had encountered downstairs, so he indicated for one of his men to check it.

The door was locked. Although the room was in darkness, there was enough daylight coming in through the window for them to get their bearings without any difficulties. What it didn't show clearly were the two one-inch holes that had been drilled near the bottom of the door, which now had hoses protruding slightly inside, having been secured there with gaffer tape earlier by the ever-resourceful Charmaine. The hoses were attached to two more small jet washers, but instead of water and creosote, these two had been filled with oil, which was now being pumped into the room without the attackers' knowledge.

'What's that humming?' asked one of Mateo's men.

'Sounds like air conditioning or something like that,' Mateo said. 'Who has the crowbar?'

One of his men pulled it out and handed it to Mateo, who stood there glaring at the man.

'Go and see if you can force the door, idiot,' he hissed.

The man raised his hands in apology and went to do as he had been ordered. He got to within three feet of the door before he fell for the first time, the oil on the tiles making it impossible for him to stand. He landed on his back, winded, with his legs in the air.

'What the...' Mateo said, instinctively going to his aid, and suffering a similar fate. Within seconds, all five men were on the floor, scrabbling for purchase and trying to get to their feet. Two of them dropped their handguns to the floor as they tried desperately to stay upright. The others holstered them in order to use both hands. They all slithered towards the shelving, the only thing they could hold on to.

'What the hell is going on?' Mateo screamed, comically sliding in all directions as he held on for dear life.

'Is that glitter?' one of the men said, shining the torch onto his oily hands.

Charmaine had added the glitter to the mix as an amusing afterthought. Some of it was glowing in the dark, which was activated by the torchlight. And now it was all over their clothing and skin, giving them an eerie appearance.

'Are we being attacked by children?' one man asked, exasperated by the traps they had encountered.

'Shut up!' shouted Mateo. 'We must find a way out of this cursed place, and we still have a mission to complete!'

'How are we going to do that?' asked the man. 'The only way out is through that window,' he added, pointing eight feet up to their method of entry.

'It's a hell of a drop,' Mateo said, looking around desperately for anything they could use. There was no rope or anything they could tie off to get down, but they had no choice. There was no way out of this room except for the window.

'Okay,' Mateo decided quickly, 'Dzeko, we'll boost you up and you have to find a way down without breaking your neck. That pile of wood isn't going to take a landing, so be careful. When you're down, I want you to find something for us to use, a rope or something.'

Dzeko looked from Mateo to his colleagues, his shoulders slumping as he realised that he was the sacrificial goat to get them out safely. It was his bones that would likely break or fracture.

'I hope I get a bonus for this,' he muttered, as he walked towards the window.

Two of his colleagues gave him a boost up, and he was able to lift himself to the window. It looked higher than he remembered on the way up and he shook his head in resignation as he reversed his position to go down, facing the wall. He hung there for a couple of seconds, looking down one last time at the pile they'd made to gain some height. That was his landing point, and he was hoping it would be soft enough to avoid serious injury. He took a deep breath and let go. The landing was anything but soft, the pile dispersed, wood scattering everywhere as soon as he landed. His body went one way and his legs another, slamming him onto the small mound of timber that remained.

Dzeko groaned in pain, but he was sure there were no broken bones, so he smiled as he lifted himself up. He wasn't expecting to see what looked like Darth Vader without a cape standing in front of him, holding a spray can—aimed at Dzeko's face. In the split second before he lost his vision and experienced the searing pain that accompanied it, he saw—in slow motion—the spray coming from the can. He knew instantly that it was CS gas and that there was no escape from it.

Before he was able to scream in pain, he felt something cover his head. It felt like sack cloth, coarse and musty, and a hand quickly pressed against his mouth. Gloved hands grabbed his arms roughly and pinned them behind his back, where they were quickly tied with zip ties. His eyes were in agony, and he was unable to do anything except allow himself to be led away.

He was taken back inside the building and up some stairs where his captors searched him thoroughly, removing all items from him. It was only then that the sackcloth was removed from his head, and he was able to breathe fresh air again. His eyes still stung like hell and his vision was very blurred, but he could do nothing about it. A metal handcuff was placed tightly on his right wrist, and he heard it attach to something metal before the zip ties were cut, freeing his arms.

One of the captors, whose blurry outline he could barely see, spoke to him from behind their mask.

'You will not shout or attempt to escape, do you understand? You will not receive a second warning.'

'Go to hell!' Dzeko spat, kicking out.

If the stinging eyes were not painful enough, the taser that struck his chest more than made up for it. Thirty thousand volts coursed through his body as he fell to the floor, thrashing uncontrollably. His head started hurting once the shock had stopped, thanks to having landed on it when he fell. He lay there, moaning in pain, trapped and unable to see, covered in oil and fluorescent glitter.

'That is what will happen if you try anything stupid again, do you understand?' the voice said.

Dzeko simply nodded, not wanting any more pain. It had not been a good day.

∽

'WHAT THE HELL is that idiot doing?' Mateo shouted impatiently. 'Pietr, your turn.'

'Damn it,' Pietr muttered as he walked gingerly to the window. 'Maybe he's still looking for rope?'

'Then you can go and help him, no?' Mateo replied.

He was lifted up and soon found himself in the same

position as Dzeko had been, only with a further drop down now that the woodpile had dispersed. He closed his eyes and prayed, before releasing his grip and falling. Pietr wasn't as lucky as Dzeko and twisted his ankle badly as he landed. He yelled out in pain.

'What is it, Pietr?' Mateo shouted, fearing the worst.

'I've twisted my ankle. It's agony!'

'Try to find Dzeko to help you,' Mateo said.

'Okay, but don't expect me to run anywhere for a while,' Pietr said. He managed to stand and support himself by leaning against the wall. He looked down, happy that it wasn't anything worse than a sprain, even though it hurt like hell. As he looked up, he almost had a heart attack as something appeared in front of him, spraying a can into his face. A second later, his head was covered, and his hands tied behind his back, whilst a hand covered his mouth. He struggled to breathe and to walk, so he was pulled along by his captors, his agony worsening. Five minutes later, he was secured in another room, along with eight of his cohorts, all incapacitated in some way or another, unable to free themselves and unwilling to risk electric shocks.

There was still much to do.

∽

18

What is keeping those buffoons? Leandra thought as she waited impatiently in the car. The phone jammer was still active, so no calls could go in or out, meaning there was no way of finding out. The short mission should have been successful by now, so her concerns were mounting that they hadn't returned yet. Drumming her fingers along the top of the steering wheel, the matriarch decided it was time to take a look for herself.

∽

'THIS IS RIDICULOUS!' Mateo shouted, banging his fist against the wall. 'Where the hell are they?'

'What do you want us to do, Mateo?' asked one of the two remaining men, still holding on to avoid slipping.

Mateo had no clue; his only shot was sending the men to find a way to get them out of this place, but he didn't want to make it obvious that he didn't know what to do next. He needed to think—and fast. They were all covered in oil and glitter, and his temperament was worsening. He did not like to be humiliated, which was precisely what had happened so far.

'We have no choice,' he said. 'There is no way they will let us leave through that door. They prepared for our attack, and they have done it well. We must leave by the window, the same as Dzeko and Pietr.'

The two men nodded, accepting his decision and hoping they would be able to leave this godforsaken place quickly. They started making their way carefully towards the window, occasionally reaching out for support. Despite the amount of oil they had soaked up between them, there was still enough on the floor to cause them great difficulty. This meant they required both hands to support each other and stay upright. They were halfway to the window when they heard the door open. As they turned to look, one of the men slipped and fell, scrambling against his colleague to try to get back to his feet. Mateo instinctively went for his gun, leaving him unsteady on his feet and unable to use it effectively.

Within seconds they were struck by what appeared to be a wooden door. They couldn't see who was responsible, or how many, and saw nothing except for some feet, strangely wrapped in towels, which was clearly helping them stay upright. There was also a glimpse of a tactical helmet, goggles and mask, so no human features were visible.

All three men were forced to the ground and trapped by the heavy door, with the additional weight of their attackers keeping them pinned. Hands appeared from the side, grabbing for weapons and anything that could cause danger. Mateo was the only one with a gun in his hand and instinctively fired two rounds, but his hand was pinned, and so the rounds struck the wall harmlessly.

'Grab that gun!' a voice shouted from behind the door.

As someone tried to grab the gun, Mateo tried to prise it away from them and pulled the trigger again, the round hitting the same wall.

'Pin the hand down!' the voice shouted urgently. A boot stepped on his hand, and he heard and felt the crack of bones in his thumb and trigger finger. The pain was excruciating, and he was now unable to squeeze the trigger. He held on, determined not to give up his gun.

His left arm was also trapped under the door, but he was able to move it and grab the bowie knife from the sheath in his boot. He managed to turn his body sideways, squeezed the knife through, and brought it towards his right hand, where he was losing the fight to keep the gun. Just as the gun was finally pulled from his fingers, he brought the knife out and stabbed towards the arm that took it. The sharp hunting knife went through the jacket of the wearer like butter and sliced their arm deeply. A painful shout followed, along with thirty thousand volts running through Mateo's arm and then the rest of his body.

It was worth it, he thought, as he shook uncontrollably then faded into unconsciousness.

∼

LEANDRA REACHED the gate and pushed it slowly open, cautious despite her team being the attackers here. She peered in and saw nothing of concern. She was just about to walk towards the building when she saw four figures walking from the side of the building towards the front. They wore tactical gear from head to toe, including masks, and carried iron bars that looked like they could do a lot of damage. Two of them high-fived each other.

Shit! she thought. What she had seen was the celebration of a winning team. And it wasn't hers.

The leader of the fearsome Qupi gang made a swift exit and headed back to her car at a trot.

'Damn those fools,' she said out loud, cursing her cousins, who had failed her so miserably. She was soon back in the car and driving away at speed, thinking hard about her next steps. Without her men, she would not be able to take back her territory or find her husband or the missing men. Her plans for a *no mercy* revenge mission had collapsed – unless she came up with a plan to reverse the defeat quickly.

They will pay heavily for this, she thought.

～

KENDRA ARRIVED at the warehouse where Andy and Mo had come to rescue Greg. As there had been no responses to her calls or messages, she was concerned that it had ended in failure, or worse, in death. She parked her car close by and went to investigate. As she approached the warehouse, she noticed the door was ajar. Taking a quick look around to see if anyone was watching, she pulled it open and peered inside. There was enough light to see the layout, and that there was nobody there. She slowly entered the warehouse, closing the door behind her, not wanting to make a sound.

Kendra had not noticed the car that had parked farther back in the road.

Leandra Qupi saw her enter and smiled.

'Finally, some luck,' she said, checking her gun and getting out of the vehicle.

∽

KENDRA WALKED towards the centre of the large space when she heard a low moan coming from one corner. She walked slowly towards it, waiting to see where the noise was coming from before reacting. She saw the man before he saw her, only just. One of his eyes was bandaged, but he had blood running down his face from a wound on the top of his head. He looked like something from a horror movie... only angrier, as he stood and walked purposely towards her.

Kendra was in no mood to fight a giant man and so turned and ran towards the door. She was frightened but elated, as it seemed that Andy and Mo had been successful with the rescue.

Why aren't they answering their bloody phones, then? she thought, as she reached the door. She was just about to reach for the handle when the door was opened by someone outside. Kendra saw the gun before she saw the woman, and she knew that her luck had run out.

'Back inside!' the woman said, pointing the gun at her head. Kendra was then grabbed from behind, as the frightening man caught up with her.

Leandra closed the door behind her and indicated with the gun for the man to take her back to the same corner. Within a minute, her wrists were zip-tied behind her back and she was forced to sit, with the pair of assailants staring down at her.

'Now, who do we have here?' the woman said. 'Search her,' she ordered.

The guard was rough as he went through Kendra's pockets, pulling out her mobile phone, car keys, and warrant card, along with the pass she used to get into the station. He did not stop until all her possessions were laid out on the floor in front of her captor, who made a beeline for the warrant card.

'Well, well, Detective March, it seems that you have found yourself in the wrong place at the wrong time, no?'

She picked up and examined Kendra's phone before throwing it to the floor, whereby she stamped on it several times to ensure it would never work again.

'Who are you?' Kendra asked, playing the ignorant cop. 'Someone reported a break-in, and I came to investigate.'

'Detective March, do not take me for a fool. I spoke with my husband every day when he was here. Do you not think he told me about you and your colleague? Does everyone in this cursed country think we Albanians are idiots?'

'I don't think you are an idiot, but I do think you are a homicidal maniac who kills for the sake of it,' Kendra said, glaring at the woman.

'You are brave. I'll give you that,' the matriarch replied. 'I will think carefully about how to punish you, but for now we must leave here before your friends return.'

Leandra nodded to the man, who lifted Kendra to her feet, pulling her roughly towards the door.

'Wait here,' she told her man, 'I will bring the car.'

She returned shortly afterwards and opened the door for the guard to bring the captive to the car. Seconds later, they were on their way.

God help me, Kendra thought, her eyes shut, praying for the first time in a while.

~

'CAN WE TAKE HIM HOME, Doctor? Is he safe to move?' Andy asked.

'Yes, but he will need to rest and give the wound time to heal. So, no more fighting with bad people, okay, young man?' Greg was still a little groggy but feeling much better than he did a couple of hours earlier.

'Thanks, Doctor, I'm very grateful,' the young boxer replied.

His face was still badly bruised but was now much cleaner. The stitches had been expertly applied and would leave nominal scars. His mental health was a different story; the scars there would take a lot longer to heal.

'Let's get you home, mate,' Andy said, helping him off the table. 'Doctor, as ever, we appreciate your assistance.'

'The pleasure is all mine. Please give Trevor my regards and thank him again for the equipment.'

Before they got into the camper van, Andy checked his phone and realised he'd had many missed calls from Kendra, along with several messages asking for his whereabouts. The last message shook him to the core.

'Shit!' he exclaimed.

'What is it?' Mo asked.

'Kendra's gone to the warehouse to look for us, where we left that gorilla unconscious.'

'Shit!' Mo repeated. 'What are we going to do? We need to get Greg home before we can do anything.'

'Don't worry about me,' Greg said. 'I can come with you.'

'That ain't happening, mate,' Andy said as they got into the van. 'We're taking you home before we go back to that place. It's not far out of the way. Mo, can you drive? I need to call Trevor and let him know.'

They were soon on the way, Mo at the wheel, whilst Andy was finally able to get through to Trevor.

'We're pretty much done here, Andy. Are you coming to join us?' Trevor said.

'We're dropping Greg off home on the way to the warehouse, Trevor. Kendra messaged me to say she was going there to look for us, and I'm a bit worried because we left one of the Albanians there when we grabbed Greg.'

'Shit, call me as soon as you get there, okay? I just tried calling, but there's no answer. Her phone seems to be switched off.'

'Will do. We shouldn't be too long,' Andy replied, hanging up. 'Step on it, Mo.'

They arrived at Greg's house a few minutes later and escorted him to his front door, where he was met by his shocked mother.

'Just go, I'll explain,' he told Andy and Mo, ushering them away.

Marge was soon underway again, with the warehouse in Dagenham just ten minutes farther. Andy was restless as he tried several more times to call Kendra without any response at all. It was like Trevor had said: it seemed her phone was switched off.

'Park here, on the left,' Andy told Mo as they pulled up before the warehouse. There were no lights on or any signs of activity, but, as before, they approached with caution. Andy carried his sword cane this time, hoping he didn't need to use it.

Mo tried the door as Andy stood to one side, and wasn't surprised to find that it was still unlocked.

'I'll go first,' Andy said, holding the cane like a club as he entered. It was now too dark for them to see clearly, so he switched the lights on, hoping again that nobody was there. With the lights on, they could see that it was safe to look around. Mo took one side and Andy the other, towards the corner where they'd found Greg earlier.

'Nothing this end,' Mo said. 'I'll take a look upstairs.'

'Don't bother, Mo, we're too late,' Andy said, picking up Kendra's smashed phone and her warrant card.

They had her.

19

'It always worries me when things are so quiet,' Rick Watts said as he walked around the office.

'Really? When it's this quiet, it generally means that not much crime is going on, so happy days,' Wilf answered, shrugging his shoulders theatrically.

'Don't be a smart-arse, Baker, you know what I mean,' Watts replied, 'those bloody cop-killing bastards are still out there and we haven't got a bloody clue where they are.'

'I know, Sarge, I'm just messing with you.'

'Well, less of the messing and more work, please, Detective. Let's find these arseholes,' Watts said, clapping his hands to urge the team on.

He walked over to Jill's desk.

'Anything back from Kendra?' he asked.

'Nope,' said Jill. 'I've tried several times and can't get through. She would've called if there was a problem, I'm sure.'

'Alright, well, if you hear anything, let me know. It's probably time for us all to head off home now. It's been a long day.

Let's get back to this tomorrow with fresh eyes,' he told the team.

'But you literally just said...' Wilf started to say.

'I know what I said, forget about it and go home,' Rick replied, waving him away. 'I get tetchy when things like this happen, so sue me.'

'Don't worry about it, Sarge. I'll bring you an apple tomorrow,' Baker replied.

Watts gave him the middle finger.

'I'll check in with Kendra on the way home,' Jill told Rick as she left.

'Thanks, Jill, see you tomorrow.'

∽

'I'M SURE SHE'S ALRIGHT,' Amir told Trevor as they cleaned up the mess at the factory.

'Thanks, Amir. I hope so,' he replied. 'How are things coming along?'

All the attackers were now safely locked up and would be moved when it was safe to do so. For this to happen, Trevor had instigated several actions that would protect the team and also assist the police with their investigations. This included the tried and tested method of drugging the captives' drinks and snacks in order to keep them pacified and easier to control.

'Yes, most of the mess has been cleaned up. The damage can be fixed later. There's no rush. We're in good shape,' Amir replied. 'We even gave them extra bottles of water and toilet paper to clean some of that crap off themselves, but they still stink.'

'Were you able to bag the firearms and other possessions and assign them to their respective owners as we discussed?'

'Yes, we made sure to keep the possessions of each captive in separate bags, which were then placed outside the room they were held in. Everything is accounted for, don't worry.'

'Thanks, Amir. It's just that I don't want these bastards to get away with it, and their fingerprints and DNA on their possessions will help the police greatly, I reckon. It's all we can do to help out.'

'What about their boss, though? There's no trace of her at all.'

'We'll probably have to go back to Fox Lane and stake out the junction again, in case she's there. Also, keep an eye on her kids. She's bound to go back there soon; their flight is booked in a few days, remember?' Trevor said.

'Fair enough. Once we've finished up here, I'll start sending the team out to do that. We'll rotate often so they can have breaks.'

'How's Martin doing?'

'They've taken him to the doctor, so he's out of circulation for a while. The doctor is loving you at the moment. That's two in one day,' Amir said.

'I'm just thankful that we have a doctor to help us out. Imagine if we had to take people to hospital. Things would be a lot more complex, I can tell you.'

'I would have found us someone else, Trev. You should know me by now. I can find anything and anyone,' Amir said, spinning around theatrically.

'And that is why you're my favourite twin,' Trevor said, smiling.

'Gee, thanks boss,' Amir replied, heading off to help the team.

Trevor sat down and looked at his phone again, hoping to see a message that Kendra was fine. It rang as he watched it.

'Is she okay, Andy?' he immediately asked.

'The bastards have taken her, Trevor. We found her belongings in the warehouse, including her phone, which was smashed. We've gathered everything and are back in the van, so I'm going to start searching for her GPS marker and hope she has it with her, unlike Greg.'

'Can you do that from the van, or do you need to come back here?'

'I can do everything here. Don't worry. As soon as I'm off the phone, I'll make a start and call you back.'

'Alright, mate. Keep me in the loop, please,' Trevor whispered, at a loss. He ended the call.

They have my baby, he choked, slumping forward, his head in his hands.

∼

ANDY WENT STRAIGHT to work on one of the computers in the van. His fingers whizzed over the keys as he brought up the programme set up to locate the GPS trackers. Everyone on the team had been allocated a tag so they could hide it on their person. Unfortunately, young Greg Petrucci hadn't, thinking he wouldn't need it at what he assumed was a safe place.

'Please, don't be like Greg, and have the tag on you,' Andy whispered, forgetting that Mo was sitting next to him.

'She means a lot to you, doesn't she?' Mo asked.

It was too dark for Mo to see Andy blushing. He turned to the elder twin and nodded.

'She does, mate. Is it that obvious?'

'Yeah, it is, and it has been for ages. I don't know why you two haven't hooked up yet.'

'It's not that simple, Mo. We both want to, but look at the sort of shit we're getting involved in. We haven't got the time to look after ourselves like that. It would feel selfish. And the criminals would use it against us every time.'

'Yeah, fair enough,' Mo conceded. 'What's that all about, then?' he added, pointing to the monitor.

Andy grinned and rubbed his hands together.

'That, my friend, is Kendra showing us all how to do things properly by having her GPS tag on her!' he replied, zooming in on the location.

'I've got mine right here,' Mo said, putting his hand down the front of his trousers.

'Not now, mate, we have a friend to rescue.'

~

'I THOUGHT you'd like it here,' Leandra told Kendra, laughing out loud. 'There is much irony, no?'

They were in the old warehouse where Kendra and Andy had been fortunate to escape death by Guran Qupi. The warehouse where Andy had lost an eye and the use of his left foot. The warehouse where Kendra's legs had been shattered by Qupi himself. Where they had both been thrown in the water to die. It was where her life had changed irretrievably.

Kendra couldn't believe she was back there. It felt like she was in a nightmare and that somebody up there just didn't like her. Luckily, this time she was not hanging, but sitting on a chair. It was dirty and damp, but a lot less painful than being hung by the wrists as she and Andy had been all those months ago.

'Not really,' she lied. 'I knew you still had the lease here, so I figured it was as good a place as any.'

'Ah, so you are a smart detective. I can see that. It makes things more, how you say... challenging. My wits against yours, no?'

'Why, are we having some sort of quiz?' Kendra asked, smiling. She was scared witless but was determined not to show it.

Leandra stood in front of her, glaring down at her new adversary.

'You think you are so smart. All of you. You think we Albanians are all stupid, in-bred peasants with nothing to offer to the world. What you don't know, Detective, is that we are much more resourceful than you will ever know. Do you know why?'

'Enlighten me.'

Leandra laughed again.

'I will enlighten you, yes. It is because we had no choice, Detective. It was survive or die, that simple. And look at us now. We come to your country and we have taken over so much territory we don't know what to do with it. We have shit upon you from a great height and you can't handle it. Well, get used to it, Detective, because we have become very good at it.'

'You like to talk, don't you?' Kendra said, trying to enrage Leandra. Emotions revealed things that would normally be kept secret.

The matriarch looked down at Kendra and smiled. Her eyes were fierce, but she was very much in charge.

'Making me angry will not do you any good, dear. I cannot get answers from a dead person.'

'What answers are you after?' Kendra asked, knowing full well what the questions would be.

'Well, for one, I want to know where my husband is, and I think you may know. Am I right?'

It was Kendra's turn to smile, with eyes just as fierce as Leandra's.

'Yes, I know that you know, very good. So, tell me, Detective, where are my husband and my men? That is my first question.'

'Pass,' Kendra replied, still smiling. She had her trump card.

Leandra nodded in appreciation of Kendra's bravery.

'Where is my money, Detective? I figure if you know where my husband is, then you know where my money is too, no?'

Kendra laughed hysterically. 'You really don't know, do you?' she spluttered.

'Don't know what? Don't play games with me. My blade is just as sharp as my husband's was.' She reached out towards the guard, who handed her a stiletto knife. She waved it slowly in front of Kendra's face.

'Your husband made a deal with the police. He could take his money and leave the country in exchange for intelligence on the other gangs and his own operations,' Kendra lied.

'Don't be absurd, he would never do any such thing,' Leandra replied, slightly hesitant.

'He took his mistress and Guran junior and ran for his life.'

Leandra glared, her face emotionless, as she thought of a response.

'Mistress?' she asked.

'Yes, mistress. One of the sex workers he brought over

from Albania. He took a liking to her from the first day he saw her. Magda, I think her name was.'

'You lie.'

'Why would I lie? You've seen the mess he left behind for others to clean up. Who else do you think is responsible?'

'Where is he?'

'The second I tell you, that will be the second I die.'

Leandra leaned towards her captive, her smile gone, her eyes fiercer than ever.

'Tell me and I will make it a clean death,' she replied. 'I promise.'

'I prefer no death.'

'I will torture you until you beg me to kill you.'

'You will not,' said Kendra. 'The moment you do anything to me will be the moment you may as well kill me, because I will say nothing.'

'Very well, tell me and I will release you.'

Kendra laughed once more.

'I doubt that very much. I told you, my life for information. If you want to find your husband, I need to live.'

'Then it seems like we have reached an impasse,' Leandra said. She handed the knife back to the guard. 'Maybe I don't care about my husband anymore, especially now he has betrayed me and his people.'

'That's not how you work, and you know it,' Kendra replied. 'You want to skin the bastard alive, don't you, and kill his mistress and their bastard offspring? You find them all offensive now.'

'Enough!' Leandra shouted. 'My patience is wearing thin, Detective. I think that I may have ten minutes of grace left in me before I start skinning *you*.'

The matriarch walked away, not waiting for a response, her mind made up.

Where the hell are you, Andy? Kendra thought. Her only chance of escape was Andy finding her... and quickly.

∿

'DAMN,' Andy whispered as he zoomed into the location of the GPS tag.

'What is it?' Mo asked.

'That's where it all happened. It's where we got caught and tortured, where I lost my eye and my foot. It's where the bastards have taken her.'

'How far is it from here? Let's call Trevor and let him know.'

'There's not enough time for them to come and help. We have to do this ourselves,' Andy said. 'You cool with that?'

'Of course. There can't be many of them left, can there?'

'I don't know, but we can find out by going there now. I have a plan.'

'You gonna tell me?' asked Mo.

'I'm sending Tim in.'

∿

20

Mo immediately called Trevor as Andy drove at speed towards the old warehouse.

'We've located Kendra, Trev, so we're gonna go and see if we can get her back now. They're at the old warehouse where she was held captive by the husband.'

'We're on the way. Don't do anything stupid, okay?' Trevor said. 'I want her back safely. Tell Andy not to risk her life.'

Trev ended the call and ran to gather the team.

Martin was still at the doctor's, along with Jimmy and Izzy, so Darren, Clive and Rory were available to help from the Walsall contingent, along with Amir and Charmaine. Zoe, Danny, and two others were tasked with securing the factory and keeping an eye on their guests.

'Don't speak to them or engage in any way. Just leave their food and drink close enough to reach but not close enough to attack you, because they will try,' Trevor warned.

After the short briefing, he and the chosen team members left in two cars and sped off.

Trevor's heart was in his mouth as he thought of his

daughter in the warehouse, reliving the nightmare she and Andy had endured. More than anything in the world, he wanted her back safe.

∼

ANDY AND MO arrived in the vicinity of the old warehouse. They parked inconspicuously a hundred metres away amongst a row of other vans.

Andy moved to the back of the van and opened a cupboard, bringing out an armoured silver case. When he opened it, Mo saw Tim, the tiny drone that Andy had used to check on the Russian gang in Hackney a few months earlier. Tim was the size of an index finger and had been developed in Norway for military use. Andy had snapped one up when it became available; ironically, with the money they had taken from Qupi. Along with the drone, he took out a controller and a headset that he would use to monitor the drone's progress.

'How will that help, Andy? I doubt they'd leave the door open for this to fly through, would they?'

'They won't, but I don't need to send Tim inside to find out what's going on. One of his cameras has thermal detection, so all we need is a window and we can get an idea of how many people we'll be dealing with. It will help to know that, won't it?'

'Absolutely,' said Mo.

'Okay, I want you to bring the drone out and hold it in the palm of your hand. When I put the headset on, I'll need you to guide me back inside and sit me down, okay?'

'Got it, let's go,' Mo replied.

They both went outside.

'Okay, ready?' Andy said, putting the headset on.

'Ready.'

Mo held the drone, his arm extended. The tiny propellers came to life as Andy began to control it and it slowly lifted out of Mo's hand, humming as it rose up vertically at speed.

'Okay, take me back inside,' Andy said, as he guided the tiny spy drone towards the warehouse that he knew so well.

Mo grabbed him by the waist and guided him slowly to the steps and into Marge, sitting him down on one of the benches.

'If you switch on the monitor in the middle, you'll see what I can see. The programme is already running. Just hit the green button.'

Mo did as he was instructed, and the monitor came to life. The image was high resolution and clear as the warehouse quickly came into view.

'I'm going to aim at the windows in the middle. From what I remember, they had us strung up by some pipes. They may do the same again.'

The drone slowed down as it approached one of many windows that had been placed above head-height. The designers had wanted light coming in, and not workers looking out. Andy steadied Tim and turned it slowly for the cameras to face the glass.

'Switching to the infra-red camera,' he said.

As soon as he did so, the view on the monitor changed to a dark grey, with lighter shades of grey around the edges. There was no thermal signature straight ahead of the window, so Andy adjusted the view first to the left, with no luck, and then to the right, where the bright lights indicating body heat immediately came into view.

'Damn!' Mo exclaimed.

'I count three people, Mo. Agreed? One sitting down and two standing. I'm guessing Kendra is the one seated.'

'Agreed. They're towards the far end of the warehouse. Can you remember what else is in there?'

'Nothing much. I know there are some offices or rooms on the first floor, accessible by a metal staircase on the side closest to the window, but the rest is all open plan.'

'So, what do we do now?' asked Mo. 'They're both standing by her, and their movements look agitated, don't they?'

'They do. We need to move fast, mate. Fancy another spin in Marge? I can only think of one thing we can do. You up for it?'

'Hell, yes,' Mo replied, heading for the driver's seat. He knew exactly what Andy was thinking. 'I have my metal pipe ready, too.' He grinned.

'Okay, I'll stay here and monitor. Listen to my instructions, okay? Don't stop until I tell you to.'

'Yes, sir!' Mo started the engine. He moved out of the line of parked vans and picked up speed as he drove towards the old warehouse. He could see it straight ahead and aimed for the dark green metal shutters with Marge.

'Here we go!' he shouted.

Andy braced for impact as he carried on monitoring the feed.

Marge was doing close to fifty miles per hour when she crashed through the shutters, which split as if they had been ripped apart by a can opener.

'Don't stop!' Andy shouted, seeing a sudden reaction from the two standing figures. 'Aim for them, but avoid Kendra, whatever you do!'

'On it!' Mo said as the van careered towards the trio, a

little slower now due to the impact. He recognised the guard with the bandaged eye and saw the woman step backwards. Both had expressions of shock on their faces as Marge bowled into the guard, knocking him to the ground.

Andy had taken his goggles off and signalled Tim to land, where he'd be retrieved later. He grabbed his trusted cane with its heavy handle and hidden sword and opened the door to the van, now stationary.

'Let's go!' he shouted, as he made his way towards Kendra, who sat open-mouthed watching the scene develop in front of her.

Brandishing the metal bar, Mo went to look for the guard he'd just knocked over. The guard was stunned and just getting to his feet. He took a knife out of his pocket as he stood, shaking his head to try to clear his vision. Knowing that he had to move fast to maintain the advantage, Mo attacked and feinted as if to strike the Albanian's head. The gangster had no choice but to raise his arm and defend his head, so he was surprised when the blow landed on the side of his knee instead.

The blow was excruciating and damaging, bringing the man to his knees, gasping. Mo then raised the metal pipe and struck him again, this time to the side of the head where his eye was bandaged, a blow he therefore did not see coming. He fell sideways, unconscious, before he hit the ground. Two blows to the head and a ruptured knee on the same day. Mo quickly retrieved a handful of zip ties and secured the heavy man's wrists. He took his knife and checked him for other weapons and belongings, retrieving car keys, a mobile phone, and a wallet.

Andy had reached Kendra in seconds, watching carefully for Leandra Qupi, who was now running towards the back door, the same door from which Kendra and Andy had been taken and thrown into the water.

'Are you okay?' he asked, using a penknife to cut her free.

'I'm fine, thanks. What took you so long?' she asked, grinning.

As soon as she was free she stood up, rubbing her wrists, watching as the matriarch made good her escape.

'I'm going after her, Andy. She can't be allowed to get away.'

Before Andy could reply, Kendra started to run after her adversary.

'Kendra, wait!' he shouted, too late to stop her. 'Damn it, she never listens to me.'

At that moment, Mo appeared, watching as Kendra started to gain on Leandra.

'What just happened?' he asked.

'Kendra just happened, Mo. She's gone after her and she won't stop until she's got her.'

'So, what do we do now?'

'I want you to call Trevor. Explain what's been happening. I'm going after Kendra to make sure she's okay.' He turned and started to run. His gait was awkward, not helped by the prosthetic foot. He used his arms to help his stability, so it looked a little odd as well as awkward, but he was quicker than he would be just walking.

'They just go off and do this shit without thinking, all of them,' Mo said out loud, shaking his head. Just as he was dialling Trevor, he saw the two cars turn up, his teammates running in quickly to help.

'Where is she?' Trevor asked. 'Where's Kendra?'

'You guys got here quick! She went running off after the gangster woman, with Andy just behind her,' Mo replied.

Trevor started after them both, before stopping and shouting instructions to Mo and the team.

'Take that bastard back to the factory and make sure his stuff is bagged like the others'. I'm going after Kendra.'

∼

KENDRA CAUTIOUSLY EXITED the warehouse after her adversary. Her memory of this area was hazy; she'd been carried on someone's shoulder while she was in agony, before being thrown into the water, so she couldn't remember much of the place at all. She couldn't see Leandra and stopped, listening for any sounds that would give her a clue. She saw the blow too late as a fist struck her from the side, but she was able to move her head slightly to make it more of a glancing blow. She took a few steps away and saw Leandra slam the warehouse door shut and then lock it with the key she had taken from the inside. She then took off her coat and stormed towards Kendra menacingly.

'It seems the gods favour you today, Detective.'

'Not the gods, the cavalry.' Kendra smiled, raising her fists as she prepared to fight.

'You will find that I will not favour you as much,' Leandra said, as she delivered a roundhouse kick that took Kendra by surprise.

'Whoa, is that some Brazilian jiu-jitsu you did there?' Kendra laughed, mocking the woman now she was aware of her temper threshold.

'You know the fighting styles, I commend you,' Leandra said as they circled each other. 'Let's hope you know how to fight, too, for your sake, eh?'

'I'll be just fine, don't you worry. Although I suggest you

just give up. Locking the door only delayed the inevitable, wouldn't you agree?'

'Maybe, but I have at least a minute to kick your ass, no?'

Leandra struck again, this time with a flurry of punches that Kendra barely managed to fend off. Her opponent was relentless and pushed forward, causing her to retreat backwards towards the water. Several blows landed, one on her head and a couple on her shoulders, as she continued to parry the attacks.

This woman can fight, she thought.

∼

TREVOR WAS CONFUSED when he saw Andy running back towards him, waving his arms as if he were trying to scare a flock of sheep.

'What's going on?' he asked, then turned and ran with him.

'Door. Locked. Go round,' Andy said, breathless. It had been a while since he'd run, and it was noticeable.

'Go!' he shouted to Trevor, who was fit and a regular runner despite his age.

Trevor needed no second invitation and sprinted ahead of him back towards the entrance. The team stood and gawked as they saw them both running in the opposite direction.

'Need any help?' Amir asked, bemused.

'Help Trevor!' Andy shouted hoarsely as he fell further behind.

Amir and Charmaine took off after Trevor. Despite the extra help, Andy carried on running; he wanted to see Kendra safe more than anything.

'Damn. Pizzas. And. Beer,' he wheezed.

∽

KENDRA SENSED that Leandra was forcing her back towards the water in the hope she'd fall in, giving her the chance to make her getaway. Knowing that help would be with her soon, she decided to stand her ground and attack instead of defending. She started kicking out towards Leandra's knees, jabbing towards her face as the she stepped back slightly to evade them.

Leandra quickly noticed the change and pressed home again, kicking and striking blows at a speed that surprised Kendra, who was starting to feel the blows more. She quickly decided another tactic was needed. If Leandra wanted her in the water, then she would oblige—but she would take her opponent with her. Kendra was a strong swimmer and knew she could handle anything in the water that the Albanian gangster could throw at her, making the contest more in her favour than it was now. She started to retreat towards the dock, Leandra following and pressing home her advantage, sensing victory. Just as she was about to kick her opponent in, Kendra lunged forward and grabbed her in a bear hug, throwing her sideways to the ground and towards the edge.

'Time to get wet,' she told Leandra, who thrashed desperately to get away. Kendra's grip was too strong, though, and as she had hoped, they rolled off the edge and into the cold water below.

Kendra let go and moved away from Leandra, who was now thrashing her arms and spluttering. She seemed to be in trouble.

'Help me!' she screamed. 'I can't swim!'

It was at this point that Trevor arrived, out of breath. He had seen them fall into the water and looked down at them.

'Kendra! Are you okay?'

'I'm fine, Dad, but our friend here seems to be struggling,' she replied, as she maintained a comfortable distance.

'Back in a sec!' he shouted. He went off to look for something to help his daughter with.

In the meantime, Leandra continued to thrash and started to drop lower into the water. Kendra decided to help.

'I'll help you. Just stop thrashing around,' she said, swimming to the woman.

She grabbed Leandra from behind and started swimming towards the edge, hoping to get some help from her dad. She grabbed on to an old iron ring that hadn't been used in years, and looked up to see Andy, Amir and Charmaine.

'You. Okay?' Andy asked, still wheezing.

'I'm fine. Find something to pull us up with,' she said, treading water as she held on to Leandra. The trio disappeared and went to help Trevor.

It was at this point that the Albanian woman decided that she couldn't admit defeat and used her arms to pull herself up, forcing Kendra down by her shoulders. Kendra was taken by surprise and let go of the ring, sinking down quickly from the force of Leandra's weight. Leandra climbed up Kendra's torso, finally reaching out with one hand to grab the ring for herself, hoping to climb up and get away. She kept one hand on Kendra's shoulder and used her feet to continue forcing her down.

Kendra realised what she was trying to do and surprised her again by diving deeper, denying Leandra any purchase and thus leaving her with nothing to keep her above the water except for the ancient ring. Surprised by this turn of events, Leandra started scrabbling up the side of the dock, trying to raise herself high enough to climb all the way up.

Kendra surfaced nearby and saw quickly that she would fail.

She swam to the side and waited patiently for her team to help her, whilst keeping an eye on the treacherous gangster. Leandra turned and saw her watching calmly, which infuriated her. She started to say something, but before she could, her hand slipped from the ring and she fell backwards into the water. Kendra waited for her to surface, cautious of her deceit. Leandra popped back up, gasping for air. Her head was barely out of the water when panic set in and the water got into her mouth. She started to choke and splutter, her arms flaying as she started to sink.

Kendra swam across and dove under, reaching out to the woman to save her... again. Leandra was in full panic mode, her arms and legs windmilling in a desperate attempt to surface. The thrashing and the dark water made it difficult for Kendra to see. She surfaced and looked for signs to indicate where Leandra was. She could see bubbles and dove again, this time swimming deeper to try to locate Leandra. She caught a glimpse of something ahead, which she swam towards. A thrashing hand appeared suddenly out of the gloom and struck her in the eye, causing her to abandon the attempt. She surfaced quickly and coughed, holding one hand against her sore eye.

'Kendra, catch!' Trevor said, throwing some electrical wiring to her that he had found alongside the building. Kendra caught it and was quickly pulled to the side by Trevor and Amir, who had joined him. Andy and Charmaine looked on. She held on tightly with both hands, closing her injured eye as they pulled her up.

'You okay, love?' Trevor said, hugging her close.

'Yeah, thanks, Dad. My eye hurts like hell, though,' she replied. Trevor gently eased her to the floor.

Andy appeared and leaned down and hugged her close. 'Glad you're okay,' he whispered.

She stroked his cheek and said, 'Thanks, Andy. You saved my life.'

'Don't be silly. You saved mine, remember?'

'Where's that witch?' Charmaine asked, looking over the side.

They joined her and searched for several minutes, without luck. Kendra saw the remnants of some bubbles in the middle and guessed that Leandra Qupi was resting at the bottom.

'I think that's the last we'll be seeing of her,' she said. 'I tried to save her, and she tried to drown me, so I guess karma kicked in, eh?'

'I don't care about her. She didn't deserve to be rescued after all she's done,' Trevor replied.

'I won't disagree, Dad. I tried, so I don't feel guilty.'

'Let's get you back home and in some dry clothes,' Andy said, lifting her up.

'Yeah, we need to get out of here quick. Who knows if there's been any witnesses that called the police,' Trevor added.

All signs of Leandra and the guard were removed from the scene, and the two cars, along with Marge, were soon away from there. The unconscious guard was placed in the camper van where Amir and Darren kept an eye on him during the journey back. He remained unconscious until they placed him in a room back at the factory. Leandra's hire car was left at the scene for the authorities to deal with later.

'Her body will turn up somewhere soon, won't it?' Kendra

asked her dad, who sat with her in one of the cars. She was wrapped in a blanket and shivering, so he cuddled up to her.

'Yes, I'm sure it will. Sometimes they get stuck in seaweed at the bottom, and it takes a while to get free from that, otherwise she'll turn up wherever the tide takes her.'

'What happens now, Dad? I mean, they've killed people, including a cop. They've left a trail of destruction wherever they've been. How are we going to deal with it?'

'I've been thinking about it too, love. The police have to deal with them. We just have to find a way of removing ourselves from the equation, otherwise what we've worked for will be scrutinised and destroyed.'

'Do you have a plan for that?'

'I do. It isn't anything complicated, but hopefully enough that it keeps everyone safe. Weirdly, it'll mean involving the factory as a crime scene, but I have a plan for that, too.'

'Glad you're on the case,' she replied, snuggling up close. 'You're more of a cop than I am.' She giggled.

Trevor laughed along with her.

'Let's not take things too far, eh, love?'

∼

21

When the small convoy arrived back at the factory, there were already signs of things returning to normal. All the obstructions had been removed from reception and the hallway, along with the cabinets and lockers in the main room. There was nothing they could do with the doors for now, but Trevor wasn't overly concerned.

'Get yourself a hot shower, love. I'll have Charmaine bring you some overalls,' Trevor told Kendra as they got out of the car.

'Thanks, I will.'

'How's it all going, Zoe?' he asked as the young boxer greeted them.

'It's all under control. Every time they shout for water or food, we give them more drugs to quieten them down. It's working just fine,' she said, referring to the crushed sleeping tablets in their guests' refreshments.

'Everything else ready?' he asked.

'Yes, if anyone comes looking, they won't see the mess, other than some damaged doors. We'll tell them we barricaded ourselves in so they couldn't get any further and then they just left. Cleaning up the creosote wasn't easy, but we managed to shift most of it.'

'Good work. So now we're all back, I want you to gather the team. We need to work fast.'

∾

FIFTEEN MINUTES LATER, the team were all assembled in the largest room, with the exception of Martin, Jimmy and Izzy, who were still with the doctor.

'You lot have been nothing short of amazing,' Trevor said as he looked around at them all, 'but we still have much to do in order to stay safe ourselves.'

'Yeah, seriously, it's amazing what you've all had to deal with these last couple of days. It was like an action movie played out in real life,' Kendra added, now warm again in her blue overalls.

'First off, we need to take our guests and dump them somewhere for the police to take them into custody,' Trevor said, 'so, Darren, can I leave the escort duties to you to sort out? You'll need to secure their possessions to their person so the police can match them up for evidential purposes later.'

'Sure thing,' Darren replied, 'how are we going to transport them and where did you want them left?'

'Luckily, our Albanian friends arrived here in a van and a number of cars, which is handy for us. Use their van to dump them all in. It'll be a tight, uncomfortable squeeze, but that's their problem. Take them, with a car following, and dump them somewhere close to a police station but away from prying eyes. Make sure you wear gloves to avoid any fingerprints and watch out for CCTV.'

'No problem, I'll take my boys for the van, one of us driving. Can you spare someone to drive the car?' Darren asked.

'I can do that,' Charmaine volunteered.

'Great. Watch them carefully, Darren. They are strong and very dangerous.'

'We'll use metal handcuffs and zip-tie their ankles when they're in the van,' Darren said, 'and we'll have our tasers and batons with us, just in case.'

'Great, thanks, mate. If you can make a start on that now, as soon as you're gone, I will be calling the police,' Trevor said, surprising everyone.

'What? Did you say you're calling the police?' Amir asked.

'Yes. We can't avoid reporting the attack here. What if there were witnesses? What if these animals tell the police where they attacked? We need to protect ourselves, and we do that by telling the truth. Or some of it,' Trevor said, smirking.

'You gonna tell us?' Mo asked.

'Of course. I'll tell the police they attacked us, but that our perimeter CCTV was spot on and gave us the time we needed to barricade ourselves safely inside, which was so good they only managed to break down a few doors. That's how I'll spin it, and they'll link it to the auction as we were the company that submitted it for charity,' he explained.

'How is that going to work, Dad?' Kendra was just as confused as the others.

'I'll tell them we were given the eyepatch in confidence to

put up for auction so that a few good causes would benefit. If they ask why us, then I'll tell them that my connections probably thought I was a good fit for it. That way, the authorities will think that another gang is behind the Albanians being captured and the warehouse doors being smashed.'

'There's a slight flaw in your plan about the CCTV, which I'll have to fix before the police ask for copies,' Andy said, 'If we give them full access, they'll see exactly what we did to these poor men, so we'll give them only the exterior footage and what we saw in the reception area until they cut the power to the cameras, which is what we'll tell them they did. Everything else will be out of action.'

'Good point, that man,' Kendra said, smiling as he blushed.

There was silence from the team as they pondered Trevor's plan. Amir, Mo and a couple of others then started clapping, nodding in appreciation – somewhat exaggeratedly but well-meant. There were also a few wolf whistles.

'Alright, alright, stop taking the piss and get cracking, we don't have much time,' Trevor said, waving them off.

The team went off to finish off their tasks. Kendra and Andy stayed with Trevor.

'That is a hell of a plan, Trevor,' Andy said, patting him on the back. 'I'm guessing there's no other viable alternative that doesn't expose our little operation here, right?'

'Not really. Fortunately, the eyepatch isn't stolen, or things may be different. The police have no choice but to take down the details of the attack, assume the Albanians were looking for whoever sent the eyepatch to auction, and then did a runner when things didn't pan out. It's nothing more than a case of criminal damage and some firearms discharges to them, so hopefully it'll be filed and linked to the more serious offences they will be charged with. Chief amongst them being the murder of the police officer.'

'Damn, that's some clever thinking there, Batman. Remind me never to get on your bad side,' Andy said.

'And don't you forget it.' Trevor laughed.

'Well, I need to get the hell out of here before all this kicks off,' Kendra said. 'Andy, where's all my stuff?'

'It's in a bag in the van, I'll get it for you,' he said, walking off.

'He saved my life, that man,' she told her dad. 'I couldn't believe we were back in that warehouse; it gave me chills.'

'I bet it did,' Trevor said, hugging her again. 'I'm just glad you're safe, love. I guess I owe that man a drink, eh?'

'Just remember that next time you get pissed off with him!' She laughed.

Andy returned with Kendra's belongings and walked her to one of the spare cars, as hers was still in Dagenham.

'You going to be okay?' he asked as she opened the door.

She leaned over and kissed him gently on the lips.

'My hero.'

He watched as she drove off, relieved that she was okay.

'I'm glad she didn't see me running,' he said out loud. 'I really need to work on that.'

∽

THE ALBANIANS WERE UNCEREMONIOUSLY DUMPED in the back of their van, still groggy from the sleeping tablet cocktails they'd been given. Darren drove the van while Clive and Rory joined the gangsters in the back, masks on, tasers and batons at the ready. The attackers were tightly bunched together, restricting their movement and hampering any thoughts of escape. They were soon on the way, with Charmaine following in one of their own vehicles to bring them back safely.

Trevor called the police the minute they were out of sight, asking for immediate attendance as they'd been attacked by armed men.

'We've been calling you for ages,' he said on the phone. I think they cut the phone lines and did something to our mobiles. We can't hear them anymore, so we think they've gone, and our phones are working again. Please, send someone now!'

The police arrived in quick time, driving up to the main entrance, where they could see damage to the door and in reception. Trevor met them outside.

'Thank God you're here, officers, we thought they'd never leave!' he said, feigning relief.

'What the hell happened here, sir?' asked one of the officers.

'We'd closed for the day, the gates locked, and everyone was getting ready to leave when we got a warning from our perimeter CCTV. We saw a bunch of men at the gate, and they started doing something to the padlock. We immediately tried calling you, but they must have cut the lines and jammed our mobiles because we couldn't get through. We literally had minutes to save ourselves and barricade ourselves in the back. I was able to keep track of them on CCTV for a short while but had to get to the back with the rest of the staff.'

'Are you the owner, sir?' asked the other officer.

'No, I'm a director. The company is owned by an overseas corporation. I'm not here that often and we only keep a skeleton staff here during the week. Most of our staff work remotely and all over the country,' Trevor said.

'How many were here today?'

'There was less than ten of us, officer. Luckily for us, this old building is well built, and they had trouble getting through the doors. They basically saved us.'

'So, nobody was hurt?'

'No, we didn't even see them. They weren't here very long, maybe twenty minutes or so? We heard power tools being used where they tried to get through the doors. Like I said, well built.'

'Can we take a look?'

'Of course, please come through,' Trevor said, guiding them into reception. 'As you can see, they made a bit of a mess here trying to get through that first door. What they didn't know was that there was another one just like it at the end of the corridor.'

'And what's beyond that?' asked one of the policemen.

'It's a training room which doubles up as a storage and locker room,' he replied. 'We barricaded the door with metal lockers, so they'd struggle to get in. They must have had a shock when they cut through the door because we'd put about ten lockers in front of the door!'

They walked through to the large room where the team had cleaned up the mess. Trevor had told them to stack the lockers near the damaged door.

'We moved them out of the way when they'd left. We couldn't hear them anymore,' he added.

'What's that smell?' asked one of the officers, his nose scrunched.

'Oh, that's some old creosote that spilt when we tipped

one of the cabinets over. We didn't even know it was in there, but it made a hell of a mess.'

'You cleaned it up already?'

'We had to. The stuff stank to high heaven and was slippery as hell. We had a right job trying to clean it up, I can tell you,' Trevor said, seeing the two officers look at each other.

'So, they got no further than this?'

'No, sir. They sounded very angry, but they couldn't get through the barricade.'

'Do you know why they were here?' one of the officers asked.

'No idea,' Trevor replied.

'We think they're linked to the murder of at least three people, including a police officer. Something to do with a jewel at an auction?'

Trevor paused before replying.

'Shit, the eyepatch? I knew that would cause us problems!' he said dramatically.

'You know about that?'

'Yes, sir. Someone approached me and asked me to put it up for auction anonymously so that a number of good causes would benefit. Because of that, I never suspected it would be anything contentious, so I did as I was asked.'

'Who gave it to you?'

'It was sent anonymously by courier, and they phoned me before it arrived, giving the name of an associate of mine from London and explaining what they'd like me to do. Honestly, if I'd have known there was anything wrong, I'd have never agreed, but I trusted the associate and the money was going to good causes, you know?'

'So, you have no idea who it originated from?'

'No, sir, I don't, sorry. All I did was send it to the auction house with the paperwork they included.'

'Okay, well, we need to take a report, so can we sit down and take some details from you? We'll need the names and addresses of your staff also, in case. We'll also need a copy of your CCTV footage.'

'Of course. Please, come this way,' Trevor said, leading them back to reception. One of the officers called the result in and reported that the attack was historic and linked to the Albanians, but that nobody was hurt.

Less than an hour later, the police had left.

'Good job you have solid doors and a good CCTV system, eh?' one of the officers had said in parting.

'Yes, sir, good job indeed.'

∽

MATEO WAS as groggy as the rest of his men, his hands cuffed tightly behind his back and his ankles zip-tied together, as helpless and uncomfortable as he'd ever been in his entire life. He sat on the floor of the van, his head bowed, his chin resting on his chest. His men were pressed against him on all sides, and he knew they were in deep trouble. He looked up towards the two men at the back of the van, wearing masks and protective equipment. They held bright yellow taser guns aimed towards him and his men, as the van trundled along to its unknown destination. All he could think of was his cousin.

I hope she got away. She will teach them a lesson they will never forget, he thought.

∽

MANFORD WAY, at the junction with Manor Way in Chigwell, is an odd Y-shaped junction with one way in and a different way out, with some greenery in between. As the police van turned right from Manor Road, it saw the suspicious van that had just been reported by a member of the public. They had seen it abandoned there just a few minutes earlier, with the driver and two other occupants fleeing in an unidentified silver saloon. The witness had deemed it suspicious enough to call 999 immediately.

The driver parked directly behind it and reported the contact to their base.

'Let's go and see what the fuss is all about, shall we?' said the veteran officer, PC Terry Mogg.

'Right behind you, Terry,' PC Will Tanner said.

As they approached the van, they heard some odd noises coming from the rear of it.

'What the hell is that?' Will asked.

'It sounded like someone coughing. We need to be careful here,' Terry said, reaching for his extendable baton.

'Juliet Bravo, can we have some back-up to this van, please? There are some odd noises coming from the rear that I'm not comfortable with. Six-nine-nine, over. It may be a van load of illegal immigrants, so if I can have some assistance, I'll hang fire before opening the back doors.'

'All received, six-nine-nine. I'll send Juliet Three to assist, along with a dog unit. Stand by,' the control room operator replied.

The two units arrived within a few minutes, and it was left to Spartan, the heavy, well-trained Alsatian, to take point when the doors were opened. Terry did the honours and moved quickly out of the way for Spartan to bark and pull aggressively on his handler's lead as he tried to attack the men inside.

'Well, they're like no illegal immigrants I've ever seen,' Will said as he attempted to make sense of it all. 'What the hell is that stench? It smells like some sort of chemical. Why are some of them covered in paint?'

'It smells like that stuff you used to paint your fence,' came the reply. 'Is that glitter? What the hell is going on in here?' asked a bemused Terry.

'Mate, you're asking the wrong bloke. This is as weird as anything I've ever seen.'

'And what's that taped around their necks?' Terry asked, once the dog had calmed down enough for them to move closer.

'They look like evidence bags filled with weapons and other bits,' Will replied.

'Juliet Bravo, can you please send more vans? Lots of them. We have twelve heavily armed men restrained in the back of this van, who will need taking to the custody suite. We'll need forensics, and firearms officers to check and make safe the guns, and someone from CID to investigate this very strange set-up. Six-nine-nine over.'

'Six-nine-nine, strange set-up all received.'

'There goes our early night,' Will told his colleague. 'We're gonna be tied up with paperwork for hours.'

'Yep, but look on the bright side, Will. When have you ever come across anything like this? It's one to tell your grandkids, the day you found a bunch of nasty armed men tied up in the back of a van. You won't forget it, that's for sure.'

'I wonder what happened here,' Will said.

'I'm sure it won't take long to find out.'

Spartan the Alsatian was still growling and threatening to

attack by the time the back-up arrived, and the men were transported to the custody suite for processing.

'Someone sure did a great job securing them and their evidence, didn't they?' Terry said as they started their paperwork.

∼

22

'Where have you been, chuck?' Jill said when Kendra opened her front door. 'We've been calling for hours without any luck getting through. Is that a bruise on your face? Are you ok?'

'Yeah, I'm fine, just knackered,' Kendra said, feigning a yawn. 'I opened the car door too fast, and it hit me in the face, that's all. It knocked me over. I had to look around to make sure nobody had seen me; it must have looked hilarious. I've been catching up on my sleep.'

She was wearing her pyjamas and holding a mug of steaming coffee, having arrived home minutes earlier. A few minutes later and she would have had a lot of explaining to do.

'What, so you switched your phone off? With all the shit that's going on? Rick isn't gonna be happy, Kendra. You know what he's like when a big case is ongoing.'

'It's not that at all, Jill. My phone is smashed to bits and I'm waiting for a new one to be delivered tomorrow morning.

I didn't realise until I woke up. I must have smashed it when I fell over.'

She pointed to the nearby table and her phone that was lying there, the screen shattered.

'Oh, well, that's unlucky, isn't it? I'll make sure Rick knows. Are you coming to work in the morning?' Jill asked.

'I might be late coming in; I have to wait for the new phone. Tell Rick I'll stay a little longer to make up for it,' she replied.

'Will do. You gonna make me a cuppa, then, or do I need to collapse from thirst first?'

Kendra laughed and walked to the kitchen, followed by her colleague.

'Something tells me that you have beans to spill, so come on, out with it,' Kendra demanded after she'd put the kettle on.

'Well, Detective March, it seems that we both had Pablo wrong. He is a scheming little git, is that one. We thought he was shy and not very assured around women, didn't we?'

'Yeah, are you telling me he isn't?' Kendra asked, surprised. She rubbed her wrists, still sore from being tied up in the warehouse, thankful that was the only injury she'd walked away with.

'He most certainly is not,' Jill said, laughing. 'That man is a secret gigolo, Kendra. He played me good and proper and got exactly what he wanted out of it.'

'Which was what?'

'Me, of course.'

Kendra noticed the soft, dreamy expression on Jill's face as she looked past her and thought of Pablo.

'Ooh, you did the dirty dance with him, didn't you?' Kendra laughed.

'That is none of your business, missy. He is a very gentle man, and I am thankful that you persuaded me to ask him out. He brings a whole new meaning to the term *"Came out of his shell,"* I can tell you!'

'Good for you. I'm happy for you both,' Kendra said, hugging her friend.

When she'd made the tea, they went to the lounge, where they talked about the case for a while.

'It's frustrating as hell,' Jill said. 'So much work has gone into it, but we've hit a brick wall. These murdering bastards know exactly what they're doing when it comes to avoiding detection.'

'I wouldn't worry. They will only get away with it for so long, and remember, we know where they're flying out from in a few days, don't we?'

'Yeah, I suppose, but I hate to have to rely on that and not on our policing skills. We should be smarter than that.'

'You know, and as much as I hate to say this, sometimes you just have to give the bastards credit that they're not as stupid as we sometimes think they are. They're evil and devious and they're learning, so we have to learn better,' Kendra replied.

Jill's mobile phone rang.

'It's Rick,' she said.

'It's all good, Sarge, her phone is broken, which is why we couldn't get through. She's been sleeping all this time.' Jill laughed. 'Let me put you on speaker.'

'Thanks, Jill. Listen, ladies, there's been a development that I can scarcely believe,' Rick said. 'The locals in Barkingside have nicked a dozen armed men who were trussed up in the back of a van, with their weapons and belongings strapped to them in bags, all neatly wrapped like presents for us.'

'What?' Kendra exclaimed. 'How is that possible?'

'Nobody has the slightest idea. They're not talking, which we expected, and they've asked for solicitors via an interpreter. Apparently, they were drugged up when they were found.'

'Who do you think is responsible, Rick?' Jill asked.

'Like I said, nobody has any clues. It's likely to be one of the other gangs who didn't like this lot messing around on their territory.'

'Wow, how freaky is that?' Kendra said.

'However it happened, I suppose we should be grateful, eh? But that's not all,' Rick continued.

'As if that wasn't enough,' Jill said.

'Apparently, there was an attack on an industrial building near Tilbury Docks where a bunch of armed men tried to storm the building. According to the locals, it may have been connected to the jewelled eyepatch, which brings us back to our prisoners in Barkingside.'

'Hang on, Sarge. The same armed men attacked a business and then somehow ended up as prisoners in the back of a van?' Kendra asked.

'Correct. According to the locals in Tilbury who went there, the attackers were picked up early by some newfangled CCTV cameras, giving the occupants time to barricade themselves in. They couldn't phone for help because the landline had been cut and the attackers somehow jammed their mobile phone signals.'

'It sounds like something out of a James Bond movie,' Kendra said. 'Did anyone get hurt there?'

'No,' Rick said, 'they had enough time to block all the

doors. The gangsters even had power tools to cut through, but there was so much stuff barricading the doors they didn't get very far and probably decided they'd spent too much time there and left.'

'And somehow found themselves captured and tied up in the back of a van,' Jill added.

'Were they left there for the police, or did they get lucky, and their captors got spooked? I'm just saying, maybe they were being taken somewhere else?' Kendra said.

'I doubt it, K, otherwise why leave their guns and belongings in bags as great evidence for the police? I'm guessing one of them will be linked to the PC that was killed, which would be a coup for the Met, wouldn't it?' Rick said.

'Yeah, that is some good PR, isn't it?' Jill added. 'So does that conclude the investigation, Sarge?'

'It does not. The dozen men in custody are the soldiers, but there's no trace of the woman. We're looking into a possible sighting at another warehouse nearby. You'll never believe it, Kendra, it's the same one that you and Andy were held captive in.'

'What? She's there now?' Kendra asked.

'No, a witness reported hearing a loud crash and when they eventually went to check a few minutes later, saw that the warehouse shutters had been smashed in. There was nobody around, but when the local units were called, they found a woman's long black coat behind the warehouse and signs of a struggle inside the building.'

'Black coat with white fur trim?' Jill asked.

'That's the one,' Rick replied.

'This is giving me a headache,' Kendra said. 'All this happened today?'

'Yes. I know it sounds crazy, but I'm guessing the trail of

death and destruction will come to a stop. She won't get very far without her men; remember, we know where her kids are and where their plane is leaving from. We won't have to wait long,' Rick continued.

'I guess that means we have a ton of paperwork to sort out tomorrow, right?' Kendra asked.

'That is correct, Detective. I thought you should know. So, I'll see you both tomorrow, bright and early, okay?'

'Sarge, I'll pop in as soon as my new phone arrives. I'll make up the hours late if I have to,' Kendra replied.

'No problem, see ya,' he replied, hanging up.

'Well, that was a hell of an update, wasn't it?' Jill said.

'That was a lot of information in a short amount of time,' Kendra agreed. 'I think I need another coffee.'

'Got anything stronger?'

∼

BACK AT THE FACTORY, the team cleaned up as best they could. Once the creosote had been washed off and the lockers and cabinets put back, it was as if nothing had happened there, with the exception of the smell, some traces of glitter, and a few discreet bullet holes that Trevor asked the team to fill.

'That smell is going to linger for a while,' he told Amir and Mo as they surveyed the place.

'Luckily, it's just in this room,' said Mo. 'The water upstairs was easy to remove as the drains for the old showers are still there. The holes in the doors are an easy fix.'

'They don't build places like this anymore, do they? It's good to know we can protect ourselves here, in case anything like this happens again,' Amir added.

'Be careful what you wish for. We know what we got ourselves into when we started this,' said Trevor. 'We're gonna make a lot of enemies along the way, so this is a massive learning curve for us. Andy will have a field day ordering more new technology to help us, but we can chip in with more obvious things, too.'

'Like what?' Amir asked.

'Like we need to hide and protect the landline from being cut again. That was way too easy. And consider replacing these main doors with reinforced security doors. I know a company that makes them especially, but keeps them looking like normal doors. That kind of thing.'

'It'll make this place into a fortress, but that's what we'll need, right?' Mo added.

'Yep, and I haven't got a problem with that at all,' said Trevor. 'The better we look after ourselves and our people, the better we'll be at our jobs.'

'Amen to that,' Amir said.

'Seriously? Amen? Since when did you become all religious?' his brother asked.

'I'm not, it's just a figure of speech, that's all,' Amir said. 'You see it on the TV all the time.'

'You mean on Cartoon Network, don't you?'

'Yes, I do. I love those shows and you know it!'

'See, Trevor?' Mo said, 'this is how you separate me from my twin brother. I like the Discovery Channel and he watches SpongeBob SquarePants.'

'Hey, don't knock it,' Amir said.

'I think that's my cue to leave,' Trevor said, raising his arms in surrender and leaving the twins to bicker.

'I BET you're glad we installed those cameras now, aren't you, Trevor?'

'Yes, Andy, I do. After all, they paid for it, right?' Trevor grinned.

'I know. That's the best part of it. I may add a few more to give us a wider angle of vision.'

'While you're at it, find a way to stop our mobile signals from being jammed. That caused us big problems, not being able to update each other.'

'I'm not sure I can, but I'll figure something out.'

'So,' said Trevor, 'the bad guys are with the cops now. Hopefully they'll have all the evidence they need to link them to the other scenes and especially the murder of the police officer.'

'Have they found the woman yet? I mean, I know we saw her disappear under the water, but could she have survived?'

'Honestly, I don't know. Kendra is adamant that she drowned, but until they find a body, I want us to stay on our toes.'

'I'll keep an eye out and will let you know if I find anything.'

'Thanks, Andy. I think we'll call it a day soon. Everyone's knackered, and we all need some rest after what we've been through.'

'Have you heard from Kendra? Is she okay?'

'She's fine. One of her colleagues popped around to see her and she'll be back at work tomorrow. She's without a phone until then, so I may pop over and stay there tonight,' Trevor said.

'Lucky you... I mean, g-good, you should do that,' Andy stuttered.

Trevor laughed out loud at his embarrassment.

'Honestly, sometimes you're like a lovestruck teenager.'

'It was a slip of the tongue, alright? No need to make a big deal out of it,' Andy said tersely.

Trevor laughed again, enjoying the younger man's discomfort.

'Get some rest, mate. You did a great job today, and I want to thank you again for saving Kendra. I'll see you tomorrow, Andy.'

'Yeah, see you tomorrow. I've got a few things I want to do here before I leave, while I remember, and then I'll head off.'

∼

KENDRA ARRIVED at work just before midday the following day, having waited all morning for the replacement phone. She and Trevor had stayed up late discussing everything that had happened, which had helped her.

'What have I missed today?' she asked Jill when she'd sat down at her desk.

'Other than what Rick told us yesterday, the only change is that the Marine Policing Unit has started searching the water near the warehouse where the woman was last seen. We're waiting on them for an update. Surveillance teams are on site at the airfield and also the brother's house where the kids are. If she turns up, we'll have her.'

'So that's it, then. Once she's arrested or confirmed dead, then the case is closed, right?'

'I bloody well hope so. There's been enough killing, fires, and weird shit to last a lifetime, if you ask me. I'm looking forward to getting back to more normal criminals, like armed robbers or drug dealers.'

Kendra laughed.

'Well,' she said, 'I have a good feeling that this will be all over soon, and you'll have your wish.'

'By the way, Rick wants to speak to you, K.'

Kendra made her way to Rick Watts' office, confident that the case was well and truly solved, and things could finally start to calm down a little.

'Morning, Rick. Jill said you wanted to see me?'

'Come in and close the door behind you,' he said.

Kendra sensed that something wasn't right; Rick's expression was as serious as she'd ever seen it.

'You okay, Sarge?'

'Not really, Kendra. I know,' he replied.

'Know what?' she asked, bemused.

'I know about your dad, Detective March.'

Kendra's blood turned cold, and she froze, not knowing how to reply.

'You should have told me, Kendra.'

'Told you what?' she finally asked.

'You should have told me that your dad owns the bloody boxing club, that's what!' he said, making an effort not to shout. 'Do you know what the implications could be if the suits upstairs found out? Or the DPS?'

The Department for Professional Standards had already interviewed Kendra recently, and she was keen not to have to speak to them again so soon. She didn't reply, not wanting to make things worse. She needed time to think of a way out of this.

'Well? Aren't you going to at least tell me why you didn't mention it?' Rick pressed.

'I'm sorry, Sarge. The bottom line is that I'm embarrassed. I don't want anyone to think badly of me, being associated with someone like that.'

She looked down at the ground, hoping Rick would believe her.

'Utter bollocks,' he said, 'don't take me for an idiot, Detective, otherwise you'll be back in uniform and reporting accidents quicker than you can say your name.'

'Sarge, my dad has criminal connections. It's as simple as that. If the bosses knew, I would never have been allowed to become a detective, let alone join the SCU.'

'Kendra, please don't take me for a fool. I've seen his record and I know that he was in army intelligence. His record was spot on, and they were surprised when he left so suddenly. So don't tell me that he was a criminal when, in fact, he was a hero.'

'Wait what? W-what are you talking about?' Kendra asked, as surprised as she'd ever been.

'See, now I'm getting pissed. If you can't be bothered to be honest with me after what we've been through, then you may as well pack your bag and piss off.'

'Sarge, I *am* being honest. You must have the wrong record. My dad wasn't in the army. He's a boxing trainer,' she replied hastily.

'Really? So, this isn't Trevor Giddings, your dad?' Rick threw the record to her side of the desk.

Kendra opened the file. The hairs on the back of her neck were raised and she felt cold again. Sure enough, there was a picture of her father in his younger days. She read on and saw Clive and Martha Giddings listed as the next of kin, her grandparents, who had raised her. His record was impressive; he had been commended several times and recruited by army intelligence early in his career, where he had served in Northern Ireland briefly and more noticeably in London, where he infiltrated the notorious Yardie gang who were suspected of buying army weaponry from disgruntled soldiers.

Kendra covered her mouth with her hand to stifle her surprise.

'Seriously, you didn't know?' Rick asked.

Kendra shook her head, unable to speak.

'How did you find this?' she finally asked.

'I have a close friend that works at MI5, and I was speaking to him about the Albanians to see if I could get some extra intel and maybe a heads-up on their operations here. We went back and forth a few times and he noticed the name on the witness report. It escalated from there quite quickly.'

'I can't believe this,' she said.

'Wow, I can't believe you didn't know. I guess it must be a bit of a shock, then. I suppose that trumps you not telling me about the boxing club.'

'Sarge, I had no clue about this. I thought you were joking. I'm sorry I didn't tell you about the club. There was so much going on I just thought it would confuse things.'

'Look, you need to sort this out with your dad. He has some explaining to do. We can discuss the boxing club at a later date. I can't ignore that. I'll keep things quiet for now until then, okay?'

'Thanks, Sarge, I appreciate it.'

'Now, I suggest you do a half day today so you can sort things out, so go and do a couple of hours' work and then go home.'

'Thanks, Sarge.' Kendra got up to leave.

'Sorry you had to find out like this, Kendra, but it's important that we sort it out from our end. You understand that, don't you?'

'Yes, I do, Sarge,' she said, before leaving.

Her head was spinning with the revelation, and she had no idea what to do about it.

∽

23

Kendra drove straight to Andy's house, tearful, angry, and confused by the revelation about her dad.

'Well, hello, Detective March, how...' Andy started to say as he opened the door. 'Kendra, what's wrong?'

'Can I come in?' she asked, wiping tears away.

'Of course!' He opened the door wider for her to enter.

They sat in the lounge, and Andy immediately went to the kitchen to make her a coffee.

'What's going on? I haven't seen you this upset for ages. It's not like you at all.' He handed her the steaming cup.

'I've never been so confused,' she said, sobbing. 'I thought he'd changed his ways, and we were getting on so well.'

'Who? What are you talking about?'

'My dad, Andy! He was in the army, and he never told me. He was in army intelligence, for God's sake!'

'Who, Trevor? Seriously?'

'Yes, seriously. I just got a rollicking from my boss who found out that he owns the boxing club and I never told anyone. He showed me my dad's army record, which showed that he was in the intelligence corps as an undercover officer.'

'Bloody hell!'

'Yes, bloody hell! How do you think I feel? He never said a word, Andy, not a word. After all we've been through recently. And now I'm also in trouble with my boss.'

'I'm so sorry, K. I honestly don't know what to say.' Andy sat next to her on the settee and hugged her closely. She put her head on his shoulder, still tearful, as she tried in vain to make sense of the situation.

'I don't know what to do. How do I deal with something like this?'

'You need to talk to your dad and ask him the questions. That's all you can do.'

'I guess so. I'm just scared that we'll argue, and it will end badly. I'm scared I'll end up losing him again.'

'Look, I've known Trevor for less than a year, but I can tell you that he's not a bad person. I'm sure he has his reasons for not telling you. Just ask him. I can call him to come here, if it helps?'

Kendra thought about it for a few seconds before replying. She was angry enough that she didn't want to see Trevor, but sensible enough to understand that she needed to confront him and find out why he had been so elusive.

'Okay.'

∼

Trevor arrived an hour later, having finished what he was doing at the factory.

'What's going on?' he asked Andy as he entered the

house. 'You were very cryptic, which tells me something is wrong.'

'Come through, someone wants to talk to you. I'll make you a coffee,' Andy said, ushering Trevor into the lounge, where Kendra was sitting.

'Hello, love, I didn't know you'd be here. Are you okay? What's going on?'

'Sit down, Dad,' Kendra said, her expression grim.

Trevor sat opposite his daughter.

'Uh-oh, that's a look I haven't seen for a while but which I remember very well,' he said.

'Do you know why I look like this, Dad? It's because I'm angry, yes, but mostly it's because I'm hurt.'

Trevor could see the conversation was heading somewhere dark.

'Just spit it out, love, tell me what I've done.'

'You've been lying to me, that's what. You've been lying to me my whole life. And just when I thought we'd put all that behind us and life was going great, it turns out you're still lying to me.'

'What is it that I've been lying about, love?' he asked.

'Well, for a start, it seems that you weren't always a boxing trainer, were you?'

Trevor suddenly realised where the conversation was heading.

'It seems like you were an army officer, which came as a bit of a surprise, I can tell you,' Kendra said. But not as big a surprise as finding out you were an army intelligence officer who worked undercover. That one was a real doozy.'

She stopped and glared at her father, waiting for him to reply.

Trevor looked at the floor, wringing his hands.

'How did you find out?' he asked, surprised that she'd found out. His records should have been well protected from scrutiny, as all undercover officers' records rightly were. In the wrong hands, the information could have done a great deal of harm.

'That doesn't matter, Dad,' Kendra said, her voice softening. 'Please, just tell me why you kept it from me.'

'Kendra, love, it wasn't because I was lying to you in any way. It's my way of keeping you safe. There's nothing sinister behind it, I promise.'

'Come on, Dad, you'd rather have me thinking you were some sort of criminally connected absent father than a national hero who risked his life to help people? Seriously?'

'I know it's hard for you to believe, but I wanted to keep that part of my life away from you for good reason. If the wrong people ever found out that you were my daughter, who knows what they'd have done to you?'

'You know I can take care of myself, so that doesn't wash, either.'

Trevor put his face in his hands for a few seconds before looking up.

'That's exactly what your mum said,' he replied. 'You are most definitely her daughter.' He smiled.

Kendra was thrown by the mention of her mother.

'What do you mean by that?'

'Your mum was the smartest and the bravest woman I knew, but telling her what I did for a living was difficult. I was terrified that the people I went after would find out I was married and go after her. And they did.'

'They went after mum?'

'They did. She was tough as nails, your mum, and was unbelievably calm when they came to the house. I wasn't there. She called the police and a friend nearby, then she hid in the loft until the intruders left when they heard the sirens. That friend was Charlie, who was my handler. He got there in time to see them leave and took a number plate down for the police.'

Kendra was numb from the revelation, and it was then she realised that Trevor had kept the secret only to protect her.

'It must have been tough to keep that all quiet,' she said.

'I haven't finished, love,' Trevor said, tearing up.

'What is it?'

'Your mum died under suspicious circumstances, which were never proven. The official report, which you haven't seen, determined the cause of death as suicide. They said she jumped from a bridge. I never believed that; never in a million years would your mum have killed herself. It's been tearing me up for years, not knowing the truth. I didn't want you to suffer the same fate, darling. Please forgive me.'

Trevor hung his head in his hands again and sobbed. Kendra dashed over and sat next to him, grabbing him tight.

'Of course I forgive you, Dad. You must have gone through hell.'

'I left the army after that, but it was a mistake because I didn't have the resources to dig deeper anymore. I was an idiot.'

'I understand. But you're not an idiot.'

He sat up and wiped the tears away, smiling at his daughter.

'I'm so proud of you, love. It would kill me if anything ever happened to you,' he said, squeezing her hand.

Andy stood by the door, not knowing whether to come in.

He'd heard most of the conversation and now understood what Trevor was all about.

'Shall I get something stronger than coffee?' he asked, meekly.

Trevor and Kendra both laughed, the tension broken and the relationship now stronger than ever.

'This time, your timing is spot on,' Trevor said. 'And yes, a beer would be great.'

∼

AN HOUR LATER, after several beers, accompanied by cheese-and-pickle sandwiches, the mood was relaxed and comfortable as the trio bounced ideas off each other for the future of their venture.

'We definitely need more cameras and tamper-proof tech,' Andy suggested.

'Stronger gates and maybe upgrade the fencing around the perimeter,' Trevor added.

'I like the idea of those bomb-proof doors you mentioned, Dad.'

'There's plenty of money in the kitty, so if you ask the rest of the team for their thoughts, we can start buying,' Andy said, delighted that he would be acquiring more toys.

'Why are you so happy?' asked Kendra. 'You've already got more toys to play with than you have the time for. Have you even taken that boat out for a spin yet?'

'As it happens... no,' Andy said. 'If you recall, we've been under attack and trying to track down bad guys, remember? I will get around to it, don't you worry.'

'Well, don't take too long. I'm looking forward to a nice

slow tour of the Thames. There are some amazing pubs alongside it when you go further west.'

'Sounds like a plan, and you can be sure I'll be gatecrashing that trip,' Trevor said, smirking.

'Of course, you will,' Andy replied sarcastically, 'and you'll probably be using your secret ninja powers, won't you?'

'On you, I will, for sure,' Trevor said, 'and you've been warned, so don't complain later on.'

'Stop it, the pair of you,' Kendra said. 'It's like being back in the school playground and trying to figure out who has the best bike, or who supports the best team.'

'It's Arsenal, of course,' said Trevor.

∾

LEANDRA QUPI'S body was found later that afternoon, not far from where she had disappeared. The police divers saw that she had been entangled in knotted wrack, a brown seaweed found in the river that usually attaches to sea walls or hard rocky shores. It appeared that the current had taken her less than fifty yards farther down before she'd become caught in the seaweed, which was why she hadn't surfaced.

Her body was identified quickly due to the ongoing murder investigation and was sent for a post-mortem. The bruises from her fight with Kendra were attributed to the seawall and her death by drowning. The police contacted the state police in Albania, along with the state intelligence service, to inform them of her death and for them to notify the next of kin.

Rick called Kendra shortly after the body was found.

'This pretty much wraps up the investigation,' he said, 'so

just the paperwork to be done and we can move on to something a lot less unpleasant.'

'I'm glad, Rick. This has been a tough one, for sure,' she said.

'How did it go with your dad?'

'It's fine, he kept it secret to protect me after what happened to my mum, so I can't hate him for that, can I?'

'No, I guess not. I'm glad it's okay, but we still need to figure out how we're going to deal with you not informing us of his ownership of a crime scene.'

'I'll put my hands up, Sarge, I don't know what else to do. I thought it would be best and that it wouldn't make any difference to the investigation. That's all I can say,' she replied, resigned to receiving a written warning at the very least, which could impact her career in the police.

'I'll tell you what, consider it a rollocking from me, verbally. There's no reason for me to reveal it now that the investigation is concluded. Like I said, there's just the paperwork and no loose ends that affect the club or your dad.'

Kendra paused for a few seconds as Rick's generosity sank in.

'I can't thank you enough, Rick. That means a lot to me,' she said. Her guilt was constant when it came to Rick Watts, a man she respected greatly. Keeping so many damaging secrets from him would keep that feeling of guilt in the back of her mind.

But keeping those secrets was essential.

∼

24

Charlie's funeral was attended by hundreds of ex-students he had helped teach and had kept safe over the years, including several British champions and one ex-world champion. It rained the entire day, but that did not stop them all paying their respects and seeing him off at the cemetery.

'This is such an amazing turnout,' Kendra told her dad as they both sheltered under an umbrella by the graveside. She held onto his arm tightly, recognising that this was a painful time for him.

'He was an amazing man, love. I can't tell you how many times he helped me out, including saving my life. He was a brother and a best friend rolled into one. I was lucky to have him in my life.'

'I'd like to hear some of those stories one day. I think it's time you told them, don't you?'

'Absolutely. We'll keep his memory alive. It's the least I can do.'

The service was concluded and Charlie's coffin was

lowered slowly into the ground. Charlie's sister Melody had flown over from France for the funeral and threw the first of many flowers onto the casket below. Eventually, only a few people remained, including the team that had been a part of the adventures Charlie had shared in the past year or so.

'Thank you for your help with the funeral, Trevor,' Melody Fenway said, hugging him. 'I couldn't have managed any of it without you.'

'It was the least I could do, Melody. He was my closest friend.'

'You know, we never spoke that often, something I regret very much—but whenever we did, he always mentioned you. He was incredibly fond of you,' she added.

Trevor nodded, finding it difficult to have lost such a close friend, so soon after losing Jacob, his brother-in-arms, and mentor.

'It's been tough, these past few months. I won't lie, but I have been blessed with incredible friends and family who have shown me that however tough life is, you should always try to find a way of making it better. Charlie did that. He made our lives better.'

'He never had any kids of his own, but always considered his students family, so it was great to see so many of them here today,' Melody added.

'Yes, he was loved. When will you be going back to France? I can help you sort out his belongings before you leave, if you like?'

'That's okay. I've already gone through most of it. He led a very spartan life, so there wasn't much in his flat. I did find a copy of his will, though. I know we must wait for probate and all that, but his instructions were pretty clear. He wanted to leave this to you,' she said, handing Trevor a rectangular box wrapped in navy blue velvet.

Trevor took the box and opened it. He smiled and shook his head, tears welling in his eyes. He showed the contents to Kendra.

Inside the box on a satin backdrop were three gold medals lying side by side, given to Charlie when he had become the armed service boxing champion three years in a row, back when he and Trevor had served together.

'These were his pride and joy,' he said, a tear finally rolling down his cheek. 'He received a handful of other medals, including the Military Cross, but he always boasted about his boxing achievements more.'

'He cared a great deal about you,' Melody said, resting her hand on Trevor's arm.

'I know just the place for these,' Trevor said. 'I'll put them on display at the club, so the boys and girls can see that he wasn't just a great trainer, he was also a great boxer. Most of all, he was a great man and a wonderful friend to them all.'

'He'd have liked that very much,' Melody said.

They walked back to the limousine that was waiting to take them to the wake.

Before they got into the car, Trevor looked back towards his friend's grave.

'Goodbye, old friend. I'll pop back soon for a beer and a chat, like always.'

∼

THE TEAM HELD a separate wake later, back at the factory, where they now had time to reflect more freely on their relationship with Charlie, along with what they had endured these past few weeks. Greg was making a swift recovery; his scars would be a constant reminder, but would eventually fade enough not to spoil his rugged good looks. Danny Baptiste looked after him and teased him about all the action he had missed.

'While you were sitting on your arse in a warehouse, we were fighting for our lives against a bunch of nasty people,' he told him more than once. Greg, though, responded well.

'You may have been fighting the nasty people, but I was keeping their boss busy to give the guys time to come and rescue me. I basically saved your arses by splitting them up, don't you see?'

And so it went on. Trevor was pleased to see them all in a positive state of mind. Who knew what was coming next?

'I think they're ready for anything, despite how young they are,' Kendra told him, proud of their achievements.

'Yeah, you're right, love. We couldn't have asked for a better team.'

After they had exchanged their stories, Trevor gathered them in the large room, where the smell of creosote still lingered.

'We lost someone very close to us, someone special, and we must never forget that. Charlie died doing what he thought was right, just as we do now, trying to make the world a better place. I just wanted to remind you of the reason we do this, folks, to help others.'

'Hear, hear,' Charmaine called out, as the rest of the team nodded in respect and acknowledgement. Trevor could see they were committed to the cause, their faces determined and their bravery unquestionable.

'We need to learn from what happened, not just to Charlie and Greg, but the attack on the factory and the club.

We need everyone here to think about that and to come back with ways of preventing it from happening again. Don't be afraid to be adventurous with your solutions. Everything is on the table,' Kendra said.

'We need to get stronger and better. That's how we'll beat the scum that are out there ruining people's lives,' Trevor continued.

The team whooped and hollered in acknowledgement, cementing their support for their cause.

'So, what now, Trev?' Amir asked, once the noise had abated.

'Now, we finish getting the factory back to how it was and prepare for the next job. We can start back on the case tomorrow; you should all go home and relax now. Come and see me or Kendra if you have any ideas, okay? Darren, before you lot leave, can we have a quick chat?'

Darren and his five Walsall colleagues walked over.

'What's up, Trev?' Darren asked.

'I hate repeating myself. It's so bloody boring,' Trevor replied, 'but I just wanted, again, to thank you and your team for all your help. Also, I want you all to consider an offer I'd like to make.'

'Oh, what's that, then?'

'Every time something happens, it seems that you're my first port of call. The first phone call I make. So, Frazer must be getting hacked off with how regular the calls have been, right?'

Trevor knew that Frazer, another old-time contact, didn't mind at all and encouraged his team to help at any time, but he was mentioning it out of respect.

'You know he's always there for you, Trevor,' Darren said. 'So, what did you have in mind?

'I think we're growing, not just as a team, but in the manner that we're conducting ourselves and working towards our mutual objectives. I think it would be a great idea if you guys relocated to London so we can work more permanently with you all.'

The team of six looked surprised at this. It was unexpected, to say the least.

'Seriously? How would that work and where would we stay?' Jimmy asked, delighted more than the others at the prospect, primarily due to his growing relationship with Rhianna, who he'd met when helping the team locate a gang of robbers.

'Well, for one, you could all learn the security products and services trade, which is what Sherwood Solutions is all about. It'll be a paid job, with a good salary and all the usual benefits. The business is starting to make money, too, legitimately, and you could all be a big part of the expansion we want to put in place.'

'So, we'd have to go back to school?' Izzy asked, disappointed.

'No, silly,' Kendra replied, laughing, 'you'd be trained in-house by specialists we'll bring in. It won't take long to learn the trade.'

'That sounds great, but where would we live?' asked Darren.

'There's lots of new developments in east London,' said Kendra. 'We could invest in new flats for you, and we can work something out whereby ownership would be transferred to you after a certain length of service with us.'

Along with the procurement of new equipment, Kendra, Trevor, and Andy had also discussed ways of helping the team out and looking after their welfare and future prospects. This was one way to do that.

'Wow,' Darren replied. His team looked at one another, their surprise growing the more Trevor and Kendra revealed.

'Listen, guys, you don't have to accept the offer. Go away and think about it. I'm just saying, it's a great opportunity to plant some firm roots and grow with us, as well as learn a trade that will always help you,' Trevor added.

'I don't need any time to think. Count me in!' Jimmy said, unable to contain his joy.

'Me too!' the rest said in unison.

'That's settled then, bloody marvellous,' Trevor said, shaking their hands one by one and receiving hugs in return.

'There is just one problem, though,' Kendra warned, her expression more serious.

'Uh-oh, I knew it was too good to be true,' Izzy exclaimed.

'What is it?' Darren asked.

'You're going to have to share the building with Mo and Amir,' she said, stifling a laugh.

They all laughed, having expected something much worse.

'Fair enough,' Jimmy said. 'I suppose we can live with that,' he joked.

'I heard that!' Amir said, strolling back into the room with his brother. Trevor had forewarned them of the offer to Darren and his team and the fact they'd also be involved. The twins were overwhelmed.

'It's the least we can do,' Kendra had told them when they had stopped dancing.

'Can we draw lots to see who stays next door to Amir?' Rory added, laughing as he slapped him on the back.

Trevor, Andy, and Kendra watched as the men exchanged high-fives and banter, all of them incredibly happy.

'You two should be very proud of what you've done so far,' Andy said quietly as he put his arm around Kendra's waist, drawing her close.

'Stop being an arse, Andy. You deserve just as much credit, okay?' Trevor said.

'Yeah, we've done this together, as a team, and we should be equally proud,' Kendra added.

'Fair enough. You can buy me a beer and a pizza to thank me for my incredible contributions,' Andy replied, jokingly.

'Amir! Andy said you can stay with him until the flats are sorted out,' Trevor shouted, taking Andy by surprise.

'What? No, he's joking, Amir. You don't want to live with me. My house is filthy, and I listen to seventies music all the time. You'd hate it.'

Trevor and Kendra laughed as Amir strolled over to talk to Andy.

'That doesn't matter, mate. It will do me good to get away from that brother of mine for a while.'

'Trevor? Kendra?' Andy pleaded, knowing full well that the laughing duo would not be helping this time.

∼

ONCE THE TEAM HAD DISPERSED, Trevor, Kendra, and Andy adjourned to the small canteen for a coffee.

'I don't know about you, but I'm knackered,' Trevor said as he sipped his drink.

'I think we all deserve a rest. Let's hope we have a few days of nothing happening,' Kendra said.

'You know,' said Andy, 'we don't give ourselves enough

credit for what we have achieved, because we haven't really had much time to reflect on it.'

'Why do you say that?' asked Kendra.

'It just made me realise that it has almost been non-stop since we started doing this.'

'So?' Trevor asked.

'So, it just tells you that there's a lot more shit out there that needs sorting out and we're not going to get much rest at all.'

They sat and pondered the observation, having never thought about it in that way before. Without saying it out loud, they had collectively realised there would be more of the same to come. The more they got involved, the more it was likely to end badly for someone on the team, maybe lots of them.

'We just have to get better and stronger,' Kendra said.

∾

EPILOGUE

The pilot waited for three hours past their scheduled flight time before he made the decision to leave.

'It's just as well they paid in advance,' he told the co-pilot. They're not coming, so let's get the hell out of here.'

They cleared a new take-off with the tower and were wheels-up thirty minutes later.

The special branch officers watched as the plane left, happy that there were no passengers on board. One of them called her boss.

'The plane left, sir. No passengers on board, just the two pilots.'

'That's fine. Get yourselves back to the office and I'll let the investigators know.'

∼

THE NEWS of Leandra Qupi's death had leaked from both the Albanian State Police and their State Intelligence Service colleagues within minutes of the information being passed to them from England. This started a chain of events that led to a rival gang, delighted at the news of her demise, moving in on the Qupi territory and smashing any resistance that remained. Many of Qupi's followers and soldiers had also been made aware and had swiftly departed, knowing what was to follow, not wanting to be involved in a vicious gang war they were likely to lose. A dozen loyal followers were killed mercilessly, leading to those left behind surrendering and offering their services to the new occupiers. The void left behind by Qupi was quickly filled, and once the dead were discreetly removed to underpin a new housing estate foundation, all traces of the family were erased.

Had Leandra Qupi's children been left behind in Tirana, they, too, would have been killed. Her brother in England knew this and kept their existence secret from anyone back in his homeland. An Interpol officer attended with a senior Metropolitan Police officer and spoke with John and Wendy Jones to relay the news about Leandra. Her brother was upset but not surprised that she was no longer of this world. He was equally upset and unsurprised when informed of the death of his family back in Albania.

'That isn't the only reason we are here, Mister Jones,' the senior officer continued. 'The children are clearly going to be at risk if they are sent back to Albania, and to be honest, there is nobody left to send them back to. You are their only surviving family, and we believe that it is in their best interest that they remain with you.'

'Of course,' Jones said, looking at his wife, who nodded in agreement.

'We will look after them. They are safe now. We are all safe now,' she said.

It was several days after the recovery of Leandra Qupi's body that Brodie Dabbs finally resurfaced. He had gone to ground quickly when he had lost the extra support from Trevor, who had been helping to guard his business interests. He was delighted at the news of her demise but recognised that she had caused a lot of damage that now needed to be dealt with.

'Damned woman,' he told his men. 'Should have stayed in Albania. Let's use her death to our advantage, eh? Start spreading rumours that she crossed paths with us and let people think we had something to do with it.'

'Won't the police have something to say about that, boss?' asked one of his men.

'Don't worry about the police, son, I have them in my back pocket for now. They'll not get in our way.'

His men laughed and confidence was restored to the gang that was now once again able to rule the east end of London without much competition.

Later that evening, one of Dabbs' trusted lieutenants went for his regular cigarette in the backyard and made one of his regular calls.

'Looks like the Albanians are history. Brodie is spreading rumours and taking the credit, and he's now saying he controls the police,' he relayed.

'Does he now?' came the reply. 'Well, he's in for the shock of his life, isn't he? I think it's time we took it all from him.'

THE END

BOOK 5 PREVIEW

'Nothing to Lose'
Book 5 of the *'Summary Justice'* series
with DC Kendra March.

. . .

Cathay Pacific CX251 from Hong Kong landed at Heathrow at 5.40am with fifteen Ghost Dragon triad gang members onboard. Three more Cathay Pacific flights followed later that day, along with two British Airways flights at Terminal 5. Each of the six flights carried a minimum of fifteen gangsters, one hundred in total. Their arrival did not go unnoticed by Border Force staff, who were diligent in checking their passports, visas, and other documentation.

'What is the nature of your visit?'

'Business.' The stock answer.

'What business is that?'

'We are here for the international security event at the ExCel Centre, at the request of our employers, Hurricane Security Solutions,' came the standard reply. The paperwork was in order and was also sponsored by judges, members of Parliament, senior police officers or other prominent businesses. All legitimate, all as it should be.

'Who am I to question a judge?' one of the Border Force assessors asked her supervisor.

'I checked online, and the security event is a large one and very popular, with hundreds of international exhibitors. I guess this company is doing something big this year, and as you pointed out, they all have the correct paperwork and sponsor letters from some impressive people. There's nothing for us here, let them pass through,' the supervisor said.

The men were all allowed through the Border Force controls and went straight to arrivals, every one of them having travelled with one small carry-on case with just their essentials. A man with a placard waited for them. *Hurricane*

Security Solutions, the sign read. The men were all directed to waiting coaches where they were whisked away to a yet-unknown location. They knew better than to ask questions and did what they were told.

The following day, a hundred more followed on similar flights, all with legitimate documentation, sponsorship and permissions. A small army of two hundred gangsters was now in place in London.

'That company must be doing well for them to bring so many staff over,' the Border Force supervisor murmured to her colleague.

'There's not much we can do if they've been given permission to be here, is there?' came the reply.

'I make that a couple of hundred that we're aware of,' the supervisor added. 'It's only a security convention, what the hell do they need so many for?'

'I wouldn't worry about it, boss, I'm sure there's a perfectly legitimate explanation.'

~

THE COACHES TOOK the men to a huge warehouse next to the Ford Dagenham assembly site, which had seen many of its factories and buildings closed over the past decade, some having been demolished. The loss of jobs had been devastating to the local population. One particular warehouse, once used to store engines before they were exported, was now a food-and-drink distribution wholesaler to the Chinese community, supplying many of the restaurants, takeaway outlets, and supermarkets. It was a hugely prosperous business that was controlled strictly by the Ghost Dragons, who had maintained a stranglehold in the area for many years.

Their share for keeping this and many other Chinese-owned businesses safe–by way of extortion–was very lucrative and they had expanded their operations over the years. Their operations were about to be taken to the next level, with their ambitious plans now going into overdrive. For those plans to work, they needed their newly arrived army.

Having planned for this day, the legitimate wing of the organisation had purchased a large number of new properties in the area, which had been built on the ashes of some of the demolished Ford buildings. They had secured a row of twelve houses in one new development along with a ten-storey block of flats in the same complex, with four three-bed flats on every floor, and which would now house the two-hundred-strong army that had arrived from Hong Kong.

They disembarked at the rear of the distribution warehouse, out of sight, and were ushered into a marquee that had been erected specifically for their visit. Once inside they were given refreshments and sent to a row of tables at the far end where they were greeted by ten seated men, each of whom had a list of twenty names that would make up their squad. From big boxes next to their chairs, the team leaders retrieved a small backpack for each of their men, containing a Glock G17 handgun loaded with seventeen rounds, two spare magazines containing a further seventeen rounds apiece, a wicked looking fourteen-inch watermelon knife—or *chopper,* as they liked to call it—and a basic mobile phone that had numbers pre-installed. Additionally, one member per squad was given an MP40 submachine gun and hundreds of spare rounds. The gun, a design originally used in the Second World War, was a trusted triad weapon and would prove devastating in the right hands. Catastrophic in the wrong ones.

The team leaders then took their teams to one side to introduce themselves and impart the instructions they had been told to give. The order was a very simple one.

'We have been waiting a long time for this. We are to prepare for war.'

~

Chapter 1

'Honestly, I don't know what you were thinking of. It's a stupid name for a boat,' Trevor told Andy, as they continued with their long-overdue trip along the Thames.

'I think it's a great name. It's fun and it's relevant,' Andy replied defensively. 'What do you think, Kendra?'

'I think I should throw you both overboard, it's like listening to a couple of bickering school kids. When are we going to get to a pub, like you promised?'

'We can stop at the Isle of Dogs if you want something soon, otherwise it'll be a while until we pass through central London,' said Andy.

Kendra looked at him and started giggling–again.

'Seriously, why can't you just accept that I look the part?' he said, adjusting his new white captain's hat to a less jaunty angle.

'It looks silly, Andy, that's why I'm laughing.'

Having spent a couple of weeks on an intensive course, Andy was proficient enough to pilot the forty-six-foot motor cruiser with its powerful twin diesel engines. A gift from a grateful hacker who had made millions thanks to Andy's tip-off, the boat had been a source of amusement for Trevor and Kendra, especially when Andy hadn't a clue how to pilot her.

'You don't sail her,' he had found out, and had corrected them, 'you pilot her.'

'You think the boat is *she*?' Kendra had said, 'with an insulting name like *Soggy Bottom*? I think she'll drown you the first chance *she* gets.'

Taking them both out for the first time was supposed to have been an enjoyable, stress-free experience, but it was turning out to be yet another humorous adventure for the trio.

'Well, as long as you're laughing, I'll take that as a win,' Andy said, puffing his chest out proudly.

'I'm just pleased we're still afloat,' Trevor added, winking at his daughter conspiratorially.

'Keep it up and you can swim back,' Andy retorted. 'Now pass me a sandwich and keep an eye out for the pub.'

They snacked on cheese-and-cucumber sandwiches, accompanied with ginger beer, all provided by Andy, as they went along at a steady twelve knots, as required by law. The past few weeks had been more relaxing than they had been used to, so despite the banter, they were enjoying each other's company along with the lack of excitement that had prevailed recently.

'It's so much more relaxed on the river,' Trevor mused, 'as opposed to the hell that is London traffic, just a few hundred feet from here. I never really took notice, you know?'

'I think we take London for granted. Yes, there is a lot of nasty crap that goes on, and yes, there is too much traffic and too many rude people. But when you take a closer look there is so much more to this city, so much good that we don't appreciate as much as we should.'

'We complain a lot about it, but I bet we'd miss it like crazy if we were away for any length of time,' Andy said.

'Well, we're here and we're doing our little bit to try and keep it crap-free, so I for one will try not to complain as much,' Trevor replied.

'Hello, what's going on here then?' Andy said suddenly.

They were approaching the famous s-bend at the Isle of Dogs, with City Airport on their right and the huge ExCel Conference Centre just past it.

'That's a lot of security,' Trevor said, as they slowed down for the approaching yellow-and-blue liveried police boat, its blue light making it clear who they were. They noticed several other similar craft within a short distance, all seemingly keeping closer to the north side than the south, along with armed police officers patrolling on foot and in vehicles on the adjacent road.

'There must be something going on either at the airport or the conference centre,' Kendra added.

'Oh, I saw something about this on the news. It's an International Security conference, they have a pretty good turnout,' Andy said.

'I've been to a couple of those but I've never seen security like that,' Kendra replied, looking up at the police helicopter that was circling the conference hall high above.

'Apparently,' said Andy, 'the UK is signing a huge trade deal with Taiwan, not just for normal trade goods but also for the newest military and cyber tech that we've developed recently. The Chinese are really pissed off about it, hence the extra security.'

'That's understandable,' Kendra said, 'many of the

companies exhibiting there are Chinese, trying to garner more deals with the west, so they can't be too happy.'

'Like I said, hence the extra security.'

The patrol boat eyed them up for a few minutes before moving on to the next craft behind, seemingly happy with *Soggy Bottom*.

'How long 'til we get to the pub, Andy? I'm parched,' Trevor said, uninterested in the activity.

'It'll be a while yet, remember we can only do twelve knots and once we get to Wandsworth Bridge we have to slow down even more, to eight.'

'So tomorrow, then,' Trevor said, shaking his head.

'No, not tomorrow, it's not that bad. Maybe a couple more hours?'

'It may as well be tomorrow.'

'It's just as well that I brought some beer, then, isn't it?' Kendra announced, pulling out two bottles from a cool bag. She handed one to her dad and kept the other for herself.

'Sorry, Andy, you're not allowed,' she said, taking a long swig.

'Damned speed limit,' he replied, licking his lips. As tempted as he was, the training was fresh in his mind, and topmost in his thoughts were the fines dished out to those who broke the law.

'You should've bought a helicopter instead,' Trevor said, smiling and raising his bottle in a toast.

'Actually, that's not a bad idea,' Andy mused.

'No!' Kendra and Trevor both exclaimed.

∼

Security inside the ExCel Centre was even more visible, with pairs of armed police officers stationed every fifty metres alongside hundreds of extra security staff. The Taiwanese delegation were accompanied by their own plain-clothed security personnel and shadowed by specialist police protection officers from the Metropolitan Police, who were employed to protect visiting heads of states or those clearly at risk of attack. The Taiwanese President rarely visited the UK, but such was the importance of the trade deal that her presence was necessary.

As the President and the Prime Minister sat facing the hundreds of press cameras arrayed in the vast room, surrounded by both delegations, the extensive leather-bound trade agreement was placed in front of each of them and the ceremonial signing commenced.

Hundreds of cameras clicked as the delegates signed the documents in front of them, before they were swapped over for them to do the same again. The camera flashes and clicks continued for several minutes as the signings were concluded, the pair standing and shaking hands warmly in front of the world's press.

One of the cameramen stood staring as his neighbours jostled amongst themselves to get the best possible shot. He wasn't there to take pictures but to witness the signing of the agreement, before reporting back to his handlers in Beijing.

And so it begins, he thought, continuing to stare at the show ahead.

∼

'See? Aren't you glad you came now?' Andy said as they sat on the wooden benches in the pub garden, the parasols shading them from the midday sun. They had found a mooring alongside The Swan in Walton-on-Thames and were soon enjoying their gourmet meals with a bottle of chilled Pinot Grigio.

'I must admit, it took a long time to get here but I'm enjoying it very much,' Trevor replied, 'so thank you, Captain.' He raised his glass to Andy, who responded in kind.

'Thank you, Trevor, the pleasure is mine.'

'We've come a long way in the past year or so, haven't we?' Kendra added, raising her glass too. 'When you consider what we've gone through and what we've achieved, having this break to recharge our batteries is the very least we should be doing.'

'Hear, hear,' Trevor said, clinking her glass.

'Luckily for us, and for the criminal fraternity,' said Andy, 'things are nice and quiet at the moment. There's nothing we can get involved in at this time, so we may as well enjoy it while we can.'

As if on cue, Kendra's phone rang.

'You had to go and say that, didn't you?' Trevor scolded.

'It's Jill, I'd better take it,' Kendra said. 'How's it going, Jill? You know I'm not back for another three days, don't you?'

Andy and Trevor watched the colour drain from Kendra's face.

'What? When?' she said, her shock clear for all to see.

'What is it, love?' Trevor asked, sensing her growing discomfort.

'Jill, we're miles from home and will be back late tonight. I'll be in the office first thing tomorrow but if you hear anything in the meantime please call me, okay?'

She ended the call and sat staring at Andy.

'What is it?' he asked gently.

'Rick Watts has been kidnapped.'

∽

Kendra was in the office early the following morning, having asked Jill to meet her there before the rest of the Special Crimes Unit came in. Jill was waiting as Kendra walked into the office, and a quick nod confirmed that they would be alone.

Jill stood as Kendra reached her desk and she could see that her colleague had been crying recently, her eyes still red and her mascara smudged. They hugged, with no words exchanged until they sat facing each other.

'What happened?' Kendra asked, holding Jill's hand.

'We're not quite sure yet, but we think Rick was grabbed off the street when he was on the way back from the gym.'

'Rick went to the gym?'

'He was training for that stupid annual fitness check that we all have to do, remember?'

'Damn thing, they're threatening to move people now if they don't pass, so it doesn't surprise me.'

'He loves this unit, K, he would have done anything to stay on it, so I'm not surprised. What I am surprised about is why they would take him.'

'Are there any clues as to why? Has he pissed anyone off recently?'

'He's pissed off a lot of people recently, or should I say *we've* pissed them off with the successes we've had,' Jill said, rubbing her temple to ease the headache she hadn't been able to get rid of.

'Yeah, but most of those bastards are inside, there must be a way to narrow it down somehow,' Kendra said. 'Can you think of anyone that would use Rick as leverage for anything? They must have kidnapped him for a reason.'

'It could be any number of things, K. It may be to distract us from a current case or to stop us from closing in. Or it could be a past case they want revenge for. Or it could be they want someone sprung from prison. I could go on.'

'What was the last confirmed location, do we have that, at least? Maybe we can check CCTV or canvas the locals to find out if they saw anything,' Kendra added.

'His wife told me about the gym, which is in Chigwell, ironically near the Metropolitan Police sports club. Other than that, we haven't received anything back by pinging his phone and we can't find his car, either.'

'Who's running the investigation?'

'That in itself is a concern: it's the NCA,' Jill said.

The team had recently had a run-in with a pair of detectives from the National Crime Agency who had resigned before they were sacked for gross misconduct. It had not been a good experience for any of them.

'At least the douchebag and his sidekick aren't there anymore, maybe it will be a more pleasant experience,' Kendra said. 'Who's running it?'

'A Detective Sergeant Jim Adair and his colleague, Detective Sergeant Jon Sisterson. They seemed like a decent pair, just doing their jobs but telling us to stay out of it for now.'

'Why would they say that?'

'In case it's something to do with a current investigation,

they don't want anything to mess it up,' Jill replied. 'We have to do something, Kendra, it's Rick!'

'I know, Jill, and I agree. But we need to keep this very quiet otherwise we could end up in the shit, okay? Let me have a think on what we can do to help.'

'Thanks, Kendra. You can count Pablo in, too, if we need help.'

'I wouldn't have it any other way, you guys are inseparable now.' Kendra smiled.

'This is messed up, nothing like this has ever happened before. Something tells me that we've stepped on some very dangerous toes, Kendra.'

'You may be right. I'm going to make a quick phone call and I'll be back in a few minutes,' Kendra said, leaving her colleague. She had to go and update Andy, as every second counted.

~

'What are they saying?' Andy asked.

'They don't even know where he was taken from, let alone why,' Kendra replied, clearly frustrated.

'What can I do?'

'If I send you his phone number and car registration, will you be able to pinpoint his last known locations?'

'I'll certainly give it a go. If he was anywhere near a CCTV camera then Cyclops will find him pretty quickly.'

Cyclops had proven a very useful–albeit illegal—way of tracking vehicles or people on CCTV by hacking the systems and utilising the existing software. Andy had used it to great effect in most of the cases they had dealt with recently, and it had proven invaluable so far.

'Great, I'll text you the info. Can you update Dad? I need to go back to work, and I'll probably be here for a while.'

'Sure thing, K. Let me know if there's anything else I can do.'

'The NCA are involved and they've tied our hands, so we need to find ways to help without them knowing it was us. If you can think of anything please let me know. I'll call you later.'

'Bye, Kendra. Take care,' Andy said, ending the call.

Trevor had told them both that he'd be at the boxing club all day, helping the twins, Mo and Amir, get things back to some semblance of normality since the death of his great friend and mentor, Charlie, at the hands of the Albanian gang leader. The youngsters had been badly affected by his death, and the twins had volunteered to help get the place going again.

When Andy called, he could hear that Trevor was out of breath.

'Have you been running, old man?' he asked, knowing he'd get a reaction.

'Less of the *old*, peg-leg. You should try it some time, you won't get out of breath running a hundred feet like you did last time.'

'I don't need to run, I have you to do that. But that's not why I'm calling, I wanted to update you on what's happening at the police station.'

'Come on, out with it, I have another couple of pounds I want to lose.'

Andy repeated what Kendra had told him. Trevor had surprised him with his tactical knowledge and then when it was revealed that he had once been an undercover operative in the British army it had all become clear. He was good at strategy because he'd had the very best training and experience.

'Alright, thanks for that. Let me know if your checks come up with anything. Are you working from home or the factory?'

'I'll be at home. I don't like the smell of fresh paint, so I want to wait a bit until I go back. There's not a lot going on there, other than the redecorating, anyway.'

'Okay, I may pop over later this evening, we can have a brainstorming session when Kendra gets off work.'

'That would be great. I'll make us a nice chilli con carne.'

'As long as it doesn't burn like the last one, we'll be good,' Trevor said. 'I'll see you later.'

As soon as Trevor ended the call, Andy was at the computer logging on to Cyclops. Kendra's text had come through with Rick's car registration number, so Andy started by gaining illegal access to the London Borough of Redbridge CCTV control room, using the trusted method of back-door entry via the weakest part of the system, the older existing cameras. The David Lloyd gym was in Chigwell and Andy started with cameras around the area of the gym that was council-run. On a separate computer, he accessed the CCTV covering the gym grounds themselves, via the gym's security office. Both systems had been upgraded in the past two years, now utilising programmes that allowed for a historic search capability.

Once Andy had input the car registration number, the search took less than a minute to give results on both systems.

'That's my girl,' Andy said out loud, patting his computer. He printed the results and called Kendra.

'Can you talk?'

'Hang on,' she said, 'let me go outside.'

When she was in the yard downstairs and free to speak, she said, 'Go ahead, what did you find?'

'He was at the gym yesterday, like his wife said. I have the car arriving at six-forty-five and him entering the gym. He was there until eight-twenty, which was when he got back in his car and left.'

'So, there's nothing untoward at the gym?'

'No. I wanted you to know that I'll now start searching the route back to his house. It will take a while but at least you know it didn't happen at the gym. Can you get me his home address?'

'Yes, I know where he lives. I'll send a text. Thanks, Andy.'

The text arrived within thirty seconds, so Andy mapped the route to Rick's house and resumed tapping away at the keyboard with Cyclops.

'That's strange,' he mumbled, 'why did he turn right instead of left?'

It took thirty minutes, but he finally found where Rick had driven to. He called Kendra back.

'Andy, that was quick. Tell me you found something.'

'I checked the route to his house, but he didn't go that way, he went somewhere completely different,' Andy said.

'Where?'

'He lives near Fairlop Waters, which would be a left turn out of the gym, but for some reason he turned right and drove to Chingford, in the opposite direction.'

'Where in Chingford?' Kendra asked.

'He drove into the car park of Chingford Golf Course,

which is where I lost sight because there are no cameras there. He didn't leave the car park so whatever happened must have done so there.'

'Shit, so someone must have called him to meet there knowing there were no cameras, knowing it's an ideal place to grab someone at night when it's empty,' she said.

'Well, they're not as clever as they think, K, because I hacked into the surrounding systems and I have a good idea about what happened.'

'Go on.'

'Thirty-five minutes before Rick drove into the car park, a white Transit van drove in there. Again, nobody walked out so I can only assume they stayed there to wait for Rick. Four minutes after Rick drove in, the van drove back out and turned right towards Waltham Abbey. I think Rick was in that van, Kendra.'

'I have to find a way of leading the investigator to the car park first, to see if Rick's car is still there,' she told him. 'What else did you find?'

'I have the van number which I need you to do a PNC check on, but I have a feeling it will come back to a hire company. Once I have the details I can dig deeper. Also, I checked the footage back at the gym and saw that the van had been there, parked up, when Rick turned up for his session.'

'So, they knew his routine and waited for him, knowing he would be coming from there to the meeting,' she added.

'Correct. And that's what's deeply worrying, K. Rick must have either known who called him, or trusted them. Is there any way you can get his phone records?'

'I don't know, Andy, the NCA are playing it tough and

telling us to stay clear, like I said. We're gonna struggle to get anything out of them.'

'Are they based at the station?' he asked.

'Yes, they've set up an incident room especially for the investigation, but nobody from the team will be allowed anywhere near the paperwork without arousing suspicion,' she said.

'Don't you have anyone who can help you?'

'Actually, I do,' she said, 'I'll call you later. Thanks again, honey bunch.' She ended the call quickly.

'That's ok... *honey bunch?*' Andy said to himself, bemused. 'Is that a good thing?'

ABOUT THE AUTHOR

Theo Harris is an emerging author of crime action novels. He was born in London, raised in London, and became a cop in London.

Having served as a police officer in the Metropolitan Police service for thirty years, he witnessed and experienced the underbelly of a capital city that you are never supposed to see.

Theo was a specialist officer for twenty-seven of the thirty years and went on to work in departments that dealt with serious crimes of all types. His experience, knowledge and connections within the organisation have helped him with his storytelling, with a style of writing that readers can associate with.

Theo has many stories to tell, starting with the 'Summary Justice' series featuring DC Kendra March, and will follow with many more innovative, interesting, and fast-paced stories for many years to come.

For more information about upcoming books please visit theoharris.co.uk.

ALSO BY THEO HARRIS

DC Kendra March: The 'Summary Justice' series

Book 1 - **An Eye for an Eye**

Book 2 - **Fagin's Folly**

Book 3 - **Road Trip**

Book 4 - **London's Burning**

Book 5 - **Nothing to Lose**

Book 6 - **Justice**

***

Boxset 1 - Books 1 to 3

***

Think you have gotten away with it? Think again!

Printed in Great Britain
by Amazon